THE

GREEN STORM

A NOVEL

BUD SANTORA

W. B. William Productions

THE GREEN STORM: A NOVEL

Copyright © 2013 by Bud Santora

W. B. William Productions
200 West 90th Street Suite 9B
New York, NY 10024
All rights reserved.
ISBN: 978-0-9911075-1-3

Graphic art and cover art by: Bud Santora

DEDICATION

This is for Mary Lou, who told
me everyone has at least
one book in them.

ACKNOWLEDGEMENTS

I would like to thank Arthur Wooten,
Greg Allen, Patty Walsh Pettit,
Rebecca Phillips, Nancy Perkins,
Elizabeth Beeton, and Scott Morgan for
all their help, feedback,
and encouragement.

GUILLORY FAMILY TREE

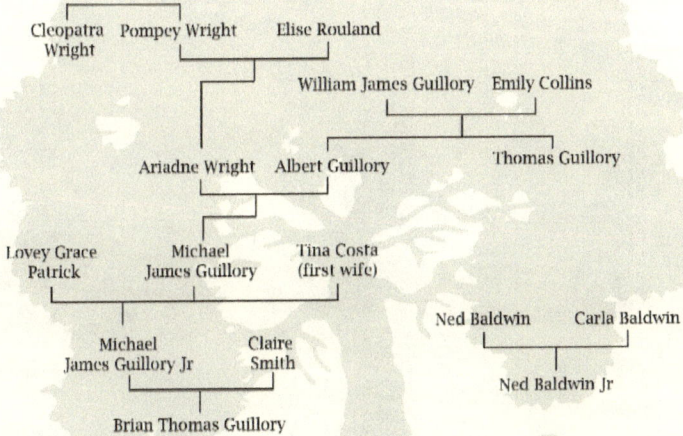

Cleopatra Wright — Pompey Wright — Elise Rouland

William James Guillory — Emily Collins

Ariadne Wright — Albert Guillory

Thomas Guillory

Lovey Grace Patrick — Michael James Guillory — Tina Costa (first wife)

Ned Baldwin — Carla Baldwin

Michael James Guillory Jr — Claire Smith

Ned Baldwin Jr

Brian Thomas Guillory

CHAPTER ONE

The Morning Before

Panting, Mike Guillory collapsed into a wicker chair on his porch after a morning run on the beach. He was still sweating after his workout due to the heat and humidity. It was early March and the morning before was so chilly he actually needed his hoodie to keep warm. After the previous night's windstorm he expected a cool breeze to accompany him on his run instead of August-like weather. Mike also noticed that the sky now had a strange greenish tint to it that reflected on the surface of the water.

He faced his chair toward the two bungalows next to his house on Plover's Island. His mother, Lovey Grace, lived next door and an old friend of the family, referred to as Uncle Ned for as long as Mike could remember, was in the house next to her. Mike threw his feet up on the porch railing just as Travis, his Rottweiler, joined him and lay belly-up next to his chair. The big dog smiled up at him, waiting to be acknowledged.

"Good morning, Travis. Looks like you're trying to tell me you want that big belly of yours rubbed."

The dog barked and wiggled sporting a large doggy grin.

"Okay, boy, but you'll have to sit with me awhile before you run off with Poo."

The black and tan bruiser wiggled again until Mike gave the dog's stomach and chest a good long massage.

Mike picked up his coffee and took a sip. "How was that, Travis? Now you and I can watch what's going to happen next door, any minute."

Travis barked in agreement and mimicked Mike's position. He put his front paws up on the porch railing next to his master's feet and looked at Lovey Grace's house with great anticipation. Mike's aunt Bridget was visiting her sister for the weekend, which meant there was going to be another pastry parade.

On these Saturday mornings she loved creating assorted pastries and breads in Lovey Grace's kitchen. Bridget lived in a studio apartment in Ridgewater, on the mainland, with only a small kitchenette. She liked to use her sister's professional grade stove to indulge her baking passion.

Lovey Grace encouraged her sibling's dedication to this art because she, herself, hated making things like cakes, pies, and cookies. Her devotion was to gardening and cleaning. She practiced and developed her skills to the highest degree. The old house was not just spotless; it was immaculate. Her garden was also perfect, with never a weed or leaf out of place. She always wore a big straw hat, a padded bib tool apron she designed herself, and garden knee and shin guards. Lovey Grace resembled a baseball catcher on a summer holiday. Her son nicknamed her *Yogi Weeda*, referencing the most famous catcher in major league history.

But Lovey Grace never tortured anyone with her compulsion for cleanliness. She simply conducted it with a silent, almost invisible efficiency. Bridget loved her sister's enthusiasm for order and hygiene because she was then free to let the flour and sugar fly. The sisters performed a whisk-and-wipe ballet every time Bridget visited. Most of the family made a point of staying away until the dance was over, except for Mike's son, Brian, who didn't mind the chaos. He would sit at the counter sampling cookie dough or licking a spoon while a cloud of flour floated overhead or a sponge glided under his elbow.

Whatever pies, cakes, cookies, or breads Bridget didn't share with her family, she used to fatten up the local wildlife. This included the squirrels from the old oak tree and the occasional raccoon or possum that wandered around the island. Mike and his wife, Claire, amusingly referred to this event as "the pastry parade."

The only island resident not invited to Bridget's confectionary cavalcade was a nasty old turkey named Trotter that lived and patrolled the old carnival ruins. All the fauna stayed away from that section because of him. No one knew how old the gobbler was and it was a mystery as to how he'd arrived five years earlier. He was either abandoned on the island one night or possibly he walked over by way of the sandbar at the northern end. Either way, Trotter was here to stay.

Mike and Travis watched the squirrels queue up, like fans at a concert, when the sweet smells from Bridget's baked goods drifted into the air. She stood on the porch with a large tray of her goodies and handed out the assortment to the fuzzy-tailed rodents.

Poo, Lovey Grace's golden West Highland terrier and poodle mix, stood guard nearby, making sure the line of small mammals were in order and no little beasts overstepped their bounds. Once the treats were distributed and they received their bounty, the visitors swiftly ran off the porch.

Mike laughed while Travis happily barked and snorted at the parade of creatures transporting big, round cookies, slices of bread, and biscuits back home to the old tree. One fat squirrel, stained with blueberry tart, juggled a scalloped piece of crust like a talented drum major, taking a nibble every beat until it was consumed.

Mike finished his coffee and addressed Travis. "Boy, want to go play with Poo now? He's on his porch looking pretty lonely. You can chase each other around your favorite spot on the beach and jump in the water. You'll need a good splash on a warm morning like this."

The Rottweiler barked in agreement and was off to Lovey Grace's house. The two dogs greeted each other good morning with a sniff and then ran to the beach. They always went to the rowboat bow that projected out of the sand just a few yards from the end of the stone path to Mike's house. Travis discovered the weather-rotted section of the boat when he was a pup. He used to sleep in its shadow on warm days or stand on top to get a better view of his surroundings, but now the Rottweiler was too large to do either. Now the old piece of marine craft was the starting point for the friends to begin their playtime.

"Good morning, Uncle Ned," shouted Mike as he saw him approaching from the beach.

The elderly gentleman waved as he worked his way toward the house. Uncle Ned Baldwin would be eighty-seven soon, but you couldn't discern it from his walk or manner. He was less than six feet tall, slim, and not bent over like most people his age. From a distance he easily passed for a man in his late fifties or early sixties. It was only his weathered (but handsome) face that gave any clue to his real age.

Uncle Ned had spent most of his life on the island except for a few years during and after World War II. He was seventeen when he left home to enlist in 1944 and didn't return until five years later when his father became ill. That next year his father passed away, so Uncle Ned stayed on to help his mother. He worked at the carnival until a fire closed the place for good in 1957. Uncle Ned never married but always had a steady female companion, the current lady friend being Aunt Bridget.

Claire came out of the house already dressed for the day in slacks and a hand-knitted sweater. She'd made it last winter, along with the other knit items for the boutique that she and Mike ran on the mainland. A family store all these years, they now sold her knitwear and other craft items on consignment.

"It's so muggy and hot this morning and it's only March!"

Claire complained. "I hope the summer isn't a killer like last year. I think I better change my sweater to something lighter."

"I know the dogs are already in the water," Mike said, using a magazine as a fan. "You can't predict anything weather-wise these days."

She rubbed his shoulders. "Mike, when you go to town, I need something from the shop. I also want you to pick up some items for tonight's dinner."

He tilted his head back and looked up at her. "I may never go anywhere if you keep doing what you're doing. Let's send the rest of the family to a movie in town with Uncle Ned and have an evening of debauchery by the old oak tree. The squirrels have been dying for a show and it's a full moon."

Smiling, she tapped the back of his head and gently pushed it forward. "Love to, but it's our monthly opera night dinner. Your mother is coming and I hope Uncle Ned and Aunt Bridget will too. They still haven't confirmed."

"Oh, tonight is *Turandot*. The massage made my mind go blank for a moment. I'm the prince of course. Are you the slave girl or the princess?"

Claire laughed. "Your mom hasn't told me who she wants to be, but I have to be the princess. We can't have you kissing your mother so she must be Liu, the slave girl. I'll have to settle all that later when I see her. Brian, Travis and Poo will be guards. Our boy will lip sync and the dogs will give a good howl or two. Better get us a couple of bottles of wine when you're in town because it's going to be a crazy night."

They both laughed and she fell into his lap just as Uncle Ned reached the porch.

"Are you guys cracking up about the pastry parade?" Ned asked. "Bridget really knows how to spoil those little creatures. Good thing we're upwind of the carnival arcade because we don't want Trotter ever getting a whiff of her treats. The last character we need tromping around here is that nasty gobbler."

Mike looked up at his uncle. "I don't think we have to worry about Trotter invading as long as you keep feeding him every time you go over there. We hear you're his best friend."

Uncle Ned laughed. "Well, we senior citizens have to look out for each other. He is nasty, but I like him and he doesn't seem to have any friends these days but me."

Mike shook his head. "I wish Travis and Mom's little Poo felt the same way about him. I've had to patch both of them up on a couple of occasions. Also, Brian wandered over by the arcade and that turkey chased him halfway home. Now he doesn't go near that place unless he's armed with his slingshot."

"Back to opera night," Claire interjected. "Uncle Ned, are you and Bridget coming?"

"Thanks for the invitation, but we're going to a French movie Bridget wants to see in town and tomorrow we're having brunch with two senior citizen friends of ours."

"A French movie and a senior double date. Gee, sounds like fun," Mike teased. "Can't wait until we retire so we can party with the elite."

Uncle Ned laughed at the comment. "Mike, are you going to the mainland today?"

"Yes, I have some errands in town to do."

"Can I ask you to help me first? I need to check things out at the Piping Plover's reserve and then go over to the arcade to clear out a few pieces of debris that fell during the wind last night."

"Sure." Mike got up out of his chair. "Give me a few minutes to shower and get ready but I have to leave no later than two o'clock to get back in time for tonight. I also have to pick up gas for my boat."

"It won't take long. I can give you some I have stored at the ferry pier."

"Thank God for that pier," Mike said. "It's really the only good place on the island to dock and launch from these days. It was a great idea when they built that for the carnival. The old ferry terminal sheds are a good safe place to park our jeeps too."

"Especially with the island shrinking," Uncle Ned added. "I remember when there were several yards of land between the Ferris wheel and the shoreline. Now that section is entirely gone. The water comes right up to the back of the arcade pavilion and sometimes floods the base of the Ferris wheel, which doesn't help the strength of its already crumbling foundation. It's a miracle that we have so much beach left on our side of the island, considering we face the ocean. We've been really lucky that the last several storms have been in our favor. If the waters keep rising as everyone predicts, we may have to pull up stakes in the next few years."

The three of them were quiet for the moment. It was Claire who broke the silence. "Can I help in any way?"

"Give your aunt a little nudge around four so she's ready?" Uncle Ned suggested in a lighter tone. "I don't want to go to the mainland after dark. You know her, the baking and the gossip with Lovey Grace. Time stops when they get going."

"Sure, I'll do my best," she laughed.

Mike headed into the house. "Let me get ready and I'll be right with you."

Once he entered the house, Claire turned to Uncle Ned. "Is the island really shrinking? How long do you think we have? Mike doesn't talk about it at all. You know how he is."

"We're losing coastline everywhere. And look how hot the summers have been. The last two winters were really mild and today is like the middle of July. The storms are getting more frequent and more lethal. Hurricanes are starting so early we're going deeper through the alphabet every year."

"Wasn't the storm last fall Wanda?"

"Good old destructive Wanda. We fortunately fared better than the mainland with that one."

"I guess when we have a Hurricane Zelda it's all over," Claire half-joked.

"It's so warm now I rarely wear my hat and gloves in winter. The only things I really need are my hip waders so I can inspect the reserve. Some of the sections are underwater now. The piping plovers' nests are floating away instead of being tucked into the dunes like they're supposed to be. We're losing eggs and the newborns are drowning."

Claire glanced at him with a worried look as he continued.

"I informed the state about the problem over the past few years. So far, beyond working with one of the officials to help start a rescue hatchery, nothing has been done. It's money or lack of it, as usual. Brian and I started building a few low-staked wooden boxes in hopes that the plovers would use them for their nests. We built ten, but we only have three residents so far. They seem to want to move to the higher ground and out of the reserve altogether. This puts them in tighter spaces where there's no protective fencing and they're in competition with the other birds. It's not good for their safety or the population growth."

"I'm so happy you're letting our boy help you."

Uncle Ned smiled. "He's a good kid. A real Guillory and a Smith too, which is a great combination." He paused a second and looked out at the sea. "Our new coastline may move farther inland sooner than they predict."

Claire hugged him. "Well, if more people thought and took action like you, the future would be better for the piping plovers, not to mention the rest of us."

Uncle Ned thanked her for her confidence but knew that the chance of any big turnaround or change was unlikely. The sea was taking over the island, a little bit every day.

CHAPTER TWO

Ridgewater Shop

By the time Mike arrived at the shop in Ridgewater it was after three o'clock. The temperature was already in the low eighties and the humidity made it feel even hotter. He entered the shop behind the store and turned on the air conditioner. No one had been there in days and the air was stale and warmer than outside. He looked at the thermometer on the wall next to the door and it registered just over ninety degrees. Mike put the bag with two bottles of Claire's favorite wine by the door so he wouldn't forget them. He had picked them up at the little gourmet shop close to where he docked his boat. She loved a particular French label that only this little specialty store carried.

Mike wasn't much of a drinker, but liked an occasional glass of wine, especially with his wife. His mom, on the other hand, preferred Scotch. She always brought it with her when she came over for dinner or to any little event that gave an excuse to celebrate with a toast. One drink was all she needed to get her going; two drinks put her right to sleep.

The shop was part office and part work area for Claire's knitting tools and yarns. She'd set up a Martha Stewart-style workbench with a selection of ribbons, labels, and wrappings next to her supplies. Above her worktable were tear sheets from magazines showing the latest knitwear and patterns. There was also a board of fabric and yarn swatches that represented a simple trend or style guide for the spring and summer selling season.

Mike sat at the desk opposite her workspace and shuffled through any invoices and bills, putting them in their proper pigeonholes. He leaned back in his chair, took out his cell, dialed, and gazed at the pictures of his family hanging on the wall above his desk.

Most of the photos, turned sepia with age, went back to the days of the carnival. The oldest picture, dated before the amusement park was built, was of the first relatives that lived on the island. William Guillory's family: his wife, Emily, and sons, Albert and Thomas, were seated at a picnic table. In the background was the house, now occupied by his mother, new and freshly painted. He looked at the picture for a moment. He knew so little about these ancestors except for their names.

The call went to voice mail and Mike left a message. He redialed and called his wife.

"Hi Claire."

"Mike?"

"Is Uncle Ned around? I just left him a message. That generation, they never leave their cell phones on. It's like they're worried the battery will run out in two minutes or it will blow up in their pocket."

"Your mother is the same way. She has a coronary if her phone rings, so when it does, it's a real shock," Claire said. "She's always changing the ringtone and then forgets what she changed it to. When it does ring again, she has no idea where the sound is coming from. I was with her when we were shopping and church bells were going off. She was frantic, wondering where the bells were coming from until I pointed to her purse. She laughed, said she hated that ringtone and changed it to something else she wouldn't remember. Gotta love her."

Mike laughed to himself as he adjusted his chair and repeated his first question. "Is Uncle Ned there?"

"He's not, but I'm on my way to your mom's in a few minutes.

I can surely give him a message or at least relay one to Aunt Bridget. Better yet, let me call your mother's landline before I leave. She always answers that."

"Can you tell him that they might want to leave earlier? The water is a little choppy, it looks like rain and the sea is a weird shade of green. There's some sort of algae I haven't seen before. Try to talk them into staying for dinner and our opera night instead of going to town. I'm leaving for the market soon and should be back before five. Anything else we need while I'm here?"

"Yes, get that great pancake mix we like and some frozen blueberries. Also don't forget to bring me the yarn labeled 'Number 7440 China Moonlight'. It's in a plastic bag and it's a soft cream color with red and gold flecks. I think I put it on the left side of my table."

"Got it. Anything else?"

"Hurry up home, honey. It does look like bad weather is on its way. The sky has that green tinge you were talking about and looks like it usually does just before a summer storm. This is the first time I've put the air conditioner on in March. The electric bill will be sky-high this month if this continues. I can feel the dampness in my old bones."

Mike laughed at the comment. "I can't wait to get back to my old lady and her sexy ancient bones."

"Hurry up, wise guy. I'm off to your mother's. Brian has been there for over two hours making hats and you know Bridget is stuffing him with cookies or pie. We won't be able to get him to eat dinner and he'll also be on one of his sugar highs."

"We'll be lucky if we get him to bed by midnight. Don't forget to give Uncle Ned my message and push them to stay for dinner. Bye, love you."

He put his phone in his pocket and gathered up the bag of yarn and the wine. He stood at the door and looked back at the picture of his great-grandfather William, and his family. Mike thought again about the fact that his father never talked about these family members he knew only from pictures.

CHAPTER THREE

The First Guillorys

The island, off the New England coast, was almost a mile from the mainland and was shaped like a slice of pie, the southern end being the widest part. The northern tip came much closer to the coast and ended in a very narrow strip of sand that zigzagged for more than three quarters of a mile into coastal marshland. The island was relatively flat except for a hilly mound populated by scrub trees, small pines, and a large oak that looked like it had been there forever.

William Guillory built a small five-room house and moved his family into it the summer of 1908. The Victorian gingerbread structure had wooden shingles that turned a pretty shade of gray after the first year. The house had a small porch facing the sea and William had built an arched trellis and a white picket fence enclosing the garden Emily tended to with love daily. Near the dunes was a picnic table with long benches. A stone path led from the porch to the sandy beach and ended with another arched trellis. Hanging from its center was a small, delicately carved wooden mermaid swimming in the breeze.

*　*　*

On a warm afternoon in late summer, Emily prepared food for her family. "Lunch is ready. Let's christen our new table with a really special meal. But hurry up before the chicken gets cold."

William and Albert moved briskly from the back of the house where they were working, while Thomas ran to the table from the beach.

"This looks like a rich man's meal," William said. "All we need is a butler and maid serving."

"We already have them. They're both called Emily," she laughed.

"I want a chicken breast and a big biscuit," Albert said.

"I want a drumstick and the biggest biscuit," shouted Thomas.

"Well boys, you can have both and you're also going to love the corn on the cob I just prepared on our new stone grill. I also cooked the chicken on it so that's going to be extra delicious too."

"This is just like the big summer picnics in town, only better because we have all the food to ourselves. What a perfect time for a family photo," William said as he headed to the house for his camera.

"Sit Willie!" said Emily. "You too boys. There will be lots of time for pictures after we eat. The food won't stay hot forever."

William kissed his wife. "Yes, dear!" he acquiesced as he sat at the table.

"Yes, dear," the boys imitated.

Emily gave them all a look and smiled. "Let's eat!"

After the lunch William retrieved his box camera from the little house and took the picture. "Everyone say, Chicken."

"Chicken."

He clicked the shutter.

Thomas helped his mother with the dishes and when they were done, he started out toward the northern part of the island.

"Wait for your brother," Emily said. "I don't want you out on the sandbar alone."

Albert answered, "I need to help Dad with the nets."

"Albert has to stay so we can complete our repairs before sunset," William said. "Thomas will be fine on his own."

Emily turned to Thomas. "You can go but don't stay there too long. It's beautiful now but a storm is supposed to come our way around dinnertime. If it starts to rain get home right away." She gave one more warning. "Please don't go too far out on the sandbar. I don't want you caught again when that crazy tide comes in."

"Don't worry, I'll bring home lots of big clams for dinner to go with more of that good corn," he yelled back as he ran up the beach.

Emily worried about her youngest son even though he was ten years old. Thomas was much less mature than Albert, two years his senior. The boy loved the ocean and also digging for clams. The sandbar was the best place on the island to do that. The center section yielded the most clams, but it was also the easiest place to get stuck when the tide came in. When Thomas was in the water he was fearless and this made her nervous. Even his parents were caught unaware a few times during clamming expeditions there.

Once out on the bar, Thomas found a horseshoe crab lying on its back and flipped it over so it was free to go on its way. Around four, after a good swim, he took a nap next to the edge of the dune grass. When he woke it was raining and windy but the tide was not in yet. He realized that he hadn't dug for the clams he'd promised to bring home.

Thomas ran out as far as he dared and started to dig. He worked frantically and tried to finish his clamming as the tide came in at an increasing pace. The boy was at the highest point in the center of the three-quarter-mile strip. As the rain became heavier, the wind picked up speed. Before Thomas knew it, he was stranded amid choppy water.

He tried to think of an easy way back and not lose all the clams he had worked so hard for in the process. He walked quickly, keeping to where the water was no more than waist-deep. The storm caused the tides to be higher than usual and soon the water was over his head. Thomas tried to swim with one arm and secure the clam bucket with his other.

But the clams were lost and he struggled to make it to shore. He shouted for help, hoping someone might have been looking for him by this time. Nobody was there to hear his calls. But something in the water did. What Thomas thought were two very large fish were gliding through the rough waters in his direction.

He heard a sound in the water that reminded him of a whale's song, only softer. Thomas kept going under as the waves became stronger with the ever-increasing wind and rain. The last time underwater, he saw a boy not much older than himself, and then a woman. She swam to his sinking body, grabbed him around the waist and kissed his lips as they both descended deeper, accompanied by her young companion.

The storm was at full force when William and Emily found themselves on the edge of the sandbar. Soaking wet, they called Thomas' name over and over. Emily discovered his shirt and shoes next to the rocks near the dunes, while his father found the boy's clam bucket floating near the shore. He persuaded Emily, who was crying and in hysterics, to return home to be with Albert.

William searched until it was too dark and dangerous to look any further. At home, while the storm raged, Emily sat frozen and silent with the boy's wet shirt held tightly in her hands.

In the morning, when it was calm, William, with the help of the police and friends, combed the waters around the island and along the coast for any sign of his son. They searched all day, to no avail.

The family was grief-stricken, especially Emily. For the next few months she barely spoke. They held a service for Thomas after two weeks, against her wishes, in Ridgewater. She refused to believe the boy was dead. She spent her time after that working in her garden or sitting at the picnic table looking out to sea, waiting for her son to return.

* * *

William was getting ready to go to town for work when he noticed Emily sitting at the picnic table gazing out at the water. He sat down next to her and put his arm around her shoulders.

"I'm leaving for town now and will be back before dusk. Albert is coming with me, unless you need him here." He waited for a response. "Is there anything you want from town or anyone you want me to give a message to?"

She said nothing and continued to stare.

He paused for a moment. "I miss him too. I loved him too. Please, let me help. Come to town with us and maybe you could visit your friend, Becca. You haven't seen her in a long time."

Emily looked down and gently squeezed his hand. "Willie, I'm okay. I just want to sit here for a while and do some more work in my garden. Go to town and take Albert with you. I'll have dinner ready when you get back."

She accompanied William and Albert to their boat on the other side of the island, then walked back to the house. She knelt down and began weeding amid the fall flowers that were still in bloom.

Late in the afternoon, Emily heard something coming from the direction of the water and looked up. Someone was calling to her. She stood up, walked to the picnic table and squinted trying to make out the shapes she saw swimming in the ocean.

Emily walked to the edge of the water and saw what appeared to be children a few yards out. She knew this couldn't be. But there were indeed young people playing in the water — children like none she had ever seen before. These children had heads and arms like humans but instead of wet hair they had shell-like helmets with clear tentacles that framed their faces and tapered down their backs. The helmets were translucent in the late afternoon light revealing a shadow of a skull underneath.

She counted three of them swimming and frolicking in the water. They looked right at her and then dove under the surface revealing large fish-like tails that cut through the water with the precision of sharp knives. The beings called out to her in words and phrases she didn't understand. The smallest one came the closest and instantly she knew it was her Thomas. He had beautiful crystal blue eyes that smiled at you, and so did this creature.

She waded into the water up to her waist without regard for the cold or her safety. Thomas swam around her then stopped, facing his mother. He hovered in the water in a way that made him seem suspended in the waves.

Emily smiled, trying not to cry as she offered this being her open arms.

She gently whispered, "Thomas? My Thomas, my beautiful boy?"

The child smiled and slowly swam closer to her embrace when suddenly a loud voice boomed from the shore.

"Emily!" yelled William.

"Momma!" cried out Albert.

In a flash, the being that was almost in her arms was gone and so were his companions. William ran into the water and grabbed his wife, frozen in position with her arms still raised in a welcoming posture. He carried her to the shore and sat her down at the picnic table.

"Albert, get a blanket from the house," his father instructed.

The boy ran off, trying not to cry.

Emily's body was cold and wet, but a warm smile lit her face.

William wrapped his arms around her. "Emily, what were you trying to do? Why were you in the water?"

Shivering, oblivious to her condition, she smiled. "My Thomas came back to me. He lives in the sea now. The storm took him away but the sea gave him back to us."

"Nothing was there. There was no one there. It was just you in the water."

"No, it was Thomas. I was about to hug him. He smiled at me with his beautiful eyes. He lives in the sea."

"It was just your imagination. The sea does have him but he is gone forever."

He lifted her up and carried her toward the house. Albert met them half way and covered his mother with the blanket as she lay in William's arms.

She smiled happily. "Thomas is back, he lives in the sea and can visit us every day." She looked at Albert. "You can play with your brother again and swim when it gets warmer. Wouldn't you like that Albert? To play with Thomas again?"

"Yes," Albert replied, as the boy held back his tears.

*   *   *

William decided they should move back to the mainland until Emily was herself again. The doctor told him his wife had lost her sense of reality due to grief. In time, with care and love, she might get better.

She needed something to do if the healing was to happen, so William cleared an area in the backyard of their rental apartment in Ridgewater. He thought her love of gardening might be therapeutic, and he was right. After a few months she stopped talking about Thomas and the sea. Emily became a wife and mother again and in the spring her new garden bloomed.

For the next year, only William and Albert visited the island. In the spring and summer they fished and together they kept up the house and Emily's garden, hoping that maybe one day, she could return.

William always looked for any signs of Thomas that he could find. He never told Emily that he also hoped to see their poor lost son. William knew that what his wife said she had seen was impossible, but part of him wanted it, no matter how fantastic it sounded, to be true.

One afternoon that fall, he was enjoying a sunset walk along the beach, knowing this was going to be his last night there for a quite a while. He had a work project in Ridgewater that was going to prevent him from getting back for several weeks. As he worked his way up the beach to the house, he saw someone on his porch. He was too far away to tell who it was.

"Hey, what are you doing?" he yelled.

He ran toward the house but the figure quickly moved off the porch and down the path to the beach. Before he could get a closer look, the stranger was in the water and disappeared under the surface. The same unusual track marks that he had seen once before, while walking on the beach, marked their way up from the surf to his porch.

William followed them. They led into the house. He checked to see if anything was broken or stolen. Everything was there except one item — a canvas stuffed dog Emily had made for Thomas when he was a baby. They had decided to leave the boy's room intact and the toy that lived at the head of his bed was gone.

That night, he walked along the beach again, looking out to sea and wondering if what his wife had said she'd experienced was real. Who was in the house and why did they take something with only sentimental value, like a simple stuffed toy dog? William never mentioned anything about the stranger or the loss of the toy. He was afraid to bring the subject up, fearing Emily would relapse.

CHAPTER FOUR

January

When it became available, William took over the lease of the space below their apartment in Ridgewater. He opened a store that sold decorative carvings and kitchen items made of wood, like cutting boards and spoons, which he displayed in the two front windows. In the back room behind the store, he set up his woodworking shop.

Emily kept busy with her new garden in the backyard and put flowerboxes in every window. She also managed the accounts for her husband. By the summer of 1918, the Guillory family's life seemed to have gone back to the way it was before the tragedy.

While Emily repotted a plant, William brought her a cup of tea. "The flowers look really big and beautiful this year. Is it this warm June weather or your daily care?"

She smiled and looked up at him. "Both, I hope. I'm trying to get as much done now because with the baby coming, I won't be able to bend like this for much longer."

William was dumbfounded by her casual statement and could utter only one word. "Baby?"

Emily walked toward him. "Yes, Willie. According to the doctor, a new baby is arriving around the first of the year. I feel it's going to be a girl this time."

"A baby? A girl?" He was still in shock but thrilled. Shaking, he handed his wife the tea, almost dropping it.

*   *   *

That Christmas was one of the best they had celebrated in years. William threw a party on the eve of the holiday for his family and close friends.

Albert, now fifteen, invited a friend named Jane Kennedy to the fete. Being a year older than him, she treated Albert like a little brother, even though she knew he had a crush on her. Her mother, Emily's friend, Becca, was also there. They had both helped William during the early stages of Emily's illness and were now the family's closest friends. Becca, a widow, brought hot meals over and helped take care of Albert when Emily was sick. He also ate dinner at the Kennedys' many times when the Guillorys first moved to town, like part of their family.

"Let's have a Christmas toast." William stood in front of their holiday tree. "To my dearest friends, who have helped us through this hard year, thank you. To my wife and son and also to my new child that is on its way very, very soon."

He looked at Emily. She smiled and touched her prominent stomach.

"Lastly, to the memory of our son, Thomas, who left us too soon."

There was a second of silence. William glanced at Emily who was trying her best to smile and not cry. They all toasted.

The apartment was small, with an open-style kitchen partitioned off from the living room by a counter and was heated by a wood stove. Two tables on the other side of the room by the big front windows faced the street. One was their dining table laid out with the Christmas dinner and the other was the table Becca had loaned them, which held the desserts.

Noah Wilson, an old merchant marine friend of William's, approached Emily, who was sitting in a rocker near the stove. He was with his wife, Ann.

Mrs. Wilson took her hand. "Thank you so much for inviting

us. This is something for the new baby I started the day I heard the good news."

Ann handed her a wrapped package with a fabric and lace ribbon around it. Emily thanked them and removed the bow, carefully rolling the ribbon up and placing it at her side. She treated the paisley printed wrapping paper with the same care.

"Oh, Mrs. Wilson, you knitted a little navy blue sweater and hat. It's so sweet and a perfect color for a boy or girl. Thank you both."

Emily received several gifts that Christmas eve for the baby and something special for herself. William gave her a brooch made of gold with enameled morning glories, her favorite flower. These same flowers covered the trellis gate to her garden on the island. Every summer morning she was greeted with a mix of color: blue, hot pink, and the occasional white in a garland over her head that was entwined in the lattice framework of the entrance.

"I adore it, Willie."

"There's also a chain so you can wear it as a necklace too," he said, pointing to the tissue in the box.

Emily found the links of gold and attached them to the pin. She handed the necklace to her husband who draped it around her throat, then fastened the clasp.

William bent over, kissed his wife and whispered, "Merry Christmas."

She closed her eyes and smiled.

The next morning was quiet as Emily made coffee, prepared eggs and bacon, and heated up some maple scones leftover from the party. After breakfast, the Guillorys walked to Christmas services through the light snow left the night before. When the church service was over, Emily and William strolled home along the same route and let Albert go to Jane's house.

Emily squeezed her husband's arm. "I want to have the baby on the island."

William's stride slowed almost to a stop. "Go back to the island? It's too cold and I've already closed the house for the winter."

"It's beautiful today and the baby can be born in our real home. Willie, can't we fix it up and stay the rest of the winter?"

"The baby is due any day and the doctor is here. What if there's a problem? I'm not sure it would be the best idea."

"Can we think about it more? I miss our house and the baby would be the first Guillory born on our island. We lost Thomas there and this baby would bring new life to the place."

Emily hadn't mentioned Thomas since she was ill. Was it William's mention of the boy in his toast the night before that brought this on? He wished her to be happy and wanted to go back to the island full-time too. But William felt Emily was safe in Ridgewater with their friends to watch over her and Albert when he was working.

"I think it's better to stay in town with the baby coming so soon."

"Yes, but the baby could arrive in another two or three weeks. The doctor wasn't that sure. They are on their own time, as he put it." She smiled. "Let's at least think about moving back."

William nodded, but concern was on his face and in his heart.

"I'll go to the island in the morning." He stopped a second, kissed her cheek, and they continued their walk home.

William did everything he could to stall Emily until after New Years with explanations from the stove being broken to the generator not working. Luckily, there was a two-day storm, which William said had broken a window and let squirrels into the house. These excuses worked until January 5, when Emily went into labor that lasted almost two days.

On the morning of January 7, a baby girl came into the world. The child weighed less than five pounds, and both Emily and the baby were frail after the delivery. Mother and daughter spent a week in Saint Peter's Hospital in the next town. William visited every day, forgetting about the shop or work. Jane helped Albert run the store and keep his mind off of his mother. Becca accompanied William to the hospital on most of his trips. She was always ready with either a hot meal or a kind word.

They named the baby January. William took dozens of photos of the little girl in the navy blue sweater set Ann Wilson had given them on Christmas Eve. Becca added a cream lace collar to the sweater and matching ribbons to the hat to make the outfit a little more feminine.

Emily rocked the baby in her arms and sang to her every evening. The child was never out of her sight. Becca offered to take care of the little girl on occasion to give the Guillorys an opportunity to go to dinner or a movie, but Emily always refused.

One day, William stopped by Becca's to talk. "I think my poor Emily is sick again. Ever since she returned home from the hospital, she hasn't been the same. She was so good at Christmas. I thought she was ready to go back to the island, but now I don't know anymore."

Becca held his hand in hers. "Losing a child is hard and almost losing another one is beyond understanding. It took me two years before I could move on after my husband died. My daughter kept me going because she needed me and that responsibility got me through it. Emily is so lucky to have you and Albert. Once she sees that January will be fine, Emily will come around and be herself again. Stay by her side, love her, and things will be better by the spring. I promise you."

"I think you're right. Everything will be better in the spring."

She squeezed his hand. "Have some coffee and a piece of my carrot cake. It can make anything better."

*   *   *

Becca was right. By Easter, Emily was much better. January was growing and getting fatter and the family finally moved back to Plover's Island.

The spring was warm, like the year before, and Emily's garden bloomed so richly that she had to put up a scarecrow in the center wearing one of her old dresses and a straw hat. This funny lady made everyone laugh but it kept the squirrels and birds from shopping for their dinner in her vegetable and berry patches.

William and Albert were in town most days, busy with work and school, but Becca visited whenever she could. With Emily back to her old self again, William's worries were forgotten.

Mother and child spent most of the days, especially the sunny ones, outside. Emily worked in the garden every morning with the baby tied to her back, Native American style. She sang while she worked in the garden and January accompanied her.

In the afternoons Emily read stories to the baby on the porch or at the picnic table. January was almost five months old, but the little girl responded like a baby much older. She laughed and made sounds that everyone was sure were words. And her eyes were like Thomas' — crystal blue as the sea on a sunny day. They seemed to smile when you looked into them.

One warm afternoon with only the sound of the breeze and the surf, Emily, in her favorite yellow dress, sat at the picnic table finishing the last chapter of *The Secret Garden*, the tale of Mary Lennox. She made sure the sheer netting over January's bassinet was tucked in and secure from any flies or insects.

The baby was still half awake so Emily sang quietly to her. Suddenly, the phone rang from the house. Emily left January on the picnic table and rushed inside to answer it.

It was Becca on the other end. "Hi, I can't talk long. I left January outside," Emily said while looking out the window. "Can I call you later?"

Becca continued to talk and Emily glanced away from the window for a second. When she looked out again, she dropped the phone.

All that could be heard as she ran out of the house and down porch steps was Becca's voice repeating, "Emily ... Emily are you there?"

When Emily reached the table, she saw that the netting was pulled aside and the cradle was empty. She looked toward the beach and saw Thomas, holding January and smiling at his mother with his big sea blue eyes.

"Thomas, give me the baby. Give me your sister. Please give me your sister."

She is coming with me. It is beautiful. She will be happy. You can come too and be with us. It is so beautiful.

Her son from the sea, her Thomas, said this to his mother, but his lips never moved. Emily felt her son's words, deep in her mind and in her heart.

His companions called Thomas from the water in sounds she didn't understand. Emily walked toward him as he maneuvered his long, limbless lower body smoothly to the water's edge. Thomas held the baby close to his chest as his scale-covered arms gleamed in the sunlight.

You can come too, he repeated. *It is so beautiful and we will all be together.*

Before she knew it, they were both waist-deep in the water. Emily cried and pleaded with her arms reaching for the baby.

But Thomas' voice and the words he transmitted to her mind were like a chant, a song that made her forget where she was. *Come with me. Come with us. It is so beautiful.*

They all disappeared beneath the surf as the sun sparkled on the surface. The only sound besides the water and the light wind was Becca's voice on the other end of the phone receiver.

"Emily! Emily! Please pick up the phone. Please!"

* * *

When William returned to the island, he brought Becca with him. There wasn't any time to pick up Albert at school. Becca left a note for Jane to meet him when he came home and to wait for her call.

When William and Becca arrived at the house, everything was as it was a few hours earlier. The front door was open and the phone receiver was dangling motionless. The bassinet William had made was still on the picnic table with the netting blowing lightly in the breeze. There were no signs of Emily or the baby except for footprints in the sand that led to the water's edge. There were also the impressions of the strange tracks he had seen before.

William looked at Becca and said nothing. His face told her that his worst fears had been realized. Emily had walked into the sea and taken the baby with her. He collapsed to his knees and stared out at the water. Becca stood at his side, gently touched his shoulder, and stared out with him.

"Becca, I tried. I did everything I could. I really did."

Becca called the police and for the next few days they searched the waters around the island for any trace of Emily and the baby. The papers in Ridgewater and the surrounding towns posted photos and descriptions of Emily and January. William even went on the radio to tell his story. The police ruled the deaths accidental drowning. But although William felt he knew what had really happened, he tried not to believe it.

They finally held a service for Emily and January on the waters in front of their home four weeks later. William and Albert borrowed a large fishing boat from Noah Wilson. They sailed far enough out to hold the funeral but still close enough to see their island and house.

William brought the priest from the stone church they attended in Ridgewater, who prayed over the small wooden boxes William made. He had carved their names into the lids. In each box were letters, prayers, and poems composed by friends and family. After the service, they slipped the caskets into the sea.

It wasn't common to have a service at sea for someone who

wasn't a fisherman or sailor, but it wasn't a common death, if it was a death at all. They disappeared, never to be seen again. William's only thought was that Emily and the baby were with Thomas, keeping him company beneath the sea.

William and Albert didn't go back to the island house until the boy graduated from high school the next year. William started a family cemetery on the island north of the old oak tree. He carved three beautiful wooden crosses with Emily's, January's, and Thomas' names and dates on them. William buried the morning glory pin he had given to his wife that Christmas and wrapped it in her favorite scarf. He put it in a little box that he had carved and inlayed with mother of pearl. For the baby, he put the doll he'd made for her in a music box. For Thomas, he took the boy's favorite book, *The Wonderful Wizard of Oz*, and wrapped it in the shirt Emily and William found the day he left them. He put the items in Thomas' tin school lunch box, decorated with pictures of cowboys and Indians.

CHAPTER FIVE

Coney Island

Over the next few years, William Guillory split most of his time between the island and the store in Ridgewater. Albert worked alongside his father full-time. He thought of doing the things other men his age did, like dating, going to parties, and just being young, but these were options he never asked for or took. His father kept so busy, he didn't notice what his son was missing. When William was Albert's age, all he did was practice his profession until he, by chance, met and fell in love with Emily.

One of William's new passions became carousel horses and the other mythical beasts that danced around the popular amusement. He saw his first merry-go-round when he sold some furniture to a client who lived near Coney Island Park in New York. William brought the items by boat and met the customer's caretaker at the dock near the park. They transported the canvas-wrapped merchandise to a waiting open truck, and when everything was loaded, William looked around in amazement at all the lights, the boardwalk, and the people.

"Pretty great, our Coney Island Park," the caretaker said in a proud, Italian accent. "It's late. You should stay the night after we deliver Mr. Thomason's furniture to the house. It's only a thirty-minute ride and we can be back by seven o'clock. I know a good, cheap place you can get a room and your boat will be safe where it's docked for the night."

"Thank you for the offer." William looked around again. "Let me decide when we get back."

When they arrived at Thomason's house, there were two beautifully carved merry-go-round horses mounted in the front yard. William was amazed to see the real thing for the first time. He had seen pictures in magazines and books but never an actual carousel horse.

On the ride back, he expressed to the caretaker how amazing the figures were. "I'm a carver but I've never seen or made anything like those beautiful horses. Where did Mr. Thomason get them?"

"Oh, he owns the factory where they make those horses. It's not far from here. I would take you there but it closed already. Mr. Thomason built most of the merry-go-rounds and decorations for the park. If you want to see more of the factory's work, you need to go to the park. They have horses, pigs, lions, tigers, and all manner of wonderful beasts. Everything is painted fancy, trimmed all around with glass jewels and mirrors. They have at least a half a dozen of the carousels on Surf Avenue and the Bowery alone. I'll drop you there after we get you a room at Clark's."

When William arrived at the park, he walked along the boardwalk, taking in all the great amusements. The entire strip was lined with penny arcades, food stands, bars, fortunetellers, sideshows, and thrill rides. Everything was lit up and decorated with exotic statues. Paintings adorned the buildings. Signs with animals, magical creatures, nude ladies, and clown faces dominated the front of all the establishments. And everything was trimmed in white lights.

William treated himself to a couple of hotdogs and a root beer. He was looking for the carousels when a sideshow in a small theater next to a penny arcade caught his eye.

The sign exclaimed: Professor Misto's Cabinet Of Curiosities. He paid a nickel to see a small assortment of wonders including the Three-Legged Chicken, the Eye of Medusa, and the main attraction, the Madagascar Mermaid. He had heard of places like this but had never been to one. After a long day of work, he needed some fun and distraction.

The chicken really did have three legs. William wasn't too surprised, having actually seen a three-legged lamb at a local farm when he was twelve. The difference was, the lamb was still alive and not stuffed in a dancing pose, wearing a top hat, like the poor dusty dead fowl.

The Eye of Medusa was another story. It turned out to be a large piece of theatrical jewelry with a big, red glass stone surrounded by a ring of plaster snakes. This mystical item was mounted on grimy, faded red velvet, and set in a large wooden box painted with scrolls, leaves, and snakes in a Greco-Roman style.

To see the main attraction, the Madagascar Mermaid, William had to go though a set of black draperies into a dark room with wooden theater seats. The back wall had another black curtain in front of a small, raised stage. When enough people were seated, a record played sounds of the ocean, accompanied by an eerie flute mixed with the crackle of the many scratches on the much-played vinyl disk.

From behind the curtain came the deep voice William thought must be Professor Misto himself. "From the deepest depths of the Indian Ocean, from the undersea kingdom of Atlantis, we bring, for the first time at Coney Island or anywhere else in the world, the beautiful Madagascar Mermaid. Don't look into her eyes too long or listen to her hypnotic song, because you will be caught in her powerful and deadly spell. Ladies and gentleman, I give you the Madagascar Mermaid!"

The ocean sounds and flute music became much louder as an old velvet drapery slowly parted to reveal a dimly lit, large glass tank filled with what looked like seaweed. They actually were thin strips of green fabric waving in a breeze from an unseen fan.

From behind the fabric sea foliage emerged a woman with a mermaid's tail, waving her arms, making believe she was treading to keep herself afloat in the non-existent water. Long red hair draped over her breasts like fake seaweed and her fish-like tail was shiny fabric with large spangled sequins sewn all over it.

William became uncomfortable at the site of this pretty girl trying to make a living as a fish. Was she a former chorus girl down on her luck? The owner's daughter? Or maybe Mrs. Professor Misto? The sounds of a woman wailing like a ghost, supposedly the mermaid's siren song, replaced the music. Then, before William could really focus on this attraction anymore, the curtain suddenly closed. Reactions from the small crowd ranged from quiet clapping and laughter to grumbles and a few muffled expletives.

This performance, as comic and theatrically unpolished as it was, created flashbacks in William's mind about what his wife had said about their son, Thomas. He remembered the imprints in the sand around his house and the ones mixed with his wife's footprints the day she and their baby daughter disappeared forever. William closed his eyes and struggled to put these thoughts out of his head.

The next announcement over the loud speaker came in a distinctly New York accent. "Thanks for comin' folks, the exit is in the rear. Watch your step goin' out and have a good evening."

William left the little sideshow and was stopped by a short, middle-aged man wearing a patterned vest in bright carnival colors and a derby hat with what looked like food stains on the brim.

The man grabbed his arm and pulled him close. "Hey Fella, did you like the show? That mermaid gal was mighty pretty and she is one of a kind. If you want, I can get you an introduction. She gets lonely in that tank and I bet she'd go for a good-looking guy like you."

William, still off-center from the performance, got his bearings and realized what this man was offering. "No thanks, I'm fine. Enjoyed the show, but I need to go."

"Ah fella, don't miss this opportunity. She said she noticed you in the audience and wants to meet you. This could be your lucky night and for only five bucks. Trust me, that lady is so sizzlin' she can turn the water in that tank into steam if she gets worked up enough."

"Thanks again, but I really have to be on my way. Good night and give Miss Madagascar my regards." William exited the theater while the stained derby man kept up his pitch.

Back on the boardwalk, he bought another glass of nickel root beer and wished it could have been something stronger after the show and that man.

He headed off to find the carousels. A man at one of the concession stands gave him directions to the grandest carousel on the boardwalk. It glowed with thousands of little lights and rotated clockwise to the sounds of an organ. The top canopy was trimmed in gold filigree and oval mirrors that flashed and bounced the lights as the structure rotated. The jewel-and-gold leaf-encrusted horses, fanciful farm animals, and mythical beasts like dragons, griffins, and unicorns, were four deep. Some pranced up and down to the music; others posed in majestic stances. Positioned among these colorful menageries were the beautiful swan chariots decorated with gilded scrolls and more glass jewels. The front of the chariots were the arched necks and heads of the crowned birds. Each was made to hold at least two people and seated in them were either lovers or parents with small children.

William bought several tickets that night and took ride after ride on the great carousels. He examined every detail of each amazing merry-go-round. He sketched and made notes of everything on scraps of paper or napkins he had in his pockets. He knew, at that moment, that this was going to be his new obsession. He bought a few miniatures of the creatures at the gift stands around the amusement park and packed them safely into his tool bag when he returned to his rooming house that night.

As soon as he was back home, William told Albert about the wonderful time he had had. The magic of it all and his father's enthusiasm also sparked the young man's interest. Albert started carving small toy versions of the carousel animals along with his father. Then they both soon graduated to the full-sized creatures. Behind the house they built a small pavilion about the size and look of a standard gazebo to house their first carousel. They trimmed it with spirals and scrolls similar to the gingerbread decorations on the little house and painted them white.

It only had three figures at first: a white horse with wings, decorated like a medieval jousting charger, an auburn-brown horse tricked out like the noble steed of an Indian chief, and a fanciful dragon painted bright green and decorated with metallic gold scales. The creature was balanced under its chest by a gold tapering tail that curled up coming to a devil's triangular point. The mechanics were all handmade and manually activated. William, being the craftsman he was, created a magical little amusement, with the help of Albert, that not only rotated but with each turn enabled the three creatures to dance up and down. They trimmed the gazebo with white lights on the roof and the four wooden posts that supported the circular structure. It also had door panels that were secured in place to protect it from the elements and curious wildlife.

William once caught the squirrels sitting on the carved wooden figures early one morning waiting to take a ride. He woke Albert so he could see this comical sight.

"Wake up and be very quiet. I have something very funny to show you," he laughed as he led his son to the window that faced out toward the gazebo.

Albert smiled and then had to put his hands over his mouth so that he wouldn't startle the silly rodent carousel riders. The squirrels sat on the ride for more than an hour. Sometimes they changed beasts and held on to the poles as if they were ready to take the ride around the amusement and catch the brass ring.

They started this first carousel in 1922 and each year it grew as William and Albert added another horse, a giraffe, a fat whimsical pig, and then a noble lion with a king's crown and a red cape trimmed in gold.

William was putting the finishing touches on a beautiful seahorse when he thought he saw something. It was late afternoon as he collected some shells to decorate his new creation. He heard his name being called from the water.

"Willie! Willie!"

The voice sounded familiar, but strange.

He looked up and for a moment he thought he saw a dark shape in the surf. The figure waved and called out his name again.

"Willie! Willie!"

He froze as he heard the voice and his name. The only person that ever called him Willie was Emily. He wasn't sure if it was the late afternoon light playing tricks with his eyes. He rubbed them and looked out to sea. But whatever he thought he saw and heard was gone. It was quiet except for the sound of the metal chimes hanging on his porch.

The image of the woman in the tank at the curiosity show on Coney Island flashed in his mind. He looked out at the water one more time, then finished collecting the shells.

William walked to his little shed in back of the house and that night, after he completed his work, sat on his steps quietly for hours, looking out to the sea as the sun set. He watched the weathered, wooden mermaid he had made a few years earlier to decorate the arched trellis that led to the beach. The carved figure swam softly back and forth as the breeze animated it.

He heard his name called again, carried on the early evening breeze.

"Willie. Willie."

He looked up and saw a figure standing on the beach. It was at the edge of the surf wearing the pale yellow dress Emily wore the day she disappeared. The figure was too far away to make out her features in the dusk's golden light. He stood up and walked toward her.

"Emily, is that you? Are you really here?"

On the edge of the dunes he could see her better. The pale dress clung to her body, revealing the contours of her breasts and stomach. Below the waist, the dress blew in the soft breeze but didn't define the rest of her figure. What William thought were strands of hair draping down around her face were translucent, slender tentacles caressing her neck like the tails of slowly moving serpents. The she-creature he recognized as Emily smiled as her eyes glowed.

"Emily is that you? Where have you been? Are you real or am I dreaming?" He knelt down into the sand too frozen in disbelief to move any closer to her.

Willie my love, I am real and your Emily but I am also something new. Our babies are with me in the sea and we are so happy. It is so beautiful there. You will see it one day with us.

"Emily, I don't understand what you are or what you say … but can I come with you now and see our children? I miss them so much."

No not now, my love. You need to stay here and be with Albert. Someday we will all be together, but not now.

She turned and slid like a serpent into the water. The last thing William saw before she disappeared was a large, gleaming, fish-like tail protruding beneath the hem of her dress.

He ran into the water only to blackout. When he came to, William found himself sitting in his chair on the porch. It was completely dark except for the moonlight and the stars. Was he dreaming? Had he really talked to his wife? Was Emily like the girl in the tank? Only real and not a carny actor's theatrical costume? He rubbed his eyes and shook his head.

"I miss them all so much," William said and began to cry. He stopped himself and got up.

When he reached the doorway of his bungalow he realized he was soaking wet from the knees down. He turned and looked out to the sea.

CHAPTER SIX

Opera Night

By the time Mike returned home from the mainland, Uncle Ned and Bridget had already left. He was hoping to see them on his way back. Mike was surprised they didn't turn around when they saw the green algae, or whatever it was, increasing in the waters around the island.

Mike listened to the weather forecast on the boat radio. The announcer reported on the strange weather but didn't seem to have a clue as to what it was. Mike had scooped some seawater into a small jar and held it up to the light. The water was a bright green.

Mike capped the sample and decided to take a look at it under Brian's microscope when he got home. It was a toy, but it worked well for basic examinations. Whatever this was, the microscope should give him some idea. He wished Uncle Ned were home so that he could show the sample to him. If anyone would have an idea what it was, it would be him.

Mike sat down on the porch. He could hear all the air conditioners on in the house but he didn't want to go inside yet. The trip from the mainland was warm and breezeless, so he wanted to cool down in his favorite chair before going inside and hitting the cold air. He pulled out his phone and listened to the sections of Puccini's *Turandot* they were going to act out after dinner — the last two scenes in act three.

The action involved a poor slave girl named Liu, who kills herself to protect Prince Calaf's name. The prince pulls off Turandot's veil after calling her Princess of Death, then kisses her, causing her to faint. The prince then tells her his real name, even though his old girl friend, Liu, just killed herself to keep it secret. Everyone comes on stage for the big finale in which Turandot professes that the prince's name is Love. The whole cast sings up a storm, cymbals crash, gongs get gonged, the end.

Mike would be the dashing prince; Claire, the evil princess who is conquered by love; Lovey Grace, the faithful, underappreciated slave girl; and Brian, Travis and Poo, the best palace guards ever. His son had been rehearsing the dogs for a few days and even made them wooden spears to hold in their mouths in addition to the hats he was making at his grandmother's that afternoon.

Brian thought the spears were a good idea to keep them from howling to the music as they usually do. The two pets loved to sing along to opera. Actually, any beautiful music made them happy, and when they were happy they howled with the greatest enthusiasm. Brian made a gong out of an old rusty wok pan cover he spray-painted gold. This was shaping up to be one of the better opera nights.

Claire walked out of the house and kissed Mike on the back of the neck.

"Have to go to your mother's. I want to borrow Lovey's Spanish hair comb, chopsticks, and some silk flowers. She holds onto items like that forever. We'll have to cut cards to see who gets to wear Grandma Ariadne's kimono. I know she'll want to use it to play Liu. Maybe I can get her to dress in one of the other carnival robes in your grandmother's trunk. They have a few moth holes but Liu is supposed to be poor, right? Wish me luck and go inside. The house is nice and cool and I made a pitcher of ice tea."

"Thanks but I think I'll sit here for a few more minutes."

Claire looked up at the clouds. "The sky is like a scary shade of green. Anything on the news about this?"

"I listened fifteen minutes ago and they're still baffled. Some say it's global warming stuff. Others think it's a freak storm coming."

"Thank God we have the back-up generator."

"And send Brian home if he is done with his craft projects for tonight. I need to find his microscope and I am afraid to go into that room of his. The last time I entered that death trap, something stuck to my shoe and a tower of boxes fell on me."

"His room is much better now. We did a major sweep-and-clean last week. Everything is secure. Nothing sticky or icky lurking on the floor or walls, I assure you."

"I'll wait for him to come back home anyway. A lot of things can grow and pile up in a week." '

"If he's finished I'll send him home." She laughed and made her way next door.

When Claire entered her mother-in-law's house, it was freezing. Lovey Grace hated hot weather and never went to the mainland if it was a sweltering day. She liked that the island was always ten degrees cooler with a good breeze, especially at night, except for today. The activity was just winding down and Brian was cleaning up the assorted materials he had used to make the hats for opera night. He was also eating a large cookie with no hands. It was a real accomplishment for a little boy with a small mouth. This oversized cookie was obviously courtesy of Aunt Bridget, who was long gone on her date with Uncle Ned. Claire dreaded to think how many cookies and other sweets her boy may have consumed while visiting.

Lovey Grace was also in the kitchen, cleaning. She was a petite woman in her early sixties and had short blonde hair, a slim figure, and big blue eyes. Both sides of the families had these amazing eyes.

She married Mike's dad in 1976. He had been a widower for three years until they met on a Caribbean cruise. His first wife, Tina, died of a stroke when she was only forty-three.

He met and married Lovey Grace on the trip. Michael senior was forty-six and Lovey was twenty years younger, but the age difference never came into play. The little woman was an old soul who happened to look like his favorite actress, Frances Dee. Lovey had never heard of the woman who was famous in the thirties and forties so Michael had her watch *I Walked with a Zombie*. Lovey didn't see any resemblance, but Michael saw those big Frances Dee eyes every time he looked into hers.

Michael's mother, Ariadne, took to Lovey Grace right away, as did Uncle Ned. Everyone could tell Ariadne was happy for her son when the couple remarried again at the Ridgewater City Hall after getting a license. Two years later, Mike junior was born and the island really came to life again.

Opera night, as the family knew it now, started with Lovey Grace and Ariadne. Michael's mother sang professionally all over Europe and throughout the states when she was young. She was also one of the main attractions at the theater in the old carnival when it opened in 1925.

Every day she sang along with opera records she played on her old crank-style phonograph. Her new daughter-in-law couldn't sing a note, so when she joined in with Ariadne, she would lip sync to the arias or chorus and act them out. Lovey made her mother-in-law laugh so hard she would have to run to the bathroom. She almost didn't make it on one occasion.

When they invited Uncle Ned and Michael senior to join them, they added a great dinner, and opera night became a regular affair. They also invited friends from the mainland. When Lovey's sister, Bridget, moved to Ridgewater, she became a regular participant too. Mike junior was the first child to join the event and it became something he participated in even as an adult. Tonight was just as exciting to him as the first time he took part.

Now it was his son and the two dogs that made opera night even more fun.

Claire elbowed Lovey. "I like the way you're teaching your grandson to eat cookies without using his hands. If he starts choking to death, can I call you?" She gestured to the crumbs all over his shirt. "Brian, how many cookies have you eaten? And please, for your mother's sake, eat the rest of that cookie with at least one hand."

"What are you talking about? I'm using my hands and this is only my third …, ah, second cookie." He grabbed a half-eaten chocolate peanut butter cookie with the same hand that he used to spread glue with his fingers.

"Only two?" she asked suspiciously. "Finish up and go see your father at home. He needs your help with something."

"Okay, I'm almost done." Brian turned and faced his mother wearing his newly made creation. "How do you like my Chinese palace guard hat?"

It was a bicorn hat like a pirate's headgear, but with part of an old paper lantern glued to the front. This section was adorned with a gold foil paper dragon and hanging down both sides of the boy's face were strings of plastic carnival beads. Above the dragon were several pipe cleaners in assorted hues with pompoms attached on top of each. It was silly, but the hat did look vaguely Chinese.

"Wow that's great," Claire said, clapping her hands. "Where did you get the dragon and those pompoms?"

"Aunt Bridget brought a box of materials she saved. I really like it too, and look at the hats I made for Travis and Poo. Theirs have ties to keep them on." Brian held them up.

The dog's headpieces were much different. Lovey gave her grandson an old flannel sleeping cap and a knitted winter hat that the boy decorated with premade bows, pipe cleaners, pompoms, and ribbons. Travis' was finished on top with a ten-inch red paper lantern and Poo's was crowned with a purple paper folding-fan with Chinese characters on it that said something unknown, but was probably a positive sentiment like "good fortune" or "good luck."

Claire smiled. She could see how proud her son was of his handy work. "Those are great too, but yours must be for the captain of the guard."

"Yes I figured since I made them I should be in charge and Travis and Poo are the army."

"That makes perfect sense," Lovey Grace piped in. "You made these beautiful hats so you should run the army. I think they could learn something from that logic in Washington. I would vote for a good milliner over a politician any day."

Claire looked at her mother-in-law and rolled her eyes. "Let's not turn this into politics." She looked at her son. "Okay, get all your things together. Time to go home. Oh and don't forget to help your father. He needs your microscope to look at something. He has a sample of this weird green seawater he wants to look at."

"Okay," Brian replied.

Claire turned to Lovey. "Have you looked out the window lately? The water has green stuff in it and the sky is that crazy color you see during a summer storm."

"I put my air on full as soon as I got up today. Been cleaning up after my sister all afternoon and looking out the kitchen window too. I haven't seen this kind of weather before, especially this time of year. I hate getting overheated when I have work to do." She wiped the counter. "Politicians are screwing things up as usual. I'm surprised the sky isn't red or purple or both damn colors."

"Everything isn't Washington's fault," Claire responded.

"Grandma says the only thing we get from the elephants is shit and the donkeys only want to give you a good kick in the ass," Brian announced on his way out the door.

Claire stared at Lovey. "Little boys have big ears. His language is bad enough, he doesn't need any contributions or encouragements."

Lovey smiled then began to laugh. "It's funny, though — and very true."

Claire tried not to giggle and changed the subject. "I need to go through Grandmother Ariadne's trunk to find some items for tonight. Can I borrow her silk kimono and your Spanish hair comb? Also, do you have any fancy chopsticks with gold or mother of pearl or something like that? I think that it will be great for my Turandot character unless you want to play her and wear it."

"I'm going to portray Liu. I'm really good at the melodramatic stuff and that kimono would be too fancy for my character. It would be much better for you as Turandot."

Claire tried hard not to laugh at her mother-in-law's modesty about her acting abilities. "If you're sure then, I'll be the princess."

"I'm sure. You do the glamour and I do the serious acting."

Claire glanced around the room. "Where's the trunk?"

"It's in my bedroom closet. I was going to pull it out after I finished in the kitchen, so your timing is perfect. Oh, almost forgot, Bridget made her fabulous trifle for dessert. It's in the refrigerator. She said she was sorry about not coming tonight but they already had plans with friends that were hard to organize and this was the best date for everyone."

"Her trifle is a really good apology, but I'm worried about them being out on a night like this."

"They'll be fine. Can you help me get the trunk? It's not heavy but the space is so full and the thing is wedged in."

The two women pulled and tugged at the old leather trunk. It wasn't the usual steamer size, but about three feet long and eighteen inches square on the sides. The old embossed luggage was custom-made to fit in the caravans used to house performers like Grandmother Ariadne during the carnival. It could be slipped under the tiny beds or on top of an existing built-in storage unit. The trunk was aged and travel-worn, but it was still beautifully detailed with fine brass handles and embossed scrolls.

They pulled it over to Lovey's bed. Claire sat on the floor and her mother-in law on a little footstool. When they opened the lid, a layer of yellowed white tissue paper greeted them. They removed the paper to reveal the garments on the inner top tray. They took out a neatly folded long skirt and white cotton blouse and laid them on the bed; then another blouse in floral pink silk that they placed on top of them.

The silk kimono was next. It was a sheer-beaded long jacket with designs of exotic birds and ornate flowers in muted shades of dark purples. It wasn't Japanese, but a Nouveau Paris creation inspired by the country. Along the large sleeves and the bottom were small beaded tassels. A few were missing and lost over the years, but they still tinkled like tiny glass bells against each other.

Claire stood and held the garment up to her body. "I don't remember this being so beautiful. I think I'm afraid to wear it tonight because I might damage it. It's also really long for me. I forgot your mother-in-law was so tall."

"Ariadne was tall even as an older woman. Michael said the Wright's were bigger than average in height, but dark, not fair like she was. Grandmother Ariadne took after her mother, who was French and an actress with the Wright troupe. I heard she had died long before they came here."

"From the pictures I've seen of Grandmother Ariadne, her style in clothing was less dramatic than this," Claire commented.

"It's her great-aunt Cleo's jacket, not Ariadne's. She wore it with black silk slacks. Ariadne said her aunt never wore a skirt or a dress. It just wasn't her style. Even when Cleo danced she wore pants, which must have been a little shocking for the early teens and twenties. There are some pictures of her in a photo album in this trunk somewhere."

Lovey Grace felt around the insides of the luggage until she found the book and opened to a page.

"Here is a photo of her wearing this same jacket. It's at some dinner they had in the 1920s before the carnival opened. She is sitting next to William Guillory, my husband's grandfather. The tall man with the funny hair is her brother, Pompey, who started the carnival." She stopped a second and pointed at the picture. "There's Ariadne sitting next to Michael's dad, Albert. Look how pretty she was. And so blonde."

"She was beautiful. I only saw the picture of her with you and Mike's dad."

"That one was taken at the old picnic table that used to be out front. It was here since this family moved onto the island and we loved the old thing, but the squirrels chewed it up so bad we had to replace it with the round table that's out there now."

Lovey refocused. "Ariadne was seventy-four in that picture and even then, she was so pretty."

"She really was," Claire agreed.

Lovey looked at the album again and turned the pages. "Here is another picture of Cleo with Pompey. It must have been a publicity photo for the show at the carnival theater. Look at that sexy pose — and with her brother!"

Claire put on the kimono, arched her back, and bent backward, mimicking Cleo's stance. "Am I as glamorous?"

She arched her back more and almost fell over. Both women laughed.

"Let's figure out what we're wearing, it's getting late and we have to put dinner together," Lovey said. "Oh, and you wear the kimono jacket. Aunt Cleo would approve."

She headed for the closet. "Let's see what else we can find. And don't worry about the trunk, I'll put it back later."

The two women spent the next twenty minutes going through the closets and boxes, pulling together their costumes for the night. While Claire was bagging everything, Lovey headed for the kitchen to get Bridget's trifle dessert and her own contribution to dinner: grilled red potatoes, peppers, and sausage.

During their preparations, they both glanced more than once out of the window. It was getting close to dusk, but the sky still had an iridescent green glow. Something definitely was coming.

CHAPTER SEVEN

Carnivals

In the spring of 1925, William and Albert received a visit from a strange group: a very tall man, a very short man, and a very beautiful woman who approached the Guillorys' home from the beach. William was by the side of the house repairing a fishing net when he saw them for the first time. The tall man was dressed in a fashionable suit with a subtle-but-large windowpane plaid and a wide, flamboyant tie with golden elephants on it. He wore fisherman's boots instead of the kind of shoes a well-dressed gentleman would wear. They weren't dull and scuffed but were highly polished with new well-arranged laces. His features were angular and slightly exaggerated, accented by poofs of red hair projecting from under his wide-brimmed, dark green fedora. It wasn't a natural ginger red, but an orange orangutan shade that came from one of those chemical hair dyes.

This tall stranger and the woman looked related, even though her hair was black. Their profiles matched, but his was large and pronounced, giving him the air of a silent film star, while hers was sharp and refined. Her hairstyle was cut short, soft, and feminine. She was in her mid-to-late thirties. Even the man's hat that she wore, pulled down at an angle, couldn't conceal her attractiveness. Instead of a dress, this dark beauty wore riding pants and high, dark brown boots with long laces. She had one hand in the pocket of a tan cotton safari-cut jacket and with the other she clutched a large brown leather portfolio. The woman glanced around the property then looked directly at William. Her dark eyes were piercing even at that distance.

The short man wasn't as elegantly attired as his two companions. He was more workman-like in appearance. He was a little person, or what was referred to as a dwarf. His upper body looked strong, even though his legs and arms were disproportionately short for his torso. The little man had a welcoming and friendly look that gave William the feeling that they would instantly become friends if he'd gotten to know him. They were indeed an odd trio standing on William's beach.

The tall man spoke first. He had a slight British accent that could only be picked up with certain words and phrases.

"Good morning! Are you William Guillory?" he asked. "I'm Pompey Wright. This is my sister, Cleo, and my friend and colleague, Ned Baldwin."

"Yes, I'm William Guillory," he replied.

"I was told by Eugene Kent, who runs Kent Reality in Ridgewater, that you own this lovely little island. We just landed south of here where the old ferry dock is situated and walked up your beautiful beach to see you on this lovely clear day."

"Yes, I own Plover's Island," William answered. He was wary of this stranger.

"We are in the entertainment business, so to speak. Circuses, carnivals, theater, and amusements of all kinds. We have been traveling this great country and the world over the last few years on the circuit. We are part of The Wright's Theatrical Company. Have you heard of us?" Pompey asked.

William shook his head no.

"Well, we came here to see you about a proposition you may be interested in," Pompey said. "Is there a place we can all sit and discuss our ideas with you?"

William guided them over to the picnic table he'd built in the front yard for his family when they first came to the island.

Pompey glanced down at the pine bench and took a seat, followed by Ned and William. Cleo didn't join them, but wandered toward the direction of the garden in front of the house.

"Mr. Guillory, do you mind if I walk around? I promise I won't steal anything. Not all carny and theater people are gypsies and thieves," Cleo said. She also had an accent but more distinctly British than her sibling. "I love your house with all its sweet decorations and especially this fetching garden."

Pompey promptly interjected. "Don't mind my lovely sister. She has always been a little forward and definitely has a sarcastic streak, William. May I call you that?"

"Be my guest," William replied. He glanced at Cleo with a boyish smile that she easily picked up on. He looked back at the tall red-haired man. "William is fine, Mr. Wright. I mean Pompey."

"Good, good! I think we will all become great friends after you hear my proposal," Pompey said. "Cleo, could you leave that portfolio with the sketches before you roam off on your explorations?"

Cleo placed the leather folder in Pompey's hands and smiled at William. "Have a good meeting." She turned and walked to the garden.

She looked down at the flowers Emily had planted years before and were still blooming due to William's care. The crocuses were just starting to show their blossoms. She stood at the arched trellis and grasped the side of the garden entrance. Cleo turned her head and looked back at the table and William. While listening to Pompey, he caught her eye. She smiled, then looked down at the flowers again and moved on to the side of the house. William watched her, as her brother talked, until she was out of sight.

Pompey opened the portfolio to reveal sketches and diagrams. He studied the papers and then looked up, directly at William.

"These are the plans for the elements of a carnival. This one is for a grand arcade pavilion with games of chance, novelty booths, penny cinemas, and wonderful curiosities to challenge the mind and delight the imagination. It will be built with a semicircular two-story corridor with octagonal towers on each end, not unlike the Looff Hippodrome on the Santa Monica Pier in California. But grander of course. The main floor will be the arcade with open archways and large, decorative-glass double French doors. The second floor will be our living quarters and offices. One tower will house our little theater of the curious and fantastic, the other a delightful amusement like a carousel or some other novelty ride, but this is still to be decided. In the center of the semi-circle, between the towers, the arcade would open to a large concrete patio with tables and a stage for an orchestra so people can dance or just enjoy the evening sea air."

Pompey took a deep breath. "These sketches are for attractions like a Ferris wheel, an amazing house of mirrors that will have ghosts, ghouls, and scary things that go bump in the night. Lastly is a diagram for a picnic area with food and drink concessions near the beach, which would include a sectioned off area where our patrons could walk and enjoy your lovely beach. Everything will be draped in lights, so from a distance the carnival will look like jewels in the evening sky. Not only will we have classic entertainments like the Ferris wheel, but a theater with the emphasis on the bizarre and amazing."

Pompey paused again, for dramatic effect. "We want our enterprise to be built on your lovely little island and we want you to be part of it."

William was silent. What excited him most was the mention of a carousel, a grand carousel, and maybe Pompey would ask him to design and build it. He listened even more closely than before.

Pompey Wright raised his hand and gestured in the direction of the southern tip of the island. "We would like to lease a section of your delightful Plover's Island, preferably the southeast end near the old ferry dock for our carnival. It would be active in the pleasant months and be closed in the late fall and winter when our troupe goes on tour. During this time we will pay for someone to secure the area, do repairs, and whatever else was needed until the spring when we would return." He pulled out an envelope. "This is a legal document, with a bid for the first year's rental of the land plus an advance of six months' security. We want you to look it over carefully and maybe we can meet within the week, in Ridgewater, to seal the deal if everything is to your liking."

William looked at the sketches and took the envelope. "Well, I never thought of renting any part of the island. Being a landlord has never entered my mind. I would really have to think about this. We've been on the island, on our own, for the last few years and now to have people living and visiting on a regular basis is a big adjustment. I also need to discuss this with my son Albert, because this is his island too."

"I completely understand. It is a big decision but this decade is a time for big challenges. Of course we would love to also employ your skills as a craftsman, and also your son's, in the conceiving and constructing of our little amusement. Eugene praised your artistry and couldn't stop talking about the lovely work you and your son, Albert, did for him and for so many others in Ridgewater. We want our carnival to be exquisite and we would need someone like you to help us make it happen."

"Thank you so much for the compliment. I did make furniture and some decorative woodwork for Mr. Kent's home. But this is a big step and I really need to think about your proposition. When do you need to know?"

"Let's see, today is Wednesday, the third of April. Can we meet this Saturday in the afternoon, about three o'clock at Eugene's office? If everything goes as I hope and predict it will, you and your son are invited to a celebratory dinner at the lovely Ridgewater Hotel that night. Then I can introduce the two of you to the rest of our little group."

"We will be in town at our workshop this weekend anyway to

finish up and deliver some furniture to a client on the east end of town, so Saturday is good."

"Perfect," said Pompey. He stood up from the old weathered table. "I have several details to take care of in the meantime. Now let's find my lovely sister and you can also show us around your charming property."

All this new information and the speed that Pompey was moving at with this proposition made William a little dizzy and nervous. But in the end, he knew that it was really his decision.

The three men walked to the side of the house and headed in the direction of the small backyard where William kept his carousel. They heard laughter and the sound of something mechanical. When they reached the gazebo, Cleo was riding the black horse with the white mane and tail. She waved her hat in the air like a cowboy at a rodeo.

Albert was operating the merry-go-round, but his concentration was on Cleo. He had never met a woman like her before. Some of the young girls he met at school or when he went to Ridgewater for the occasional dances and social functions were pretty, but not like Cleo. Even his first boyhood crush, Jane, paled in comparison to this older woman. It seemed that both Guillory men were enchanted by her.

Pompey had picked up on the men's attraction to his sister right away. It was one of the reasons he brought her to the meeting in the first place. This wasn't the first time he had used Cleo's beauty and presence to enhance a situation.

"What a delightful carousel," Pompey exclaimed. "It only needs a little music to make our Cleo's ride complete. Ned, give us a tune, my good fellow."

Baldwin smiled, dug into his back pocket, and pulled out a harmonica. He played the old circus waltz, *Over the Waves*, befitting the seaside location. Pompey and Ned both swayed to the classic song in perfect unison, which made Cleo laugh even more. William and Albert were amused too. They had never had any experience with people like this. There were a few eccentric and interesting people in Ridgewater but rarely did anyone they know speak in such superlatives or use grand gestures. Pompey pulled a small box camera from his bag and took a picture of his sister as Ned finished the song and put his instrument back into his pocket. Albert rushed to help Cleo dismount her steed, but she had already leaped off and was heading toward him.

Pompey gestured to the carousel. "William, did you create this masterpiece?"

"Albert and I built it."

"I am so impressed. I knew your island was the perfect place for us."

Pompey turned to Cleo who was approaching the men with Albert on her arm. "My darling Cleo, I assume you had a marvelous ride? I haven't seen you so giddy in a long time."

Cleo put her hat back on and adjusted it to the perfect angle to accent her face. "Mr. Guillory, I have to thank you and your son for letting me experience your darling carousel. It is truly a work of art and in such an unexpected setting. Where did you get your inspiration? The craftsmanship, the colors, and the details are all so perfect. We have seen many great carousels in our travels but very few as amazing."

William smiled at her. "Thank you so much. I'm glad you enjoyed your ride. You have the distinction of being the third person to ever do so. We started it a few years ago and it's been kind of a secret between Albert, the squirrels, and myself."

Cleo glanced at some bushes behind William and saw three squirrels spying on them. The group turned and everyone chuckled at the mischievous rodents with the fuzzy tails. The squirrels looked at each other as if discussing the group and looked back even more intently.

William laughed. "Those are our best customers for our little hobby. As for an inspiration, I went to Coney Island in twenty-two and the sight of all the wonderful rides and amusements made my mind up for me. I knew it was what I wanted to do. Then Albert caught the bug and we have been working on it for three years now. It gets bigger every season."

Pompey got even more excited. "Your impressive amusement must be part of our carnival. Your carousel will go in the second tower opposite our arcade and little theater. You can scale your merry-go-round to fit the tower and we can get a calliope to accompany the fortunate people who will get to take a ride on it. This is the perfect match to round out our Ferris wheel, arcade, hall of mirrors, and other attractions. Your craftsman's eye will grace all the details of our little island leisure and I hope when we meet on Saturday all will be in agreement so we can start our magnificent enterprise."

William really started to feel good about the morning's encounter. He loved the idea of his carousel being featured and the opportunity to work on a carnival and all it entailed. This was the most challenging and exciting thing that had ever happened to him, especially as an artisan. He contained his excitement and tried not to look too agreeable and accommodating until he had a chance to talk to Albert. This could be the best or worst decision they would ever make.

Pompey extended his hand to the two men. "Well, my dear William and Albert, we will take our leave and stroll back down your lovely beach to our waiting boat. Until Saturday then, my dear new friends and possible colleagues, *adieu* and good day."

William and Albert shook everyone's hands and accompanied them to the beach. The trio waved goodbye again as they turned and walked down the sand. Pompey still waved over his head, even though his back was turned to them, until they were several yards from the house. William put his arm around his son's shoulder and they walked back to the house. They had a lot to discuss before the meeting on Saturday.

CHAPTER EIGHT

Celebrations

By Saturday, William and Albert had decided that leasing the land and being part of the new carnival was what they wanted to do. The celebration dinner was great fun with Pompey, his usual flamboyant self, making toast after toast about the future. Cleo, for the occasion, wore a sheer-beaded long kimono jacket with designs of exotic birds and ornate flowers in muted shades of dark purples and matching silk slacks. The jacket was trimmed with tiny beaded tassels that tinkled like little bells when she walked or made an arm gesture. In the candlelight, the purple outfit looked almost as black as her hair. She was the most opulently dressed of anyone at the affair, but she didn't seem to stand out because it matched her persona. No matter what she wore, Cleo was the most beautiful woman in the room.

They met Pompey's daughter, Ariadne, for the first time that night. She was also attractive, but no match for her aunt. She was seventeen, fair, tall, and blonde. Her height was obviously inherited from her father, but her coloring and features were decidedly from her mother. The late Mrs. Wright had died when the girl was only five while their troupe was traveling through Hungary as part of an acting company out of London. Ariadne's mother was French, not English like her father and aunt. The company performed unusual plays with mystical and supernatural themes.

Some of the stories were authored by Pompey and supposedly based on true-life encounters he'd experienced during his travels. When Albert innocently asked how Mrs. Wright had died, Pompey quickly changed the topic. The manner of her death was never brought up again.

His colleague, Ned Baldwin, was definitely Irish from the sound of his thick brogue. His wife Carla, also a little person, joined them for the dinner. She was fair with blue green eyes and jet-black hair and, like her husband, friendly and genial. Carla had a wonderful laugh that inspired you to tell her something humorous so you could hear it over and over again. Even though Ned was in Pompey's employ, there was never any hint that he or his spouse was his subordinate. They liked to talk, laugh and entertain with the same enthusiasm as Pompey.

Both Ned and Carla were from Cork and they left home when they were in their early teens to join the circus. Their parents were normal size and the circus seemed the best option for little people who had any ambitions beyond being farm laborers. They met while working in the same circus when they were both eighteen and the two were married ten months later.

A couple years after that, they met Pompey in London while doing a comical magician's act with a funny bearded man. Wright was performing scenes from great classic plays, in addition to telling tales of horror and the supernatural. Cleo was also part of the act but would alternate nights with Pompey's young wife and hold title signs, play scenes opposite him, dance, or just add a touch of glamour.

The act received mixed reactions. In places like Italy and France, rural theatergoers were greatly offended by what they perceived as sacrilegious. Stories of vampires, witches, and the like didn't go as well as scenes from Shakespeare or Voltaire. Pompey was always striving to put together a traveling show with novel and unusual attractions. It was important that the show was a success because he had a young wife and baby to support in addition to his young sister.

The Baldwins and their magician colleague hit it off with Pompey right away and became part of his fledgling company. Ned liked being Pompey's friend because of the excitement. Sometimes the troupe's journeys were pure fun, other times a lot of hard work, and a few were dangerous, but always an adventure.

Listening to their stories, William realized that Pompey's company had been traveling together for a long time. In addition to the Wrights and the Baldwins, there were two more couples at the dinner. There was John, the fat-but-agile magician with a black beard that was striped in white and covered his colorful tie, and his companion, Madame Regina, a thin middle-aged woman with strange small tattoos on her forearms that were later described as runic symbols. She was a fortuneteller and seer and John's talent was his ability to fit into small spaces and disappear, which seemed unlikely considering his considerable girth.

The act started with the large man making Ned and his wife appear and disappear inside an assortment of decorated boxes or from behind his constantly choreographed, twirling cape. The entertainment climaxed with Ned and Carla assisting the great bearded magician as he stood on a box half his size. With the twirl of his great cape and a crash of the cymbals, he was gone, with only his cape left lying on the top of the box. Ned and his spouse then pantomimed looking for him under the cape and around the box with great dismay, but to the crowd's amusement.

Finally they'd open the front of the box and the bearded gentleman was half his original size and dancing a jig. It was obviously a mechanical puppet of the man inside the box doing all the dancing. The audiences, in on the joke, would roar with laughter.

Ned then would close the box and hook Carla to a harness. The little lady would ascend into the air like an angel holding the cape outstretched. She'd hide behind the garment, the cymbals would crash, the cape would fall, and she'd be standing with arms raised high and on the shoulders of the now full-sized, John the magician.

The other two guests at the dinner were not part of the troupe, but locals hired to be involved in accounting, sales and the daily business of the carnival. Brother and sister, Alan and Miriam Cather, were quiet and seemed overwhelmed by their outlandish dinner companions. He was an accountant and she was his assistant. Miriam's other job was to see to the needs of Pompey, Cleo, Ariadne and the rest of the group. The town wanted a local or two involved in the inner circle of the carnival for at least the first year as part of an agreement with the mayor of Ridgewater.

Pompey also had to be willing to hire Ridgewater craftsmen and laborers, beyond William and his son, to construct the carnival and new dock and be part of the daily operation of the enterprise. This agreement was going to cost Pompey a good deal of money, but it didn't seem to worry him, nor did he ever complain. William had no idea where people like this acquired the kind of capital they were spending on this venture. Maybe entertainment was more lucrative than he had imagined. He was just happy that he and his son were now part of it.

Pompey had arranged the seating at a table in the hotel's only private dining room. William sat between Cleo and Pompey. Next to them he strategically placed Albert with his daughter, Ariadne. Then there was Ned and Carla, and John and Madame Regina. The Cathers rounded out the table.

Albert was having a good time and happy to be next to someone as pretty as Ariadne. "I love your wonderful names. They are so unusual. How did you come by them?"

The bearded magician overheard his question. "Hear, hear for John, a good English name!"

They all toasted immediately, except for the Cathers, who seemed to be unaware of the reason for the salute. They slowly mimed a toast and went back to their meal.

Ariadne leaned in to Albert and smiled, making him blush. "My father would be the best one to answer that question. Daddy, why do we have such grand names? Albert would like to know." She touched his arm.

The young man's face turned redder as Pompey answered. "What better name to have than a grand one?" he laughed. "Cleo and myself had parents with an historical sense of humor. They loved ancient history, so I became Pompey and my dear sister, Cleopatra. Tragically our namesake's lives ended badly, but they had a great time in the process of getting there." Everyone laughed as Pompey looked back at Ariadne. "My daughter, on the other hand, was named after the offspring of the great king Minos. She was in charge of the labyrinth and helped the love of her life, Theseus, kill the Minotaur. I hope some day my Ariadne meets her Theseus and helps him through the mazes of life, find happiness and have a wonderful time in this world."

"Hear, hear!" toasted John again.

Albert continued to blush which made Ariadne giggle. "Daddy, where does the name Albert come from?"

"Ah, Albert means noble and famous like our good Prince Albert, beloved of Queen Victoria, England's greatest sovereign." Pompey then turned to William. "My good man is that your lovely son's namesake?"

William looked up at him smiling. "No, nothing so royal. My son is named after my dear wife Emily's oldest brother, Albert John Collins."

"Hear, hear for John," the bearded Magician toasted again. "And Albert too. Hear, hear!"

Everyone laughed and toasted. "Hear, hear."

William talked with Cleo through most of the dinner. She asked about fishing, carving, and his life on the island. She seemed fascinated by his seemingly simple existence.

"How did you manage to stay in one place all your life? I go crazy if I am not always traveling to new destinations. The only time I was anywhere for more than a year was when I was a child and had no choice. We spent the first years of my life in London, where I was born and we've been on the road ever since. Pompey decided he finally wanted a home base and that's why we are here. Traveling shows are dying out and movie theaters are taking over. There are fewer and fewer houses to play except in the big cities, and that is shrinking too."

Her smile faded as she looked at the ice water in her wine glass. Pompey had snuck a little gin into it from a flask he kept in a secret pocket, that he had in all of his coat jackets. She picked up her glass and took a large sip. Cleo knew her brother had spiked her water and was actually happy he did.

William really hadn't spent any time with a woman, especially one like her, since Emily. Sitting and talking with Cleo made him happy and awkward at the same time. He wasn't a young man anymore and the attentions of a beautiful woman made him feel uncomfortable. Was this just about the carnival and business or was she actually interested in him and his life?

William broke the silence. "Sounds like you will be missing that life. It must have been wonderful meeting all those people, seeing all those places. And I didn't know the theater profession could yield you such great fame and profit. Your brother seems to have no problem with money."

He looked down as her hand touched his.

"Pompey and I have been ..." she paused, "lucky when it comes to money. Fortune has been good to us."

Cleo's half-smile was more sad than happy.

"Well I hope that fortune smiles on your — or should I say our — carnival too." He lifted his water glass slightly and gave a toast, hoping John didn't see so it could be just between the two of them.

The dinner and festivities ended just after midnight. Everyone shook hands and patted backs as they moved to the lobby. Pompey wished everyone a good night and announced that they would all meet again on Monday to begin their great carnival project.

Cleo grabbed William's arm and kissed him lightly on the cheek and whispered, "Goodnight, William."

Ariadne saw this and kissed Albert too, but in a more abrupt way, adding a girlish giggle. The night was more company and conversation than the two Guillory men had had in a long time, not to mention the kisses good night. Monday would start the adventure and beginning of the carnival and this night marked the first chapter in the history of the Guillory, Wright, and Baldwin families on Plover's Island.

CHAPTER NINE

Dinner and a Show, Plus Rain

Just before dinner, Mike and Brian went to the boy's room to use the microscope. The area was in good order, relieving Mike's fears of falling boxes or something sticking to his shoe. They put a sample of seawater on the glass slide with a little eyedropper and looked at it under the scope. The liquid was relatively clear but it seemed to be made up of tiny particles that were brilliant green. They were too small to see clearly, whatever they were. The flicks of emerald darted around in the sample. They appeared to be greater in volume than they actually were as they grouped, dispersed, and then regrouped. The pattern of the organisms was repetitive, implying a system or plan.

"I wish your microscope was stronger," Mike said in frustration. "It's good, but it's still a toy."

"I guess I need a better one for my birthday, which is sooner than Christmas. Or order one next week online." The little boy took a look into the scope. "They sure are fast. They're glowing too."

Mike took a second look. "Yes, they are! What in hell are these things?"

"Even the jar is glowing," Brian yelled.

Mike looked at the sample jar sitting on his son's desk and it was glowing like the drop of water on the slide.

Mike stood up. "Wait here."

He picked up the jar, went into the living room, and looked out the window. The sea now had a pale green luminosity that seemed to move and fluctuate. He looked at the sample in his hand in amazement as it did the same thing.

The glowing phenomenon was more apparent now that the sun was down. Something new was in the sea and it made him nervous. Mike wished Uncle Ned were there because he might have seen this kind of thing before. Mike took out his cell phone and was about to call him when he heard Claire enter the house with his mother.

"Mike," she hollered. "Can you hold on that call and help me? My arms are breaking and I'm about to drop this box."

"I could use some help too," Lovey said, out of breath.

Mike put his cell in his back pocket and went to help them. He grabbed the box from Claire and she draped the costumes over the closest living room chair. He put the container on the floor next to the garment bag then went over to his mother and took the large glass pedestal dish she was holding.

"Put the trifle in the refrigerator, son. It's better cold than room temperature. I have to put this pan in the oven. Everything is done, but I need to keep it warm."

Lovey Grace looked over at her daughter-in-law who was about to go to the bedroom.

"Claire, can you turn your oven on for me? I always have trouble with all those buttons and computer things."

"Okay, but let me show you how to turn it on again. If that ancient stove of yours ever goes to appliance heaven, you will have to buy a new one. They all have the same computer buttons, lights and bells on them, even the real professional models that cost thousands of dollars."

"Show me, but I won't remember," Lovey assured her. "Besides that oven of mine will be working when you are an old lady, my dear."

"I hope so," replied Claire. "Mike, who were you going to call?"

"I was going to ask Uncle Ned if he heard or knew anything more about this weird weather and the color of the water."

"Well, if it has happened here before, he would have seen it," Lovey Grace stated. "Uncle Ned was born on this island way before we all existed. But calling him won't work because he left his cell phone at my house. I saw it on the table near the door when we came over, and it's no good calling my sister either. She never leaves her cell on."

"Neither do you Mother. You also never check your voice mail," Mike replied.

"Cell phones, voice mail," Lovey Grace said exasperated. "It all makes me crazy. Call me on my home phone. I always answer that."

"You should get use to using your cell phone," Claire advised her. "It's better and you can use it everywhere."

"I know, I know, I carry the thing all the time. It lives in my purse."

Mike's mother walked to the window, looked out, and then turned around with her hands on her hips, which meant she was about to pontificate. "As for this weird damn weather, it's probably something to do with an oil spill down south. Plastic bottles, nuclear plants, chemical dumping, whatever. I'm surprised there are any fish at all and we aren't all glowing green. The government officials talk all the time, but no one does a damn thing. Even when I moved here in the seventies, they were bitching about polluted water and the environment. Still, nothing is better, and by the looks outside tonight, probably worse. Let's get dinner ready. That's something we have control over. Then we can have some fun and dig into my sister's trifle." Lovey Grace paused a second. "Son, I need a drink."

She went over to the box Claire brought in and Mike had set by the chair. Lovey Grace pulled out her bottle of scotch and handed it to Mike.

"Please pour your mother a good one and not too much ice."

*　　*　　*

Dinner was just after seven that evening and Claire cleared the table with the help of her mother-in-law. The two women then retired to the bedroom to change into their costumes. Mike and his son did the dishes and got themselves ready too. Brian, with some effort, put the hats he'd made onto Poo and Travis. The two dogs weren't as keen on the idea as they were earlier in the day. Travis shook his head and Poo scratched, but both settled down and gave in to the idea of wearing them. For the moment.

Mike set up whatever props they needed and dressed the coatrack in a feather duster and an old bathrobe to represent the emperor. He put an old raincoat and knitted winter cap on a kitchen chair to be the old king, Calaf's father. When everything was set up, Mike pulled out the records and put the vinyl labeled *Act Three* on the crank phonograph. The old rosewood and brass machine stood in the back of the living room, to the left of the double doors.

Lovey Grace emerged first from the bedroom. She was wearing a tattered silk robe from the trunk that was more European gypsy fortuneteller in style than Asian. Her head was wrapped in a rainbow scarf at least four feet long and piled as high as she could get it to stay. Lovey's arms were covered in bangle bracelets and on her feet were little white socks. She made up her face with white powder, black eyebrows, and bee-stung lips. Poor Poo growled at first, then whimpered when he finally recognized her.

Claire entered next, wearing Aunt Cleo's kimono jacket. She also had on little white socks with gold evening mules. On her head, she wrapped a long metallic sheer scarf decorated with chopsticks, a big Spanish comb, and some leftover carnival plastic beads Brian didn't use. Claire was made up just like Lovey Grace with the white powdered face, tiny oval lips, and arched eyebrows.

The two women stood together and asked in unison, "How do we look?"

Mike glanced at Brian. "Well, son, I guess the circus is in town and it's time for the show."

Claire laughed at Mike in his everyday gray terrycloth robe, big floppy knitted hat, and a tin foil serving tray tied to his chest with two crisscrossed lengths or rope. "I guess we all work for the same circus."

"Okay, everyone in their places," Mike directed. "Brian, you, Grandma, and the dogs stand by the front windows. Claire is on this side of the room and I'm by the record player until I come in later for my big scene."

"Wait!" yelled Brian. "I need to give Travis and Poo their spears or they will start howling to the music right away."

He secured them in the grip of each of their jaws. Poo's slanted to the floor due to the canine's short stature and length of the staff.

Mike looked at everyone. "Are we all ready?" They paused until he gave the cue to begin. "Son, walk in with Grandma and drag that chair with the raincoat on it. That's the old king. Claire you enter right after that and everyone who's singing should begin."

Mike ran over to the old phonograph and started the music. Brian grasped the old king chair with one hand, his grandmother's arm with the other, and dragged them to the center of the living room. The two dogs started to move, but Mike was able to signal them to stay put.

Claire entered next, hamming it up with a glamorous strut and arms outstretched like a silent movie vamp. Lovey Grace did her best melodramatic acting and Brian looked stern, threating his grandmother with his wooden spear.

Claire started miming to Lovey Grace, alias the slave girl,

asking her to give up the prince's name, but she refused again and again. Claire ordered Brian, the guard, to torture her. So he poked his grandmother with his spear. This started to upset the two dogs and Mike had to order them to stay.

Finally, Lovey Grace as the slave girl, took the butter knife tucked in the rope belt around Brian's waist and stabbed herself several times with more than enough drama and vigor to kill three slave girls. She fell to the ground with a thump.

This was too much for Travis and Poo. The canines dropped their spears and ran to the side of Lovey Grace, lying in a heap on the floor. The dogs nudged and licked her face then Poo sneezed from the taste of the white powder. Claire started laughing, followed by Lovey Grace, who was rolling on the floor with the two excited dogs climbing all over her.

Mike shouted, "Okay, time for a break then we set up for the next scene."

It took about ten minutes to start again. Mike played his big kissing scene with princess Turandot, alias Claire. She playacted a quick faint into his arms, then revived just as fast when he told her his name. The music soared to announce the last scene when the princess revealed that the prince's name was Love. Everyone sang. Travis and Poo dropped their spears again and howled to the music until it was over with a smash of Brian's homemade wok gong. Poo became so excited he peed on the hardwood floor, almost hitting the Persian rug.

With a roll of paper towels in hand Claire declared, "Time for everyone to take a bathroom break before dessert — and honey, please take the dogs out now."

Travis and Poo managed to free themselves of their headdresses as Mike quickly took off his bathrobe, slipped on his hat, and grabbed the large flashlight on the table next to the door. "Come on boys, let's take a walk."

He opened the front door and the canines ran past him and out onto the porch. The hot, humid air that greeted them was so damp, Mike felt it through his shirt. The three made their way to the beach and were greeted by the strangest occurrence.

Through the darkness he could see what appeared to be a light, thin rain but only over the sea and ending at the water's edge. Actually, the tiny drops of moisture were more like a fine mist. They glowed like the water did earlier, but this wasn't the most unsettling aspect that Mike and the dogs witnessed.

It was the realization that the thin, glowing veil over the ocean was ascending instead descending. And in the distance he could see funnels of light that rose up like tornadoes. They were thick, symmetrical, and continued climbing until they dispersed into the clouds.

CHAPTER TEN

The Dream of Emily

William stood on the beach in front of his house and looked out at the water. The fog was dense, but he liked the solitude and the way the haze wrapped around him like a blanket. On mornings like this, his thoughts were of Emily and the children he had lost. Was Emily right about what she had seen? Was everything she said about Thomas real? And were January and Emily with him now? These thoughts haunted William when he was quiet, like this.

Keeping busy with his work, Albert, and now the carnival, saved him from these constant fears that he could never discuss without sounding as mad as his poor lost wife.

This was the day the Ferris wheel was arriving by barge from the mainland. It was ordered from the Eli Bridge Company in Illinois the week after the celebratory dinner. The wheel was forty-five feet tall, had twelve passenger seats, and was constructed to be portable so that it could travel by rail or truck. It was a popular Ferris wheel used in several fairs and parks across the country. Pompey wanted it as soon as possible so they could customize the decoration to go with the theme of the carnival.

Pompey approached William from the beach and did his usual sunny greeting that seemed out of place on such a gray day. He was there to discuss the designs William was creating that would decorate the great wheel. It was very important to Pompey to keep it in the spirit of the rest of the carnival.

"Good morning, my dear William. What a foggy day it is, just like my lovely London." Pompey got right to the point and held up a tube of rolled blueprint paper against his chest. "I want to talk to you about the Ferris wheel that is coming today."

Pompey had clearly explained to William his creative wishes the Monday after the celebration dinner, while they had lunched at Mario's, the only Italian restaurant in Ridgewater.

* * *

"William, this is the plan for the Ferris wheel that is being delivered in the next few weeks. I hired professionals from the company to set it up once it arrives. The framework is mostly steel and quite simple in design. I want it to be decorated with scrolls, leaves, and fanciful beasts painted in metallic gold and bright but tasteful colors. I liked how you added the simple nautical touches to your house and also your wonderful carousel. This is a seaside attraction, so everything should reflect that, but in a grand and fanciful manner. We should also add more lights than it comes with so it can be seen from miles away, like a spiral beacon to lead customers to our enterprise. This diagram has all the specifications and sizes of our new Bridge wheel."

Pompey placed the rolled blueprint of the wheel by the side of his chair and pulled two books out of his leather bag.

"I want you to have this Italian book of design covering the last three decades and this old science book. In it I found brilliant sketches and prints of undersea life. There are living things described and pictured one would believe only to exist in myths if they weren't documented. The design volume I bought in Italy years ago, and I think it will inspire you. I want an organic, but ornate look for our carnival that is bold and fresh and will be appropriate for our seaside surroundings, but still have a familiar link to the past. I hope these books will inspire you." He paused for a second to let William digest what he had just said. "Is this something you think you can take on for me?"

He reached his arm across the table and laid the books in front of William.

William flipped slowly through the pages. "I'll try. Give me a little time to come up with some ideas and sketches. Ferris wheels and carnivals are not furniture or wooden horses."

"Just think of the ride as a window frame, like the ones in your lovely home — except it's just a really big round window frame. Also imagine the carnival as the grand space to compliment your carousel and the other wonders we will build for the public's enjoyment."

This made William chuckle. "Okay. I'll think of it as a really big window frame. I'll do my best."

"Go to your lovely island and study the books. Take a long walk on your beautiful beach, pick up shells, rocks, run your fingers through the sand, look out onto the water and see what it all says to you. Go back to your worktable, peruse through the books again, and sketch out your ideas. It will all come to you. All the details for the basic structures are in the works. Our crescent-shaped main structure and the foundation of the patio will begin at the end of the month. The other rides and attractions are being worked on too. When they are ready we want you to enhance them with your designs."

Pompey looked at his pocket watch. "Now I must go and arrange for our four caravans to be transported to the island. They are currently behind the hotel. My lovely Ariadne and Cleo share one, Ned and Carla are in the second, John and Madame Regina occupy the third, and I have the last one. We decided to treat ourselves and stay at the hotel for a few weeks. We will be living in our cramped little quarters for the next few months until the rooms over the arcade in the pavilion are completed."

"I wish I had extra space in my house," William said. "I would gladly put you all up, but we only have two bedrooms, a little living room, dining room, and kitchen. We could double up if it were only men, but I don't think the ladies would be comfortable."

"Never worry, my dear man, about our accommodations. We would never think to impose. Besides, theater folk are an eccentric group with our own strange ways. We wouldn't want to loose your friendship just when we have made it. Go back to your island, be inspired, and let me know as soon as you have something to show me."

*   *   *

Weeks had gone by since the lunch and Pompey wanted to see what William had designed.

"I would love to show the workmen your sketches and ideas," Wright said.

"I have gone through your beautiful books, studied the blueprints for the wheel and the other attractions, sketched several ideas … but none seem good enough. I need one more week and I think I will have a solution for you."

Pompey was quiet for a moment and then smiled. "A week it is."

Then he handed a roll of vellum to William, who knew it was more blueprints and diagrams. "These are some updated plans I just received for the grand pavilion and some of the smaller buildings that will house the other attractions and the concession stands. I want to wait until we have our concept designs before I commission the patio and the glasswork. Maybe seeing more of the carnival will inspire you to come up with your concept."

William took the plans. "Thank you, I will go over them as soon as you leave."

Pompey dug into his bag and pulled out a narrow fabric bag and offered it to William. "Here is some more inspiration; a nice bottle of red wine from the Isle of Capri. Maybe a glass or two will spark your imagination and open up your creativity. I know here in your country it's against the law, but this is just a gift between you, your island, the sea and me. Create wonders and I will see you in a week. Ciao, my dear friend."

Pompey turned and walked down the beach in the direction of the old dock on the southern tip of Plover's Island. His wave goodbye lasted until he was out of sight.

* * *

The week had almost passed. William studied the books, sketched, and walked on the beach. He did all the little exercises Pompey recommended for inspiration, but nothing seemed to bring him that perfect concept he needed for this project. Spending time by the water's edge, picking up stones and shells was relaxing, but didn't inspire him at all.

It was late in the afternoon and the sun was just beginning to set, causing the light to turn gold and then rosy. In his kitchen, William paused from his doodling and looked up at the bottle of red wine Pompey had given him. It was a risky move to be the presenter of such an illegal gift, but the man lived on the edge. In reality, since the ban in 1920, drinking was more widespread than before the law. It was easy to get a drink even in a quiet town like Ridgewater. The beverages that were usually available were something more likely to poison you than be a luxury item like the beautiful bottle of Neapolitan wine sitting in front of him.

Maybe a relaxing drink to help him focus was what was needed. He was all alone, so who would know? William grabbed a teacup from the shelf because there weren't any wine glasses in the house. He poured a few ounces, made a toast into the air, and took his first sip. The deep red liquid tasted fruity, but very dry. The warmth spread through his throat and ended in an even warmer glow that radiated through his chest and stomach. He wasn't a drinker even when it was legal, but this gift from his new friend tasted wonderful and made him more relaxed.

William poured himself some more and started going through the old books. Before he knew it he fell asleep with his head resting on a print of a fantastical looking creature that must have been a jellyfish or at least an ancestor of the medusa or hydra varieties. The fish, if you could call it that, was all translucent domed chambers and snakelike tentacles. The plate was tinted a pale shade of green and posed in the center of the page surrounded by sketches of smaller but still fantastical relatives.

Sleepy, the second William closed his eyes he felt a soft breeze from the direction of the front door. He slowly opened them and lifted his head. The figure standing in the doorway was blurry at first, but as his eyes adjusted to the warm rose-gold light silhouetting the being, he discerned the shape of a woman and the garment she wore. William recognized the dress. It was the pale yellow cotton frock Emily was wearing that last time he saw her. It was also in his dream. Could this be what he was experiencing now? This wasn't his Emily but the Emily from the sea that haunted his sleeping thoughts.

He saw her smile as she glided up to the table. She was wet and the pale yellow dress clung to her body like it did in his dream. The damp, hair-like tentacles undulated as her head moved closer to his face. She kissed him, touched his neck and shoulders with a caress that was both strong and gentle at the same time. William was paralyzed. He tried to lift his hand to touch this Emily's arm, but as in a dream, he couldn't move. First, everything spun in slow motion, then, in a flash of time, he was standing next to the figure. The wetness of her dress penetrated his shirt. The Emily from the sea pulled his body close to hers and kissed him again.

She looked down at the books and smiled at the images of the denizens from the depths of the ocean. She whispered something into his ear as she kissed him a third time. In another blink, they were both standing at the water's edge. The red-and-gold sky was now accented with hues of purple.

He couldn't move unless she willed it. The creature that resembled his wife was both terrifying and beautiful. William wanted to break free, but his body gave in to the creature's powerful hold on him. He kissed this Emily, then closed his eyes and surrendered to her.

Time blinked again. When he opened his eyes, he was under water. His body was meshed to hers as they swam deeper and deeper until the light of sunset on the surface disappeared and they were in complete darkness. William felt the cold and began to lose control of his breath. Was he drowning? He flailed his arms and legs, trying to desperately break free. If he died in this dream, would he also die at the table he knew he was really sleeping at, with his cheek pressed against the pages of the old book?

The creature Emily pulled him even closer and kissed him deeply. When she pulled away, a large bubble grew around his head. His fight to breathe eased, his body and will once again gave in to this being. He looked around, only experiencing blackness, until light emanating from indiscernible forms moving toward them came into sight. They were lit from within and looked like the wings of angels or butterflies, but without bodies. These large undulating shapes softly flapped in the water. Other, larger beasts were now also visible, but only from the light that reflected from these angels without bodies.

William saw a pod of great whales swim by and a school of smaller fish danced around them in a spiral, barely touching their bodies, as they moved toward the surface and disappeared from sight.

Soon the sea around them was filled with creatures that were self-illuminating and invisible at the same time. The crustaceans and undersea vertebrates in the book Pompey had given him were common and uninspired compared to these wondrous animals. Most glowed blue, white, and pale green; some pulsed a deep red.

William looked through their forms as they passed in front of each other. Some caressed them while others poked at his body in what he thought was just innocent curiosity.

This continued until he heard a deep harmonic tone that created waves of sound visible in the deep water. The parade of fanciful sea aliens suddenly dispersed and creatures like his Emily swam around them. There were six beings like his wife. Three were female and three were male. William could see the gender distinction in both their size and bodies. The men were much taller and with broader chests and slightly larger heads. All the females were appealing, even with their fish tails and serpent hair.

One male approached, kissed Emily, and then suddenly turned to William and smiled at him. Its eyes were blue. The same translucent, watery blue he remembered as the color of his dear son Thomas' eyes. He was amazed that something half-human and half something else could be so attractive. Even the males, like his son, were arresting to gaze upon. The non-human parts of these beings were hard to identify as fish or crustacean. They were some other variation he had never seen before.

Thomas' head was encapsulated in a translucent nautilus shell-like helmet that framed his face and revealed an inner humanoid cranium. The headpiece tapered at the back of the neck, then continued down the spine in overlapping sections. The plated segments widened at the middle of the back and narrowed again where it reached the base of the tailbone.

Growing from the center of this back plate was a dorsal fin that also narrowed at the small of the back. The lower part of Thomas' body was a smooth, legless metallic sheath of scales. It had defined, muscled thighs and buttocks and ended with a large caudal fin instead of feet. Arteries in their tails lit up as luminescent liquids pulsed through them, revealing patterns similar to the human circulatory system. These tubes of light glowed through the back fin and coursed through the helmeted skull.

Both sexes had snakelike tendril hair, but the women's locks were much longer and better defined. These slender appendages also trimmed the dorsal fins and lit up with throbbing luminosity. When they communicated with each other, veins and arteries pulsed inside the shell helmets in waves of blue and green.

William thought, *What magnificent monsters these handsome creatures are.* Thomas looked at him and smiled. William knew that his son from the sea had read his mind and was pleased.

Thomas was no longer a boy, but a powerful being at least six-and-a-half feet tall. The features of these beings that were still human-like were present in the face and upper torso. Their skin was the color of normal flesh, but paler. They looked like the most perfect athletes. Muscular stomachs and arms, small symmetrical breasts on the females and broad chests on the males defined their exceptional beauty and almost dismissed the fish-like details of the rest of their forms.

The human aspects transitioned at the lower pelvic area into scales that changed from flesh color to translucent then to a metallic turquoise-green and gold. They had no other discernable man-like features. William knew these must be the mermaids and mermen of legend and his loved ones were now part of this mythical race. He couldn't even imagine how or why they were able to transition like this.

His son from the sea hugged him when Emily released her grip. Thomas looked into his father's eyes and a stream of images and words flooded William's consciousness.

He told his father of the day he was caught on the sandbar during the storm and pulled under. While his lungs filled with water, a woman, now his kin, saved him with her kiss and brought him to this beautiful place. He described his conversion from man to merman is a series of images that showed his childlike body unite with an arthropod-shaped species. Its clear tentacles merged with his head and spine, creating the distinct shell headpiece and began his evolution from a human boy to a being of the sea.

Thomas spoke to his father through these thoughts and images. *I miss you and still love you as much as the day I left. I miss Albert, too. Mother, January, and I live in a beautiful place we want to show you. You can live here too when you choose to come. Let us find my sister and see our city. It is so beautiful.*

William responded, *I love and miss you all. Albert and I think of you every day. I see what's become of you, but how can it be? You're human and yet different. How could we become something else?*

Emily spoke. *We are not different. We were all the same once. This is the first home for all mankind. Some of the first of our kind left and became the people of the land. They forgot the sea and our home, but when they come back we will welcome them and it will be like it was in the beginning.*

William looked at Emily. *Why have you been hidden for so long? And if we are all the same, why don't we know of you?*

It's best for us and for you. We know your ways and stay where we can live in peace. As long as our ancestors on the land do not threaten our homes, we will be invisible to them. It has been that way since the separation and will stay so until we think it has to change. We are the sea and it is where we will always be.

William was silent, knowing the separation could only last a limited time. His world had changed and advanced so much within the last century.

Thomas took one of his father's hands, Emily the other. Together they swam deeper into the sea, followed by an entourage of their fellow beings. Beautiful life forms in a variety of shapes and sizes lit the way.

The first sign of a city was a tower-like plant of a gigantic scale. It moved with the currents that made the structure sway from its base anchored to the edge of a cliff at the entrance to a canyon. From the roots grew a narrow stem that blossomed into a ball-shaped chamber. This was covered in a web-like, woven dome that, like everything else in this undersea world, was self-illuminating. Inside the vaulted canopy were mermen.

As William got closer to the tower he could see that these beings inside were also rooted in the center, attached by tendrils and tubes. The mermen were part of the plant's architecture and function, not just dwelling inside its dome. They moved their bodies and arms in unison, like weavers at a loom. Bulb-like sections inside the dome raised and lowered, changing degrees of light emissions as the mermen touched them. William knew whatever they were doing was beyond his understanding. The mermen sentries waved them on as they passed the great structure.

William could tell they were getting closer to his loved ones' new home when more plant guard towers appeared and in a variety of sizes and shapes. Volcano-shaped chimneys projected steam, gases, and light toward the surface. When they moved past the towers, William could feel their heat, which counterpointed the freezing water around them. The deeper they swam, the bigger the bubble that enclosed his head grew, until it encompassed his whole body. Emily and Thomas no longer held his hands. They guided William's bubble chamber like a clear beach ball. Sometimes he rolled over and over as they descended until his chaperones made him upright again.

Everything became brighter as they entered a great underwater mountain range. Sharp, jagged cliffs dropped off as they descended into the huge canyon. The overhangs were covered with the plant-like towers and giant tubeworm colonies that constantly fed on the millions of floating particles. Even his son and wife fed on these glowing entities as they descended deeper.

The surrounding mountains of this great canyon were made of limitless sizes and chunks of rock and crystals. The variety of stone and minerals reflected a whole range of changing colors and flashes of luminance. He had only experienced this world of light and color in a small way when he saw the spectacle of the boardwalk on Coney Island and the huge animated signs in Times

Square. The cliffs reminded him of the soft sparkle of the metal-beaded fabrics on draperies or costumes performers wore at the circus, for stage shows, or in the movies. The deep water reflected them into numerous points of light.

At the base of the canyon was the city. It looked like a group of huge, interconnected jellyfish anchored at a central hub — a gigantic structure of chambers with a main core that seemed to grow into the center of the earth and extend for miles. This glowing green nucleus rotated its millions of sections slowly, emitting waves of intense light and sound. Everything seemed to be fed by the power of this core that vibrated with intense yellows and oranges.

Even William could feel the rejuvenation in his body as they came closer to the city. Surrounding the great metropolis were more tower-like vents propelling gases, heat, and light. Beyond that were vast sections of fantastical plants rooted in the savanna that spread along the ocean floor.

Thomas and Emily smiled at William. They said in unison, *Isn't it beautiful? Isn't our home beautiful?*

They paused and looked down.

Emily spoke. *We will go to our daughter now. She is so beautiful and will be happy to see you again.*

They took a quick detour and sharply descended. When they reached their destination, William could get a real sense of the scale of this undersea metropolis. It was bigger than any place he had ever been to. The biggest city on land was small in comparison and it was obvious to William that this world and its inhabitants were much more advanced and more in tune with their environment than mankind.

The three stopped at a section along the outer hub. It appeared to be a large chamber with a series of smaller rooms inside. Everything was clear, as if it was made of glass, but all the walls pulsed with light and undulated as if they were breathing. The movement gave it the appearance of being inflated. It reminded

William of soap bubbles in a bath that joined and overlapped each other, constantly moving as they floated on the surface.

On the other side of the wall was a group of smaller, juvenile mermen. William wondered, *Is this a school?* He chuckled to himself and then realized that his son and wife also laughed at the pun.

The merchildren swam up to the wall and some went through the clear illuminated barrier. Everything was fluid here, even the walls of this great city. They gathered around him, laughing and poking at his bubble vehicle.

One little girl kissed Emily. She brought the child closer, and William knew instantly that this must be his January. Her eyes lit up and images of her on the beach with her mother and brother depicting the last moments of the child as a human were transmitted to William's thoughts.

The little girl swam through his bubble chamber then kissed and hugged him, but the joy of this sweet moment was short. The life-giving capsule burst from this action and William began to flail in the deep water. He started to drown and convulse from the pressure of the depths. His body spun and floated upward at an ever-increasing speed. He could see that his wife and son tried to reach him but without success. Then he blacked out.

When William came to, he raised his head in complete darkness. When his eyes adjusted, he knew he was back in his house, at the table covered in books and sketches.

He touched his body and clothes. He was wet. No ... damp. Was he in the water or was it his own sweat? He felt around for a light until he found the lamp on the console near the window.

He moved back to the table and picked up the bottle of wine. It was close to empty. He concluded that this beverage did its intended job. What he imagined was both amazing and frightening and all too fantastic to ever be real. In this dream his lost family was happy and that made him happy too. He had this wondrous dream of them and it was a spark of inspiration that made him ready to create.

William filled the kettle with water and took down a coffee mug from the cupboard. It was then that he noticed the sand on the floor. Did he go outside and into the water without remembering? This wine must have been stronger that he thought. What was real that night and what was just a dream? William wasn't sure as he picked up his pencil and started to sketch.

CHAPTER ELEVEN

Gaudi, Glass, and Balloons

The morning the foundations of the pavilion were started, Pompey Wright held an intimate groundbreaking ceremony. The Guillorys, the Wright troupe, the mayor, the men that began the work, and some local press were in attendance.

Pompey opened the festivity with a short speech. The mayor spoke briefly, then helped Cleo break ground with the silver-plated shovel they had ordered for the event. Everyone toasted with a non-alcoholic cider and the ceremony ended with a few photos taken by reporters.

Later that morning, William met with Pompey on his porch, just as it started to rain.

"Pompey, when I looked at the book you gave me I saw buildings and sketches by a Spanish designer named Antoni Gaudi. His designs, along with a dream I had, gave me the key to how we want our carnival to look."

Pompey smiled. "The best and worst things can come from dreams, but they are always a spark for creativity. Even the bad ones."

William nodded in agreement. "Gaudi's architecture reminded me of sandcastles and my dream of the creatures of the sea. Not the regular marine animals we eat or keep as pets, the ones of legend and myth, the denizens of the deepest parts of the ocean."

"Tell me about this dream in the greatest detail."

William wanted to talk about his inspiration, but hesitated to reveal the part of the vision that dealt with his lost family. He had to be specific, but also vague in his description of this very personal vision.

"I imagined beings that were half-man and half-fish, of a city made of sea creatures that were self-illuminating and ever changing in shape and context. I dreamed of fantastic gossamer animals that floated in the water like balloons and kites do in the air. Their beauty and scale were not to be believed. I think I owe it to your book with the drawings and scientific studies, but also to that bottle of wine you left me that day. After a few glasses my imagination took off."

"That is a great wine. I wish I could get more. I have to investigate the opportunities to do so if it helps the creative juices in such a positive way." The red-haired man laughed and adjusted his seat. "Tell me more of these marvelous balloons, monsters, and sandcastles. How do you envision them as part of our carnival?"

"I liked the textures the Spaniard used and the addition of glass and ceramic. This gave me the idea to use sandcastles as an inspiration. His buildings of stone and concrete took years to create. Ours could use the same ideas, textures and materials on the smaller structures and use plaster, canvas, glass, and wood on the larger ones."

William pulled out his first sketch from a large portfolio. "Pompey, here is the artwork for the Ferris wheel decoration and the additional lighting. I added a more decorative framework to the foundation area. The entrance will be built and sculpted to resemble a nautilus shell covered in colorful designs of glass and shell, like Gaudi, with steps inside leading you up to the passenger gondolas. The ticket booth will have a scroll-framed window and above the shell booth will be a painted smiling mermaid inviting you to take a ride. Attached to the base of the wheel and floating even higher than the Ferris wheel will be helium balloon sea creatures made of shaped bands of wood and sheer painted silks. They will float in the wind like the magnificent monsters of my dreams. We can fill the whole island with these floating marine fauna in balloon and kite form. People will feel like they're under the sea while witnessing the mythical denizens of a fantasy world float over their heads."

Pompey responded by leaping up and giving William a hug and a big kiss on both cheeks. "Wonderful! Inspired!" He quickly sat back down again. "Continue, show me more."

William pulled out additional sketches.

"Here is an overhead view of the bottom-of-the-sea design for the mosaic grand patio in front of the pavilion. This drawing shows my idea for the windows and doors for the pavilion and the two towers you had designed. Each window of the arcade and the towers will be stained glass and have a different scene with a fantasy sea beast in the same simple style of the mosaics."

Pompey leaned closer and listened quietly.

"The windows at the top of the towers will have matching sea motifs in bright colors to reflect the light inside. I am still working on the designs for the carousel and the theater, but I think this is a good start. The book you gave me helped a great deal, especially the work of the Spanish designer. I have been dreaming about oceans, sandcastles, and sea creatures every night since my first dream."

Pompey looked at the sketches, said nothing for a few seconds and then jumped to his feet. "Beautiful! Perfect!" William stood and Pompey hugged and kissed him even harder than he had the first time. "My good man, I suggest you keep looking at my book and take a long nap this afternoon so you can have more of those wonderful dreams. Let me know when you're finished. I must go over to the crew at the pavilion, and I also need to contact my friend who is a genius with glass. Can you make copies of all the window designs so I can send them to him?"

William was a bit off-center from all the hugging and his first

French diplomatic kisses. "I'll work on that right away."

* * *

William took Pompey's suggestion and sketched all afternoon, stopping only to work with Albert on some details for the carousel expansion. By twilight he had fallen asleep in the wicker chair on the porch. A soft, warm breeze caught a few of the drawings and carried them to the edge of the garden.

A silent figure skimmed with the ease of a serpent to the opening of the white scroll trellis. It caressed the arch, pressing its face against the small vines and flowers that necklace the garden gateway. The figure, Emily, looked down at the pieces of paper and picked them up. She studied the drawings with her luminous eyes and smiled. She moved up and onto the gingerbread porch and gently placed the pages on the table next to where her William slept. Her hand touched her husband's hair, and with the utmost care and delicacy, she brushed it off his forehead. Emily slowly bent over and kissed the sleeping man's cheek.

This caused William to move his head and adjust his body in an abrupt motion. Startled, Emily darted to the water, leaving only a trail of wetness and sand on the porch. She knew that if he saw her that moment, his illusion of her as a dream would be gone and the secret of their family would be revealed. It was better for it all to be a vision in his mind until the time was right.

He opened his eyes but wasn't sure if he was still dreaming. He smelled a sweet sea perfume and looked down at the glistening moist sand and water near his chair, trailing off of the porch.

William walked to the water's edge. He wet his hands, scooped up some seawater, and splashed it onto his sleepy face. He looked out at the water and the stars until it was completely dark and Albert called him back to the house.

CHAPTER TWELVE

The Green Storm

The fine mist developed to rain droplets as it continued up into the night sky. Mike stood frozen as he watched this phenomenon and felt himself get wetter the closer he came to the water's edge. The two dogs ran up to the thick wall of moisture, wet their noses, snorted, then moved back in caution. Travis and Poo smelled something in the watery cloud they didn't like. Mike tried to discern the glowing funnels of light in the distance. Were they tornados, waterspouts, or an optical illusion?

He moved back toward the house and signaled the canines to do the same. Travis and Poo retreated backwards as their general instincts were alerted. They knew that something was wrong. Mike looked above his head and saw greenish-gray clouds that tumbled in the sky, moving to the opposite horizon in the direction of Ridgewater. The air smelled like moist, dead grass. The ascending mist did not relieve the humidity and denseness of the atmosphere; it just made it heavier. The night sky was lighter than it was when they left the house just a few minutes before. The three reached the porch and the huge funnels in the distance looked brighter but it was still hard to make out their details.

"Claire, Mom!" Mike shouted as he cracked open the front door. "Look at this scary damn weather!"

The two women and Brian approached the entrance. Claire said nothing and just stared, wide-eyed.

Lovey Grace was about to speak when the boy exclaimed, "Holy shit, Grandma!"

Instead of correcting him, she agreed. "Holy shit indeed!"

"Mom, have you ever seen anything like this?" Mike asked. He turned to his wife, who was frozen at the doorway. "Honey, turn on the TV. See if there is anything in the news."

Claire rushed to the television.

Lovey Grace pulled Brian inside. "I'm going home right now to turn all my air conditioners on. I only left the one in my bedroom going. I don't want the awful damp stink in my house."

Brian called Travis. "Come inside, boy."

The big dog ran into the house, bumping into Lovey Grace in the doorway.

"I'm getting my things and going home with Poo."

Mike pleaded with her. "Mom, stay here tonight. I'll turn your air on. If this gets worse, I want us all together."

"No," his mother declared. "If this is the end of the world, I want to be in my own bed with a big glass of my scotch, a good book, and my honey, Poo."

He pleaded again. "Please stay?"

Lovey Grace went into the kitchen, followed by Poo.

Mike joined Claire, who was surfing channels on the television. "Any news? There has to be something. It looks like this storm or whatever it is goes all the way up the coast and is moving inland."

Claire clicked through channels until she landed on the cable show broadcasting from the largest city north of them.

A weatherwoman was pointing at a blue-screen map of the area. "Seems like there is an unusual spring storm based several miles out to sea off of our coast that is spreading, bringing mild precipitation, heat, and high humidity with it. There's also severe lightning and some tornado sightings have been reported."

The weatherwoman cut to a cell phone video that looked like what Mike and the dogs had witnessed. The recording was shaking and the audio was hard to understand, and it was from too far north of Plover's Island to be what they'd just experienced.

"Several similar reports and videos have been posted online, but authorities have yet to comment on any of them. Please stay tuned and we'll keep an eye on this storm for you. If we get any updates, we will let you know so your morning commute will go smoothly."

Mike muted the television. "I'm going online and see if I can find anything else." He headed for the bedroom.

Brian yelled, "Grandma fell and it's raining."

Mike turned back. "I thought she was in the kitchen. Brian stay inside with your mother."

Lovey Grace had left the house carrying Poo under one arm and a large covered basket with the other. As she walked down the porch, it started to rain downwards. She slipped on a wet stone along the path between the houses. Poo fell out of her arms and danced around her body, trying to help her up.

Mike ran to his mother's aid, followed swiftly by Travis. The big Rottweiler nuzzled Poo while Mike grabbed Lovey Grace's arm and helped her stand up. The rain fell in large, heavy drops, then in sheets until they were completely soaked. Travis grasped the basket in his mouth, carried it onto the porch and put it down by the front door. Poo followed. When Mike and his mom reached the door, Claire helped them in, then slammed it shut.

"Damn slippery stones," Lovey Grace cursed. "I think I knocked my hip out. Please get the basket from Travis, it still has some dessert in it. Thought I would save some for my midnight snack but I think we all need another a drink, don't you? I know my hip does."

"Should we call the doctor?" Claire asked as she helped her to a chair. "And what's this green stuff on your blouse? Is it from the rain? Let me get some towels."

Claire ran to the linen closet as Lovey Grace pointed to the dogs. "They have it on them too. Look at poor Poo, all tinted green like an old ladies' hair on Saint Patty's Day. What the hell is going on? They've really screwed up the world now."

Brian ran in from his bedroom. "It's crazy in the backyard. That big old turkey Trotter is really jumping around like a nut and he never comes this close to the house. The squirrels and birds are acting weird too. Dad, don't let Travis or Poo out again, they might get into trouble."

Everyone silently stared out the windows as the rain hit the ground even harder. It created large splashes of pale light that glowed lime green, then not at all.

Claire passed out towels and gave Lovey her white terrycloth robe with a Hyatt logo on it. Mike had changed into dry clothes, toweled down the dogs, and handed his mother her drink. Meanwhile, Claire gathered everything that was wet and stained and immediately put it all in the washer.

Lovey Grace just sat in her chair, nursing her drink.

"Claire?" Mike called out. "Save one of those items. I'm going to look at it under Brian's microscope. I want to see if that green stuff is the same as what I sampled from the ocean."

"Use mine," Lovey Grace said. "Then throw the damn thing out. My good blouse is ruined because of the crap they pump into the air. I should send the bill to the damn EPA."

Poo, now clean, climbed up on Lovey's lap.

"Give your Mommy a big kiss, sweet Poo Bear. You look your golden self, again." She hugged the little dog tightly.

The rain continued all night. Flashes of neon green and white lightning flashed in the darkness, followed by the loud drumming of thunder. That night, Lovey stayed on the pullout in the living room, afraid to go out into the rain and of being alone.

Dawn came, but there was no sun. The sky was filled with dark, green-gray swirling clouds and thunder boomed in the distance. Flashes of iridescent green lightning between the clouds created alien shadows against the billowing shapes. The sea was active, but not stormy. The waves that lapped upon the shore, seemed thicker, with less appearance of surf or foam. It was greener too, and if the angle was right, traces of light could be seen on the peaks of waves. One aspect of the morning was positive, at least — the rain had stopped.

Lovey Grace insisted upon helping Claire make breakfast, even though her hip was still hurting.

Claire pleaded with her. "Please sit down. I've got this. Do you want an aspirin to ease the pain?"

"I'm fine. It's just a damn bruise. I have some Percocet at home if it hurts later. I never used it up after my operation and I think it's still within the expiration date. One of those and I am good to go. The drug never made me sick like the doctor warned. I just get mellow and the pain goes away."

"If you want to help, arrange the plates and silverware for me. You can do that sitting down. Everything is on the table ready to go."

"Okay, okay, I'll take it easy. I did kill myself last night during opera night to protect the identity of the man I love, but of course the bastard told the princess his name anyway after I did the deed," Grace said in a deep voice. They both laughed.

Mike and Brian, eager to find out more news, discovered that the TV wasn't getting a signal and the satellite cable was out. Mike tried to get the computer to pickup a wi-fi signal, but no luck. His cellphone was also dead. So was their landline. He tried Claire's phone, then his mother's, but nothing worked. They still had power, but how long would that last? The old generators they'd had for years automatically kicked in whenever the regular electric went out, a real necessity when living on an island.

Mike and his son went to the boy's bedroom and put a section of his mother's stained blouse under the microscope.

"Looks similar to what was in the sample from the ocean but more concentrated and thick. It isn't as clear and watery."

"Maybe because it's dry?" Brian suggested.

"No, it's still wet and sticky on the fabric. I can see things moving and joining then pulling apart, like when you see cells dividing."

Brian made a face. "Like on the science channel show that was about crappy germs and virus stuff?"

"Sort of like that but these are shaped like crabs without arms or legs, just tentacles."

"Let me see, sounds gross." The boy pushed his father aside and looked into the microscope. "Holy shit, you and Grandma had those things on your clothes and on your bodies?"

The boy quickly looked at his father's head and pulled his hair until the man shouted.

"Take it easy! I don't have anything there now. I washed it last night."

"I better go check Grandma, Travis, and Poo for germs," Brian said as he headed out of the room.

"Hold on, son, let's keep this to ourselves. No need upsetting your mother and grandmother. You can quietly look over Travis but don't scare anyone until we know what is going on. Promise me?"

"I promise." Brian went to the backpack hanging on the door of his closet. "I need to get my magnifying glass but I will be discreet."

Mike laughed. "Discreet is the word of the day. Now let's go have some bacon and eggs."

Mike tried to disguise his concern at what he and his son had just discovered. This green slime from last night was in the rain and also in their hair and all over them. Mike felt a sudden chill that stayed with him until he kissed his wife and mother when he reached the kitchen table.

After breakfast, Lovey Grace was calmer, so Claire walked her home. The older woman talked nonstop on the short walk to her house, but Claire could sense she was not herself.

"Claire, first thing I want to do is check my windows to make sure none of the green stuff seeped in through the cracks and ruined my new drapes. Then I want to check and see if my phone works. You never know, we had a storm years ago and every phone was out but mine."

"Look at your poor plants," Claire said as they passed Lovey's garden. "It's a mess like ours and everything died. Look, your roses and the vegetables that we just planted the other day are gone."

"Maybe it's that acid rain thing they talk about? I thought that was fixed a few years ago. I didn't know that it had green stuff in it that would ruin our gardens and my favorite blouse."

"This is different and something else," Claire told Lovey as they climbed her steps. "I hope we can get a news report."

Mike and Travis walked over to Uncle Ned's to use his shortwave radio. Mike also wanted to check his uncle's house for any damage. It was fine, except that his garden was destroyed like the other two. Everything was flattened by the heavy rains and covered in the green wash that pooled in the puddles and seeped into the ground. Mike found the key under the front doormat and entered the house.

He did a general check of the windows and found the radio in the bedroom. The radio had its own little crank generator that gave power during blackouts. Mike powered up the generator, turned the radio on, and spun through the channels. He didn't pick up any transmissions until he found a signal at the end of the dial. He tried for thirty minutes to contact whoever was transmitting and then gave up. He packed up the radio so he could try later.

Mike sent Travis back home and decided to check the rest of the island on his own. He walked up the beach to the old carnival picnic grounds. There were two benches left and the remnants of the decorative marine sculptures still dotted the area. His father and grandfather had sold or removed most of the figures after the carnival closed.

He went to sit at one of the picnic benches, but it was stained with the same green substance that covered him when they were caught in the rain the night before. It didn't look slimy, just very wet. Mike walked past a partially broken and decayed whale sculpture. Only its smiling head was left. In the carnival's heyday, all the walkways were lined with huge plaster monsters like this. Mike reached the old seashell ticket booth at the front entrance to the carnival. Its colors were faded and cracked, but it was still impressive. The canvas walls that separated the park from the path to the dock had been gone for years. Only a few random support posts still existed.

Most of the plants and grass in the area were dead or dying. Whatever was in the rain really affected them the most. He didn't see any dead animals. In fact, the local squirrels were more rambunctious than ever. The birds on the beach seemed fine too. This must have been some form of acid rain with something in it that killed just vegetation.

Mike walked back to the pavilion area to see if the remaining structure was still sound. It was only a hollow shell and should have been torn down a long time ago to prevent any accidents. He stood in the middle of the once beautiful mosaic patio and checked whether any stray boards or glass had dislodged and created a hazard. He walked to the edge of the patio perimeter and was met by the only resident of what was left of the carousel tower.

"Good morning, Trotter, you nasty old bastard. You seemed to have weathered the storm okay last night. My boy said you were raising hell in our backyard. You know that is a no, no, old bird."

Trotter didn't do his usual noisy song and dance, but moved catlike from his tower lair. He tilted his head forward and dropped his tail for balance. His eyes glistened a dark shade of red. Mike felt an instant uneasiness. He moved slowly away from the pavilion carousel tower that was framed by the skeleton of the great Ferris wheel behind it.

Mike walked backward toward the concrete-slab remains of the old octopus ride. The ancient attraction had been replaced by a tilt-a-whirl in the thirties, but that was gone now too. Suddenly, the turkey ran at full speed toward him. Mike picked up a few stones and hurled them at the bird, but Trotter kept coming. Just as he was about to reach Mike, the turkey was hit in the side of the head by a stone that came from nowhere.

"Take that, you old fucker," Mike heard someone shout from behind him.

Mike turned to see his son a few yards behind him, with Travis at his side. Trotter retreated into the tower.

"Terrible vocabulary, but a great shot and timing," Mike shouted. "I'm glad you had your sling shot with you."

"I never come over here unarmed. Trotter is always on the attack. Oh, my vocabulary is fine. Got an A on my last test. It's my swearing that needs some work."

"Well since you saved my life I won't bring it up with your mother, but you have to cool it on the swearing. As your grandmother might say, 'It doesn't sound refined.'"

Brian laughed. "Grandma would never say that."

Mike knew his son was right. "Well, then Great-Grandmother Ariadne, she would agree with me."

Mike looked back at the carousel tower and then to his son. "What was with Trotter? I know he has always been mean, but just now I felt like I was being stalked by a raptor in *Jurassic Park*. He didn't do his usual gobble-gobble, wave-his-tail routine to protect his territory. The old bird was ready to kill me. That was the first time I've ever been afraid of him."

"All the animals on the island are screwy except our dogs. They were going crazy last night when the storm started too. I had to shoot at two squirrels that were going to attack Travis and me. Then a big seagull dive bombed us and almost crapped on us.

There were also some small birds flying into the side of the house and knocking themselves out."

"'The word 'crazy' is perfect to describe last night and today. I looked around the island and most of the vegetation is dead."

"Some new weird looking stuff is growing in the garden and on the side of the porch. It's all green and purple."

"I'll take a look when we get back."

"Oh Dad, I forgot why I came to get you. Mom said Grandma is sick. When she took her home, she had trouble breathing and had pains all over. Mom wants to see if we can get a doctor or something."

Mike picked up the radio he had placed on the ground. He wiped the bottom with a rag he had in his back pocket to remove any of the green substance. Mike threw the piece of cloth away and followed his son back to his mother's house. He moved as quickly as he could to keep up with Brian, but felt a little out of breath, which for a runner like himself was unusual after a short walk. The air was still so thick and heavy. His chest felt like it did when he tried to breathe in the steam room at the gym.

CHAPTER THIRTEEN

Enrico Foscari

A little over a week had gone by since the demonstration of the first kite and balloons. The test was a great success. The huge silk jellyfish balloon and the smaller kite version floated over the island until sunset. They could be seen in Ridgewater and the sight of the two marvels in the distant sky caused quite a buzz for the carnival. The other nine balloons and five kites were being completed at the two sailmaker shops in town. All employees worked full-time to finish the fabric elements. The air bladders that kept them afloat were being made at a balloon factory two states away. As the finished air bags were delivered, they were assigned to their structures and covered in silk or metallic fabric. Then the balloons or kites were assembled. It was the last week of May and much had to be done in the few short weeks left before the carnival opened.

Pompey worked with his construction crew to get the third stories of the pavilion towers constructed and the framework for the mechanical roofs built. This was an idea he had come up with after the balloon and kite test. He wanted the towers to be even more spectacular than before, giving the chandeliers that lit them more of a featured role.

He successfully got one of the architects to work out how the roofs would open. If Pompey wanted something to happen, he usually figured out how and who could get it done. Performing was his first love, but this gift for getting anything he wanted accomplished was his greatest talent.

William and Albert worked inside the temporary tent they had put up to house the four nautilus shell gondolas that sat on the inner part of the carousel. They constructed the sleds with flat sides carved in low relief to look like the beautiful baroque seashells. The design spiraled outward, then continued into the elegant bodies of sea horses positioned in the front part of the sled. Inside were leather-padded seats on opposite sides that held four riders, two on each side. All gondolas were still in the basic stages, with only the beginning of their applied relief designs. But even at this level they were amazing.

Ariadne sat in the gondola Albert was working on while they ate their lunch. "These are going to be wonderful," she said. "I can already tell what they will look like. I want my father to see them when he comes by today. He went to pick up Mr. Foscari at the ferry. He is the famous glass artist from New York who is creating the windows for the pavilion and also the chandeliers for the towers."

"I would love to meet him and talk about what he is also doing for the carousel. The scenic panels around the crown will be made of stained glass like the windows. The sections in the center covering the calliope will be the same and backed with mirrors. The roof will have decorative windows revealing the tower and the chandelier above."

Ariadne stood. "It's going be so beautiful and just as grand as my favorite merry-go-round in Paris at the Luxembourg Gardens."

"We'll need your expert opinion, then, when it's complete," Albert said.

Pompey entered the tent with a short dark gentleman in his early forties. The man was dressed in a suit jacket and denim work pants. Pompey and he were speaking rapidly in Italian. They stopped as soon as they reached William, who was working in the gondola next to Albert and Ariadne.

Pompey waved and blew a kiss to his daughter, then turned to William. "I want you to meet my dear friend, the famous and talented glass artist, Enrico Foscari. He has come from the great city of New York to see the carnival setup and especially you. He loves your concepts."

William extended his hand. "It is an honor to meet you, Mr. Foscari."

Enrico held on to William with both hands. "It is my honor, my artistic friend. Please call me Enrico. I am so thrilled about this project. It is *bello pazzo*. I can't wait for you to see my drawings for the windows and the crazy chandeliers. This is the most exciting challenge I have had in years."

William smiled. "Thank you. I am so happy someone with your skill will be working with us."

Pompey put his hand on William's shoulder. "I want you to walk the carnival with Enrico and I. Then we can go over the designs and timeline with a nice bottle of something relaxing. But first I would like you to say hello to my daughter, Ariadne, and William's son, Albert. You haven't seen my little girl in so long."

They walked over to the next gondola and Enrico extended his hand to Ariadne. "*Ciao, bella ragazza.* The last time we met you were a baby and now what a delightful woman you have become."

"Thank you so much, Enrico. I mean Mr. Foscari." She blushed when he kissed her hand. "I would like you to meet Albert Guillory, co-designer and builder of the carousel."

Enrico smiled at Albert and took his hands in his. "*Ciao, bello ragazzo.* Your father and you are true artists."

Albert, understanding only half of the greeting, replied, "Thank you, it is an honor."

Enrico, still holding Albert's hands, asked, "What are these beautiful creations? Did you design them?"

Albert was unable to point or gesture. "They are the nautilus shell gondolas for our carousel that I based on my father's sketches. I hope they will be as spectacular as his ideas when they are done. Everyone is working so hard."

Pompey smiled and then took Enrico's hands, releasing poor Albert from the Italian's grip.

"Let us first take a walk to the pavilion and then to the other attractions that you will enhance and glorify with your glass creations. Then we can go to my caravan and look over your sketches. Goodbye, my lovely daughter, and you too, my boy." Pompey paused and made an announcement to the others. "Back to work, everyone. Only one month left before we open."

Pompey retrieved William from his work and, along with the Italian, walked out of the enclosure. Enrico smiled and waved at Albert until they were out of sight.

Albert turned to Ariadne. "Nice man, but a bit strange. It must be that he is Italian or European or just from New York. I never met anyone from any of those places before. Are they all so informal and touchy?"

Ariadne smiled. "It's not the Italian, Europe, or New York City, it is the man."

She leaned into Albert and whispered into his ear. "*Omosessuale nelle sensibilita.*"

Albert looked puzzled having no idea what she just said. "Okay."

"His dance card is different than yours."

Albert, even more confused, continued his work.

The three men spent the rest of the afternoon talking about all aspects of the carnival that Enrico was involved with. At the end of the day they went into Pompey's small-but-elegant office. This was also where he hid his stash of wine and other spirits.

It was a Bertram Hutchings Voyageur caravan that he called his drawing room on wheels. The exterior looked like a cross between a small railroad car and a cartoon house. Instead of a row of windows like a train car, it had two double ones with diamond-patterned panes on each side of a narrow door. The outside was covered in synthetic leather in burgundy and dark gold. The interior contained a convertible sofa bed, wood paneling, desk, bathroom, and tiny stove. This was also to be used as the main carnival office until the pavilion facilities were ready.

"Before we sit down, let me get something."

He lifted the bottom of the daybed up and revealed a mini wine rack under it. Pompey retrieved three bottles and put them on the table. He then closed the curtains and turned on the small lamp next to a dual finial German clock on the compact mantel to the right of the front window.

"No need to draw any attention to our next activity."

William laughed. "You mean so we don't get raided by the feds?"

Enrico added, "Such a strange country where everyone indulges but no one admits it. Even good wine is a sin. My country, with all its faults, lets you at least enjoy a nice *vino.*"

Pompey opened a bottle and poured everyone a glass. Unlike William's teacup, he had the appropriate glass for the right wine, even in such small quarters. He was a true believer in packing the correct essentials for travel and the perfect wine glass was just as important as the right shirt, tie, or shoes.

"Let's start with a nice Prosecco in honor of our guest."

William looked at the tall thin glass. "I haven't had champagne in years."

"It is like that, but Italian from the Veneto region. You will like its lightness, with just the perfect amount of bubbles," Pompey explained.

"A perfect drink to have when meeting with friends and business associates," Enrico lifted his glass. *"Ad una grande impresa!"*

They raised their glasses as Pompey repeated Enrico's toast, "To a great enterprise!"

Enrico opened his bag and pulled out a handful of sketches on transparent velum. He placed them in a disorganized pile on the table opposite the burgundy sofa bed they were sitting on. He separated the drawings into four groups. The first to be discussed were the sketches for the windows of the pavilion.

"These drawings were easy. All I did was follow your designs with the magnificent, crazy monsters and beautiful patterns you created. What a mind you have to see such things beneath our waters. I was born in Venice, but could not have imagined these creatures. I have worked with plant, animal, and geometric shapes, but never ones like these. *Bravo, genio.*"

He toasted William and drained his glass, which Pompey promptly filled.

Between the end of one bottle and the beginning of the next they discussed the scenic panels for the carousel, the theater, and the bulk glass pieces for all the mosaics Enrico was supplying and producing. William also asked about vendors Foscari could recommend for the mirrors and the specialty glass for the maze.

They discussed Pompey's new idea for making the house of mirrors about the bottom of the sea instead of it being the usual haunted house attraction. He wanted it filled with glass plants and sea life like William's sketches.

When the three men got to the topic of the chandeliers, Pompey opened the third bottle of Prosecco. By this time William was very light headed.

"Here, my *bello* William, is my idea for your chandelier. These undersea marvels you designed lent themselves beautifully to my glass."

Enrico handed him a sketch of what looked like his jellyfish core of the fantasy city but much more hydra in appearance than William imagined.

"Each curling, grasping arm will be developed and shaped by me. They will then be assembled and attached to a metal frame. Inside will be the light source. I know you asked for the chandeliers to be in bright colors, but I think frosted white and clear will be the most versatile. This way we can change it to any hue we wish," Enrico said.

Pompey toasted and took sip of his drink. "That will be wonderful when they rise from the center of the domed roof and into the night sky."

William laughed and needed to hear that again. "It must be the drink, but I thought you said the chandeliers will lift into the sky from the open roof of the towers. I knew the roofs opened but not that the chandeliers would rise up."

"I did, I did say that," Pompey calmly stated as he took another drink.

Enrico jumped up and hugged and kissed him. "My crazy, red-haired, beautiful friend. If anyone can accomplish that it will be you. *Salute!*"

"Now I know I'm drunk because I actually believe you can do it too," William slurred. He tried to stand, but was only successful on the second try. "I would love to hear how?"

"Simple. The sections of the roofs of the two towers will mechanically open like the petals of a flower. I then will have men on cranks with a series of pulleys and cables turn them until the two chandeliers rise into the sky, rotate, then lower down again over the carousel and my theater. They will throw dazzling light throughout the carnival and the carousel, and they will create the most magical effects during our theater performances." Pompey took the last sip of his wine.

With that statement William had to sit down again, just missing Enrico's lap. "Hell, I really have to see that, but not tonight. I think I need a short nap followed by a pot of coffee. Still have work to do."

He managed to stand up, hug Pompey, then Enrico, and carefully worked his way out of the caravan.

"What a sweet man," Enrico said. "I like him even more, a little drunk."

"I think this carnival has been a wonderful challenge and boon for my dear William," Pompey replied. "He has lost a great deal over the last few years and this is his chance for a new beginning. William is a talented craftsman who was making furniture and playing with carousel designs as a hobby until we gave him a way to channel his craft into something extraordinary."

"The carnival will be a magnificent success for us all," Enrico said. "That's if we can all finish this insane amount of work in the next month without killing ourselves. It will be crazy, but I love crazy. I think you will have to smuggle some more good wine in to get us all through this and help keep everyone happy in the process."

"I just remembered, I have something good hidden behind the clock," Pompey grinned. "Let's have one more toast. A taste of old Scotland, okay?"

Enrico smiled. "One more toast then I will need to take a swim. The night is delightful and I haven't been on a beach since I left Venice. I always loved to swim at night after partying at the Lido. A nice nude swim was the best way to end the night."

"Sounds good, but I will go with you so we don't lose you to the ocean. I have to get you back to town before the last workmen's ferry leaves. As for nude, this isn't the Lido and I have some very proper swimsuits in my trunk."

"Will that handsome boy Albert be on the ferry too? I would so like to talk to him again."

Pompey laughed. "That boy is my daughter's property, even though he doesn't know it yet."

"Well the boat will be full of workmen and the night is still...."

"I guess I will need to escort you back to your hotel. I have my open room and an appointment in town after lunch anyway. You need you to create beautiful glass, not a big scandal." Pompey smiled and shook his finger at his friend. "Wait until you get back to New York, my dear Enrico."

They both laughed as Pompey proceeded to get the liquor from behind the clock.

CHAPTER FOURTEEN

Tangos and Carousels

The night before the opening of the carnival, William entered the Theatre of Curiosities looking for Pompey, who had sent a message via one of the workmen that he wanted to give him a preview of the Undersea Maze of Mirrors attraction.

When William entered the back of the house, he saw Cleo dancing on the stage. The workmen were gone and she was rehearsing her tango number by herself. She was blocking the steps and seemed frustrated. Pausing for a moment, she looked up and saw him standing in the back of the theater.

"William! Hello!" she shouted. "Can you help me, please? I need to practice my steps for the tango act I'm doing with Pompey and I haven't been able to get any time to rehearse with my brother. Can you be a dear and stand in as my partner? I promise I won't step on your foot."

William laughed. "I don't know how much help I would be. I haven't danced in years and I've never done the tango!"

"Don't worry about it. Please, I just need you to be Pompey for a few minutes so I can block my steps properly. I'll lead you through. It will be simple," she assured him.

"Okay, but I am more worried about stepping on your feet than you stepping on mine."

Cleo walked over to the old phonograph, cranked it up, and placed the needle arm on the record. As the music began they got into position and William put his arm around her waist as she started to count.

"Okay, now follow me. Step one, right front, two, left front, three, right side, four, left back."

William tried to look at her and his feet at the same time. Cleo counted out the tango terms softly. Then she called out the term *gaucho* as she whipped and hooked her leg around William's thigh. This move startled him and he lost his balance and grabbed at Cleo. They fell backwards and landed on the floor with her on top, facing a pinned William below. They looked at each other for a second then Cleo began to laugh. He could feel it throughout her body. This made him laugh and they both rolled over until William was on top.

He looked into her eyes. "I told you dancing wasn't one of my skills. I guess I did more than step on your foot."

They were still for a moment and Cleo kissed him lightly. He smiled, stood up, and extended his hand out to her. She reached for it and he pulled her to him. William held her closely to his body.

"I can do the waltz," he said with a smile as he started to lead her slowly around the stage.

The tango music had ended so William hummed a waltz and the couple continued to dance.

Pompey had entered the theater earlier, unseen, and witnessed most of what had happened. He smiled to himself. This was something he definitely approved of.

Pompey interrupted their moment. "William, I'm so sorry to be late. I see my lovely Cleo has kept you company."

"He has been kind enough to help me with my rehearsal since I can never get any time with you," Cleo said. "When can we rehearse, my dear?"

"How about right now? William can we meet at the maze in, say, thirty minutes?"

"Sure, I need to check in with Albert first at the carousel

anyway."

"Thank you so much for the help, William," Cleo flirted and then walked to her brother's side.

"You're welcome. Have a good rehearsal and I'll see you in the morning." William looked over at Pompey. "And I'll see you in thirty minutes."

He started to leave and then glanced back at Cleo. "Good night."

She gave a small wave as he left the theater. Pompey started the record with the tango music and took her into his arms.

"Cleo, Cleo, my lovely Cleo."

Then they began to dance.

*　　*　　*

Ariadne was riding on her favorite carousel horse, Guinevere. The calliope stopped and she dismounted. She picked up her embroidered handbag and pulled out a wrapped gift tied together with a silk ribbon. Clutching the bundle, she ran up to Albert, who was working at the center of the merry-go-round. He saw her reflection in the mirrored panels and turned around smiling.

"Did you enjoy your ride on good ol' Guinevere? Do you want another one? The carousel is all yours tonight," Albert said.

"Oh yes, of course. But first I have something for you. It only arrived this afternoon."

She handed him the gift.

Surprised, Albert smiled. "Thank you."

He opened the small bundle with great care. He took the time to untie the ribbon and roll it up as his mother had always done. Then he opened up the mauve cloth covering to reveal white tissue paper. Unfolding it, he discovered small brass engraved plaques. Each one had the name of one of the figures on his carousel. There was Wyvern, the dragon, Happy Harold, the polka dot pig, and Guinevere.

Ariadne could tell he was pleased. "After we decided to name the menagerie on your carousel I knew they needed a plaque for each to make it official. So I had them engraved in town. I was hoping they could have been ready sooner so they could be mounted for the opening, but I feel it may be too late now."

"It's not too late. We can do it right now. Can you help me?"

"Of course. What do you need me to do?"

"Just hold the plaques in place while I attach them. Oh, and thank you again." He quickly kissed her.

William arrived at the carousel just as Albert and Ariadne were attaching the last plaque.

"Look, Ariadne had these plaques made for our carousel menagerie and now each one has a proper name. Isn't it a wonderful idea?"

"Wonderful! And perfect too. Everyone who takes a ride will always remember their favorites by their name, the next time they come to the carnival. We should show your father. They could be sold as souvenirs to our customers. It would be a perfect memento." William turned to Ariadne. "Thank you so much."

"You're welcome, Mr. Guillory."

William placed his hand on his son's shoulder. "Albert, I forgot to ask about the calliope song cycle. Did you have the operator set that before he left? We want some good old patriotic tunes playing tomorrow."

"All set. They'll be playing all night and when they set off the fireworks."

"I need to go over that display with Pompey when I see him in a few minutes. Now I think it's about time for the two of you to get some sleep. Tomorrow will be a long — and I hope great — day for us all."

William stepped off the merry-go-round platform. "Good night, you two."

Albert turned to Ariadne. "I can walk you to your caravan if you can wait a few minutes. I have one more thing to check, then

I can shut the carousel down."

"I can wait."

He looked at her, took her hand and then kissed her. And then kissed her again.

CHAPTER FIFTEEN

Mermaids and Mirrors

William walked beyond the center arcade area where there were three smaller tented attractions featuring John the Magician, Madame Regina, and Carla's ballerina act. These were set up separately from the pavilion to give more room for arcade games and nickelodeons. These attractions would not be open all the time because of the performer's multiple duties.

Madame Regina's tent was in the center. She told fortunes by reading the Nordic Rune stones and tarot cards. She also had a crystal ball that was tricked out by Ned with mirrors and smoke. When she tapped the lever under her draped table, a canister released smoke that filled the clear glass orb and tiny mirrors inside spun, reflecting a ghostly light.

The type of reading was usually determined by how much the customer was willing to spend. Madame Regina billed herself as a Romanian gypsy princess whose lineage went back to the thirteenth century. She usually held an object from the customer in her hand when she called upon spirits from the past to give her guidance.

In truth, she hailed from Wales. Madame Regina was Regina Humphreys Pugh; the Pugh was added when she married the handsome half of a tap dancing team billed as Peerce and Pugh. To her misfortune, it wasn't the better half and they were only together a few months before he abandoned her.

After that, she headed to London, where she met John the Magician, who was eccentric and more than a few pounds overweight. He hired her to assist him in his act. They fell in love and worked together until he developed the new comic routine with Ned and Carla. Regina was never able to divorce Pugh because he could never be found. But John didn't care. He was happy to be with her in any arrangement.

In addition to the technical help Ned provided for Regina, he was also skilled at theatrical stage effects. He even learned to use filmstrips, lighting, smoke, and mirrors to create ghostly effects for his act with John. Ned also built and animated the puppet magician in the act that Carla and he did with John when they first met.

The other two tent venues were similar to Madame Regina's in their supernatural, mystic, and macabre offerings. John, when not doing his magician's act, would wear a medieval monk's costume and present a display of mystical objects. Most of the items were billed as ancient coins, jugs, and small statues from the time of the crusades. They were supposed to have been recovered from the tombs of the Knights Templar.

The featured object was billed as the mask of the Green Man from Le Mans Cathedral in France. It was described as the symbol of man's link to the earth. This mask was no real icon or relic, but a rubber-and-paste concoction with light-up eyes that animated when John chanted something that he said was Celtic but sounded more like Pig Latin. The mask was another one of Ned's little masterpieces of trickery. The audience loved it all and was happy to pay the five-cent admission.

Carla occupied the third tent and was advertised as the world's smallest ballerina. In the center of the draped enclosure, Ned, wearing a tuxedo, greeted the customers as they gathered around a small circular stage. He collected their money and gave a short speech, telling the mini dancer's story. Once the tent was full, Ned opened the curtain and little Carla began to dance on point to an abbreviated version of Tchaikovsky's *Sugar Plum Fairy* from the *Nutcracker Suite*. When the dance was over the customers were escorted out of the tent to make room for the next group of paying customers.

Beyond the trio of attractions was a spinning ride in the shape of a giant octopus. It had eight tentacle legs with a seashell shaped car at the end of each one. When the cephalopod rotated, its head went up and down while the shell cars spun in place, rotating with it.

The head and legs of the octopus consisted of a metal framework covered in painted canvas reinforced with mesh underneath to help prevent it from tearing and collapsing. The seating for the ride was carved wood, similar to the carousel gondolas, and had fabric cushions for comfort.

A few yards away, in the shadow of the octopus ride, was the Undersea Maze of Mirrors. This attraction was Pompey's version of a haunted fun house, but with an undersea theme. Enrico created blown glass plants and sea creatures to decorate the inside. Pompey challenged Ned to come up with some of his best tricks, especially with film and lighting for this amusement.

The little man became fascinated with trick photography when he saw the Méliès shorts and some of the work of Spanish filmmaker Segundo de Chomón in France years before.

Ned figured out that by projecting into mirrors at different angles he could create various ghost-like effects. They were making smaller 16mm projectors by then, so it was easier to adapt and conceal them. He placed the projectors in strategic places in the maze so that the ghost of a long-dead pirate or a monster fish made of bones appeared and disappeared on a glass wall when needed. The illusions were on timed film loops that played over and over during the attraction. He also used slides and old lantern projectors in the same way.

When you entered the first corridor, the bottom of the sea greeted you. The labyrinth was a series of tunnels that led throughout the attraction. As patrons entered, they were surrounded with the deepest depths of the ocean and all the plants and inhabitants that resided there. The illusion they experienced was that of being inside a wondrous submerged city with all its dangers and beauty. There was no real water, just deep blue green lighting that made the mirrored walls seem to appear and disappear at any moment and challenged the customers to find their way through.

The most interesting aspects of the maze were the three zoetropes and a rotating room at the end of the attraction. The zoetropes were not the nineteenth century toy, but large spinning chambers that appeared in three sections of the maze. Lights dimmed every few minutes and a two-way mirror revealed a rotating cylinder with slits in it. The patrons would then see an animated image of a ghostly apparition through the slits as the cylinder spun. The sound effects and the scary sight lasted a few seconds and disappeared. The brave customers then continued their way through the labyrinth.

* * *

William arrived at the Undersea Maze of Mirrors attraction, but no one was around. While waiting, he had the odd feeling that someone was watching him. In fact, he had felt this sensation since he'd left the theater. But he sensed it even more now that he was alone in the dark, with only the lights from the attraction to illuminate the area.

Pompey where are you? he wondered.

He waited one more minute then entered the front door of the building.

"Ned? Ned, it's William. I'm at the front. Are you around?"

The only responses were flashing lights and spooky sounds. At the entrance was a ticket booth that looked like a Jules Verne-inspired diving bell. What would have been the glass viewing area was the ticket window decorated with fancy rivets and scrolls. He turned left through a metal plate doorway and walked down the first mirrored corridor.

William was greeted by endless representations of his own images. The lighting was blue and animated like the reflections of water. Some of the mirrors he passed were distorted and twisted his body into bizarre shapes. In one mirror he was fat, and another thin. The last mirror made his head huge and his body the size of a child's. The farther he ventured down the hallway, the darker the lighting became until he felt like he was truly under the sea.

William called Ned's name again, but still there was no reply so he walked down the next corridor. This section was constructed as an eight-sided tunnel made of glass panels and riveted metal bands. It gave the patron the illusion of being in part of the undersea city. A garden of glass and fabric undersea flowers, coral, and plants flanked both sides of the hallway. The shadows of various marine life forms swimming over his head were mysterious and unsettling. The mirrored walls constantly changed from transparent to opaque as the lighting fluctuated in its intensity.

At the end of a corridor William was suddenly faced with the first zoetrope effect. The lights dimmed and a translucent figure of a pirate ghost appeared as a flickering, staccato apparition.

William felt cold for a moment, not knowing if it was the fright or an air effect. This animated figure was accompanied by the most comical cries, shrieks, and pirate jargon. Then, thankfully, it ended. He felt his way, pushing on mirrored panels until one swung open giving him the freedom to move ahead.

He passed down two more hallways. On both sides were the ruins of what he assumed was Atlantis and the wreckage of a pirate ship. Pale ghostly images of sea creatures like the ones in his dreams floated by. Some resembled his balloons and kites but on a much smaller scale. They had more elaborate detailing and were lit from inside.

In addition to the undersea world, the corridors featured trick tilting floors and fake exits to hallways that he could see went somewhere, but he was unable to enter.

William continued until he approached another of Ned's nightmarish cylinders. The lights dimmed and the strange underwater sounds and music were heard, but the flickering image that appeared was now a female form. At least, the upper part looked like a woman. The lower portion was something else. It was hard for him to tell in the dim lights.

Once his eyes adjusted, he was shocked to see that this figure resembled the Emily from his dream. What looked like a shark passed through and around what he took to be his wife's image. The shark's staccato shape was repetitive and continuous. The Emily figure moved more asymmetrically. A voice came from the female figure that said something that sounded like his name but was difficult to hear over the roar of rushing water, loud bubbles, and organ music. Before he heard his name again, the illusion was gone, the lights came up and a mirrored wall slid back giving him access to the next corridor.

He continued down the next hall and called Ned's name again.

Ned emerged from behind a mirror panel and stepped over some blown glass coral and sea urchins. "Hey, William. Where's Pompey? Wasn't he supposed to come with you for your tour? I wish Pompey didn't ask Enrico to do all this glass flora and fauna. I have to watch my every step. Don't ever tell him but there are a few purple blown glass tubeworms without their tubes. Had to hide that area. Thank the Lord for theatrical lighting."

William laughed. "He was meeting me, but the rehearsal with Cleo must have taken longer than expected."

"Well how do you like our Undersea Maze of Mirrors, my good man?"

"It was pretty frightening and spooky as far as I got. All the dark lights, shadowy sea monsters, and ghosts are certainly as scary as the old haunted house effects. Do we have insurance if you give some poor person a heart attack? That flickering image contraption will probably give me a nightmare."

"Oh, my zoetrope machine. I love that. It's just a toy, just a big spooky toy. Wait until you see the rotating room at the end. It has mermaids and ghosts bouncing off all the walls."

"Maybe next time. What I saw tonight was enough for now. Especially that strange woman who calls out your name while the shark swims around her. How do you coordinate that with the right person's name? Does an operator work from some sort of list they sign at the beginning?"

Ned was at a loss. "I don't know what you mean. There isn't anyone like that in the zoetrope. The only women are the mermaids in the rotating room and they are plaster figures on wires. The first one is supposed to be the ghost of Black Beard the pirate. The second is an animated shark and you didn't get far enough to see the third, which, is a school of fish skeletons. I wish we could figure out how to call out a person's name. That would really scare the life out of them."

William smiled but said nothing.

"I guess we got you good if you're frightened enough to see and hear things that aren't there, my dear William."

The two men walked back to the front entrance while Ned proudly pointed to and described every aspect of the attraction. William could see how excited he was with his creation. When they arrived at the entrance, Pompey was still not there.

William shrugged his shoulders. "I guess I'll go back to the theater and tell him not to come. I need to make some notes for Albert and the operators in the morning. We all have to be up at sunrise, even though we don't open until ten. Tomorrow is a big day for all of us. Good night, and thanks for the scare."

Ned returned the goodbye and walked back into the maze building as William worked his way to the theater. Most of the lights of the attractions were off now. The moon was behind a large cloud and gave little illumination to the island. William decided to return to the pavilion via the beach. It was safer and there wouldn't be anything like rigging ropes, stray boards, or rocks to trip over.

He was walking at the water's edge when he sensed something behind him. The clouds that blocked the moonlight moved and it was clearer to see. He turned and saw the figure of his Emily about twenty feet away at the edge of the grassy dunes.

"Emily?"

The being retreated into the tall dune grass then suddenly appeared in front of him. It was Emily, the Emily of his dreams. She wasn't wearing the pale yellow cotton dress. Long tubular hair-like strands slithered around her face and caressed her shoulders and breasts like slender translucent serpents. She smiled and projected his name though her thoughts, *William.*

He gazed wide-eyed at the figure in front of him. Without the yellow garment from his dream, every aspect of his Emily from the sea was revealed. This wasn't any dream and he knew that. She was truly a creature, this was happening, and she was real.

He paused, looked at her, then extended his hand. "Why were you hiding and why were you following me? I could feel your eyes all night."

She slid slowly toward him. Emily's hair constantly danced. Her skin glistened in the cool blue light and her lower body of scales tapered smoothly to a tail fin with an illumination of its own. She glided close to William's face, kissed him lightly and spoke with words, not thoughts.

"The woman, do you love her?"

He knew from this question that she had indeed been watching him all evening.

William looked at her. "Cleo is a friend. My only love was my wife but the Emily I knew died." Tears ran down his face as he stared directly into her eyes. "Who are you? What are you?"

Emily saw the tears and felt his fear and revulsion at what he saw in front of him.

The smile left her face. "It is me and I am your Emily, but new and better." She paused. "You can love the woman now but you must come to us when it is your time."

She slithered around him, touching his body with her long fingers and razor-sharp nails. She scratched him, tearing his shirt and breaking the skin. When Emily faced him again, she ran her fingers along his neck and he could feel the pain of her touch.

Emily repeated, "You can love her until your time comes to be with us again."

She kissed him hard, holding his face in her hands. She looked at him. His eyes were tightly closed. Emily turned toward the water and disappeared into the night.

William heard the splashes and he knew she was gone. He fell to his knees. What he thought was a dream, a symbol of his love and loss, was now a nightmare too unreal to comprehend. The scratches on his body, and the imprint of her fishlike form clearly visible in the sand confirmed what had just happened.

William went home instead of going to the pavilion. Still in a daze, he couldn't talk to anyone. His wife and family were half human and half a thing from the depths of the ocean. And she had also acted in a way he had never experienced before. The Emily of his dreams and life was soft, loving, and kind. This being tonight was frightening and jealous.

How could he deal with this? How would he get through the rest of the night, tomorrow, and his life with this knowledge he couldn't reveal to anyone without sounding insane?

CHAPTER SIXTEEN

Crazy

By the time Mike reached his mother's house, groups of small birds were flying in erratic patterns overhead. Brian turned to his father with concern, but said nothing. Travis looked at his master and rubbed up against his leg. A squadron of small birds attacked a gathering of piping plovers foraging on the beach. One even got its claws into a little plover and was mauling him as they rolled in the sand. Another group flew suicide mission into Lovey Grace's side windows, causing the glass to crack on one of them. A seagull flew down and picked one small bird from its formation mid-air and tore it apart.

"Brian, help me close Grandma's shutters."

The boy climbed up onto Mike's shoulders and they worked their way around the house closing shutters that couldn't be reached from the ground. "Son, when we get inside, look for cardboard or something to cover the cracked window and the ones over the doors until I can find some wood. Thank God Uncle Ned convinced us to install storm shutters on the houses. We can close his and ours after we see Grandma."

The three entered Lovey Grace's house to find the living room and kitchen empty. They walked to the bedroom, but Mike stopped the boy and the dog.

"You two stay out here. If your grandma isn't feeling well, she won't want too many people around. Keep an eye out for Trotter to make sure he didn't follow us back. And turn on Uncle Ned's radio so you can scan the channels for a signal. I know he taught you how to use it." Mike paused. "But the first thing I need you to do is to cover the cracked window and the little ones over the front door we talked about. Grandma should have some gift boxes in the closet and there should be scissors and tape in the kitchen."

Brian sensed the seriousness of the moment. "Sure Dad, I've I got it all covered." Brian turned to the dog. "Boy, keep a watch out for Trotter while I get to work."

Travis went to the front window, propped his front paws on the windowsill, and peeked through a crack in the shutter. The big dog's eyes were transfixed on the pathway and beach. Travis hated the turkey ever since the beastly fowl attacked him as a pup, when he innocently wandered to the pavilion area.

* * *

Little Travis had been playfully pursuing a squirrel he'd encountered at the back of the house. By the time he lost the fuzzy-tailed rodent, he was at the site of the old Ferris wheel behind the pavilion. The pup was sniffing around educating himself about this unfamiliar place when, without notice, he was attacked from behind. Trotter took a small chuck out of the tip of Travis' tail with his lethal beak. Travis had never felt a pain like that before and it was an unwelcome sensation. So far, his short life was about kisses, hugs, treats, and play. Mike never got his new pup's tail docked when the breeder suggested it. He felt it was unnecessary and cruel. Now this crazy bird had taken the end piece off of his beautiful wagging tail.

Travis turned quickly and behind him was this thing with mean eyes, feathers, and his blood on its beak. The pup had no idea what this monster was. He ran home as fast as he could and into the arms of his master. Mike bandaged his poor bloody tail and made it feel better. Since that event, the bird was the dog's one and only enemy. Travis and Brian never ventured to the pavilion without each other for backup.

*   *   *

Mike entered his mother's room and saw Claire sitting on the bed holding a damp cloth to Lovey's forehead. Poo was at his wife's feet waiting for his turn to comfort his Lovey Grace. Mike's mother was breathing in short, labored inhalations and he heard the faint sound of wheezing.

He stood next to the bed and addressed his wife in a whispered tone. "How is Mom?"

"She has a little trouble breathing and all her joints started aching."

Lovey Grace spoke up. "Hi, I hear you and I'm not dead yet. It feels like the damn flu but who catches that in the spring?"

Mike looked at his mother with the greatest concern.

She could read his mind and before he had a chance to speak, she declared, "It's not a heart attack and I would know. I helped your father through three of those."

"Do you want an aspirin or tea and honey?" Claire asked.

"No aspirin, but there is a bottle of Percocet in the top draw of this nightstand. I'll take one of those and a shot of scotch in a little hot water. That will do the trick. I can get some sleep and I should be fine by dinnertime."

Then she changed the subject with a barrage of questions. "How is the island after that lousy storm? Is everything dead like our gardens? Have you been able to get in touch with Ned or anyone else? Are the phones still out?"

"The storm, acid rain, or whatever it was, pretty much killed all the plants and grass. Nothing was down though, and all the buildings are intact. Also, Trotter attacked me. He was ready to do me in if our Brian didn't save me with his sling shot."

"I hate that bastard turkey," Lovey Grace exclaimed. "Son-of-bitch isn't even good enough to kill for Thanksgiving. If Ned didn't have such a soft spot for that monster we could have shipped him off to turkey heaven — or hell, in his case — years ago."

"I think he would have a hard time getting into either, that's why he has lived so long," Claire laughed.

"Enough about that guy," Mike said. "To answer your last question, the phones are still out. I picked up Uncle Ned's shortwave radio to check for any signals."

Lovey winced in pain as she adjusted herself in bed. "Why is it so damn dark in here? It can't be night already."

"No, it's only two o'clock. I had to close all your shutters because the birds are going crazy. They flew into your kitchen window and cracked it. Brian is taping it now along with the little door windows. Since last night nothing has been routine."

"Damn, first it's the storm from hell now it's *The Birds*. What's next, locust?" She looked up at Claire and painfully adjusted her position in bed again. "Please get me some water so I can take my pill, and don't forget the scotch. Make it a big one."

Claire looked at her seriously. "Do you think that is wise? Percocet is very strong, but with whiskey? Throwing up could be added to your aches and pains. I'll get you a little whiskey in hot water with some sugar in it."

"Okay, Mommy, whatever you say," Lovey replied in a little girl voice.

Mike smiled and kissed his mother while Claire went into the kitchen. "Love you, Mom. Listen to Claire and get some rest."

"Love you too." Lovey Grace moved again to get comfortable, but not without more pain and coughing.

As the day progressed, there still was no contact from the outside world. Mike and the boy had little success with the radio. They closed and secured the storm shutters on all three houses. Mike found some pieces of plywood for the doors and some one-by-threes for the front windows. He secured the glass panes with tape and covered anywhere a crack or hole could be found. The last thing he wanted to deal with was a bite from a rabid squirrel or a crazy seagull attacking them in bed in the middle of the night.

Claire constantly checked on her mother-in-law. Poo had climbed up onto the bed and lay by his mistress' side. The little dog used his paws to knead and massage his Lovey Grace in an attempt to ease her discomfort. He had to be taken, reluctantly, for a bathroom walk outside, but was quickly allowed back on the bed to be next to his owner. Fortunately the pills and scotch did their job and she slept the whole afternoon. Claire and Mike took turns staying at her house to be there if she awoke.

By dusk, there were signs of more changes on the island. The dead plants and grass had become compost for new budding greenery of an unknown nature. These plants had progressed rapidly since the morning. By evening they were in full bloom and spreading toward the beach and the three bungalows.

The sky never lost its glow and spirals of illumination on the surface of the water replaced the tornado-like funnels from the storm the night before. They looked like pinwheels of light swirling clockwise beneath the waves and deep below the surface.

The erratic activity of the wildlife on the island quieted down, so Mike felt safe to sit with Travis on his porch. He watched the rotating light pulsate in the distance as it highlighted the crest of the surf that lapped thickly onto the shore. The air was almost too heavy to breathe, but he needed to stay outside for a while after being cooped up in the house for so many hours. Whatever this phenomenon was, he knew that they had to make some move soon before it got worse.

Mike worried about the malady that afflicted his mother. The green goo that stained their clothing; was it the cause of her illness? Would he get sick too? Claire and the boy were fine, but was that due to them not being caught in the rain? The dogs got wet but showed no signs of any illness. Travis was more alert than ever. Whatever made his mother sick made Travis brighter and stronger. He hadn't spent any time with Poo except to see the little dog comfort his mother.

Getting sick terrified Mike because who would keep things together? He may have to go to the mainland to get a doctor if his mother became worse. This meant leaving them all alone to face whatever was happening.

The sea looked lethal and he didn't even know if he could get to Ridgewater. Was the water poisoned? Would the boat make it or sink and kill him? This was the first time in his life he didn't know what to do. He always had support from his father and Uncle Ned. He knew Claire could handle a situation if he went to the mainland, but what would that be now? Since the storm, everything was an unknown variable. This wasn't a normal hurricane, flood, or natural disaster. The green skies, the glowing light, all the dead plants, and crazy animals were not something he could leave his wife, child, and sick mother to deal with on their own.

He looked down at Travis and stroked his head.

"What the hell is going on, boy? Why aren't you sick? Why aren't you and Poo going crazy like the other animals?"

The big dog looked into his master's eyes and he seemed to hear him say, *I don't know Mike. I can feel something different, but I don't know what it is.*

CHAPTER SEVENTEEN

Lovey Grace

Mike rose from his chair, left his porch, and walked to his mother's house, leaving Travis to keep guard outside. It was his time to replace Claire. Mike did his best not to show his wife how frightened he was. When he entered, his mother was still sleeping. Claire turned and her look gave him a feeling of sadness. She stood and hugged her husband and they walked to the bedroom window.

"I'm really worried. Mom isn't any better. She woke up in a lot of pain, so I gave her two of the Percocet to ease it. I didn't know what else to do. Lovey Grace is a trouper and for her to show she is in that much pain means it's bad."

"I'll go get a doctor now. My boat is okay and is still at the old dock."

"It's almost dark and what if you can't get to the mainland? We don't know what's out there. And besides, we need you here. I need you here."

Claire was thinking the same things he had been. Could he even make it across the water — if it still was water? If he made it across, could he even find a doctor? They knew nothing. Ridgewater could be a town full of sick people just like his mother.

Mike looked at Claire. "We have to do something. I wish we could look up the symptoms. Do we have any medical or first aid books? I never look in a book anymore when you can Google it."

"Nothing, all we can do is help her with the pain for now. I think we should wait until morning. Help might show up. It has only been a day and maybe the phones will work again."

He kissed her lightly. "You go home and take care of Brian. Travis is on the porch and he will walk with you in case anything acts up. Fortunately it's been pretty quiet, but keep the dog by your side in case one of those crazy birds or squirrels or whatever tries to get into the house. I'll check the phones here and then Uncle Ned's radio all night until I find something."

He walked to the bed and looked at his mom. "Claire, when did you say you gave her the pills?"

"About thirty minutes ago, but we have to be careful not to give her too much. The dose is very strong and it says no more than two pills every six hours or they could cause liver damage. If she wakes up and wants more, just put a damp cloth on her forehead and make sure she is comfortable. When the time has passed you can safely give another dose."

She paused and looked up at Mike and took his hands.

"I know it's not our style, but maybe we should do some late-night praying, too. Can't hurt."

"I'll try anything." He smiled and kissed his wife.

After Claire left, Mike sat in the floral print chair by the bedroom window. He stayed there for several minutes, looking at his mother while flashes of his life filled his head. He saw himself on that same bed cuddled up against his mother while she read him a storybook or an article from the newspaper or her favorite, *The New Yorker* magazine. They laughed at the cartoons and Lovey Grace explained the ones he didn't understand. He chuckled when he got the joke and even when he didn't. Lovey Grace read to Poo now and showed the same jokes in the magazine, but she laughed to herself.

He left the chair, walked to the bed, opened the nightstand drawer, and took two of her pills. He may need them later if he became sick. Mike tried to be quiet, but Lovey Grace woke up and moaned in pain. Poo, at her side, whimpered and increased the speed of his massaging paws.

"Mike is that you?" his mother asked.

"Yes. How are you feeling?"

"Not good. I need another Percocet. The pain is really bad."

He poured her a glass of water. "Drink this and I'll get you a cold cloth. You can't take more pills yet because it will make you feel worse."

Mike left for a moment to rinse a cloth in cold water. When he came back, he placed it on his mother's head. He knew they had to get to the mainland.

Mike sat on the bed and took her hand.

"I'll take the boat to Ridgewater and get a doctor back here in the morning. Get some more sleep and I will give you another pill as soon as you wake up."

He stayed at her side until she fell asleep again.

Mike looked at Poo and whispered, "Boy, take care of our mom for a while. I'll be in the other room."

The little dog looked him in the eye and, like Travis, seemed to communicate, *Don't worry Mike, I'm here.*

Mike worked hard to control his desire to cry when he left the bedroom. He knew he had to get to town for his mother, but the thoughts of the danger in doing this repeated in his mind. Was the glowing ocean poisoned? Would he die as soon as he touched it? Would a boat make it to the other shore? All these questions were a mystery, but what other choice was there? If he did nothing but wait, Lovey Grace could die, and so could they all.

He checked the landline phone and both his cell and his mother's. Everything was dead. Mike sat at the shortwave radio and slowly turned the dial. All he heard was static and more static. After about twenty minutes, he picked up something that was faint, but sounded like a signal. He barely made out a voice and then it was gone. Was anyone out there? Civil Defense? The state patrol? Anyone?

Mike went to the bedroom to check on his mother. Thankfully she was sleeping soundly. Poo was still massaging her with his paws. The poor little dog must have been so exhausted, but he continued kneading her side. Mike went back to the radio until his eyes closed and his head almost hit the table. He took a break and stretched out on his mother's couch.

*　*　*

A sound came from the sea. It didn't so much resonate in the air as it did through the ground. Poo felt it before he heard the deep tone. It was more like a whale's song, but steady, without change or modulation. The little dog was frightened at first, but the sound felt warm and relaxing as it pulsed through his body. Poo sensed Lovey Grace stir beside him and she slowly sat up in bed and looked at the window.

A light illuminated through the cracks in the storm shutters that wasn't there before. This cool glow stretched to the bed, creating a faint striped pattern. The sound continued as she got out of bed. Poo didn't sense she was in pain as she moved. The light and sound seemed to have eased all that.

Lovey Grace stood and looked at the little dog. *Time to go to the sea. Time to go to the sea.* She repeated this phrase again and again.

Poo heard her but she did not speak. She talked to him with her mind and body through the sound. The little dog sat up on the bed and was about to bark, but something told him he should be quiet. Lovey Grace slowly walked to the window and then headed out of the bedroom. Poo followed behind her into the living room past Mike, who was sleeping on the couch.

She looked at her son and smiled. *Mom is going to the sea. I love you. I will see you soon when you join me.*

Then Lovey Grace looked at Poo. *Stay, my little man. Stay here with our Mike.*

Poo tried to cry but he couldn't make a sound. He disobeyed his mistress and followed her out and down the steps to the beach.

He saw the light from the water pulse gently as they reached the water's edge. Assorted birds watched, but nothing moved, attacked, or even took flight. When Lovey Grace's feet touched the surf, several shell-covered arthropods emerged from beneath the surface. They were larger and more fantastical than horseshoe crabs and gleamed in the water. Long, translucent tentacles projected from under their segmented shells and touched her. When Lovey Grace was waist-deep in the green water, they surrounded the woman. One creature's arms attached to her back and it climbed gently up onto her until its form encompassed her head and neck.

The clear fingers caressed her face as she turned to Poo, who was sitting at the water's edge. *Goodbye for now, my little Poo Bear. Mommy is going to her new home. Take care of my family until we all see each other again. I love you, and stay here with our Mike for now.*

She turned toward the spiral light and the sound and then walked into the ocean until Poo could see her no longer.

The little dog tried to enter the surf, but the strange arthropods stopped him with the caresses of their long appendages. Their touch was not harmful, but soft and pleasant. He felt his Lovey Grace repeat her request through these creatures' touch. He sat near the water until the light dimmed and the sound was gone.

CHAPTER EIGHTEEN

Opening Day

All the wildlife of the little island, including the mischievous squirrels, abandoned their normal routines to watch all the last-minute preparations. Small booths and tent structures lined the long walkway from the dock to the front gate. Some of these stands were populated with concessioners selling trinkets, drinks, food, and sweets. Others ran games of chance like the milk bottle throw and the wheel of fortune, assorted dart and balloon games, and nickel pitching. They were independent contractors who leased their space from Pompey Wright and weren't part of the carnival crew.

Once patrons arrived at the front gate, they were greeted by a twenty-foot arched entryway topped by a sign trimmed in hundreds of lights titled Wright's Carnival of Curiosities. In the center was the logo of Pompey's company, a golden mask with curled up edges like a paper scroll, outlined in lights.

On each side of the arch were stretched canvas walls painted with fanciful images of sea life and scenes of the ocean. They were lashed to steel-framed supports that protected the scenic tarps from the wind. At different intervals, each vertical steel support was crowned with sand-and-glass textured starfish finials. On both sides of the gate were clamshell-shaped booths selling entry tickets. This pass gave access to the carnival and most of the attractions, except for the inner theater pavilion show. When a customer wanted to ride the carousel or Ferris wheel, all they had to do was get their ticket stamped by the person at that booth.

Floating over both sides of the gate were groups of fish-shaped balloons attached to cables. A fine and almost invisible cable joined the aquatic balloons to each other, creating a unified school of brightly colored sea creatures. This sight was sure to make the customers look up as they entered the carnival.

Once past the gate, customers were greeted by another long walkway. On both sides of this stone path were sand sculptures of mythical mermaids, whales, giant lobsters, clamshells, and sea serpents. The figures were made of plaster, sand, glass, and canvas and were much lighter in weight than they appeared.

Everywhere you looked there were kites and balloons floating in the sky over the park, guarding the magical landscape. Anchoring the balloons closest to the pavilion and amusements were tented canopies with seating. These gave shelter and rest to anyone who wanted it. Pompey planned in the future to build large wooden gazebos next to the picnic area to serve a similar purpose.

As the patrons ventured farther, the grand pavilion was to their left and the entrance to the picnic and beach areas to their right. The pavilion patio had tables and seating framing the outer perimeter of the circular mosaic. The central area was left open for dancing. The main theater was closed until evening, but the outer open-theater stage had a small orchestra playing music continuously.

Inside the pavilion were two small concession stands at each end of the building. They served mostly drinks like coffee, tea, soda, and snacks to the people sitting on the patio or playing the coin-operated amusements and games. Two uniformed waiters served drinks to the patio crowd during the day and one extra man was added for the evening.

Two photo kiosks were set up at the carnival near the pavilion. They had layered canvas-and-wood fantasy scenes of the ocean that customers stood in front of to get their pictures taken for a nominal fee. The tableaus had holes cutout so the patrons could poke their heads through and make believe they were mermaids, King Neptune, pirates or comical fish.

Pompey spent the first day touring the carnival grounds and greeting the customers. At one o'clock in the afternoon he was at the photo kiosk with the mayor of Ridgewater, posing for a picture.

"Your Honor," Pompey said, "you and your lovely wife stand in front of the seashell and I will peek my head from behind this old pirate ship. First let me replace my fedora with this bicorn hat with the skull and cross bones on it. We have several props available to our customers to wear for their photo souvenirs."

He placed the politician and his spouse in front of the tableau, then attracted the attention of the photographer who operated the kiosk.

"My dear man, get the mayor and his lovely wife the king and queen crowns and those beautifully decorated sashes — plus a good handful of these colorful beads."

The attendant accessorized the mayor and his wife as instructed.

When all was ready, Pompey announced, "Now everyone say Seaweed!"

The photo was taken, followed by several more with the couple together, one each with Pompey and a few with some of the onlookers watching the proceedings. When it was over, Pompey handed the mayor two tickets to his show for that night at the pavilion inner theater. He also passed out a few to some of the customers walking by. Pompey knew it was a good idea to paper at least fifty percent of the house for the first and second show.

While working his way to the pavilion, he noticed Albert sitting at a table holding an ornate box.

When Pompey reached him, he put his hand on the young

man's shoulder. "Albert, my dear boy, how is business at the carousel? Are we packing them in?"

"Oh, hello, Pompey. I was just taking a break to hear Ariadne sing at two o'clock. And the business is great at the carousel. We have had a steady crowd since we opened."

"Fabulous! And thank you for reminding me that my daughter is singing soon. With all the craziness, I almost forgot."

Pompey sat down at the table, looked around, and turned his attention back to Albert. "What do the people like best about the ride? I bet it's your wonderful creations. They're so amazing."

"Everyone likes the fantasy animals, but what they seem to enjoy the most are the effects from the overhead chandelier. Riders look up in amazement at all the light and colors pouring through the carousel's stained glass canopy. It's like a huge round church window over their heads. Most of the customers haven't even noticed the brass ring to win a second ride."

"I will have to tell Enrico tonight when he arrives. Wait until the real show gets going this evening. They'll be in for a marvelous surprise."

"The crowd will love the fireworks. My father said something about the tower roofs opening up and the chandeliers rising into the night sky. I can't wait for that. The crowds will go crazy."

"Let's hope so," Pompey said. He raised his hands to reveal fingers crossed on both. "Who is your little gift for? I hope my lovely daughter. You must know she is very fond of you."

"Yes, it's for Ariadne. It's a thank-you for the plaques she had made for the carousel animals."

"The plaques are a superb gift and a very good idea. She obviously inherited my business sense." He paused a second. "I don't want to sound like a prying father, but how do you feel about my daughter? All she talks about is you."

"I am very fond of her, but she's so beautiful and talented. She would be bored living on a little island like Plover's."

Pompey gently gripped Albert's arm. "She may have my

business acumen, but like her dear mother, she would love the perfect home and family with the right person, anywhere. Ariadne has experienced a lot in her young life and knows more about what is important to her than a person much her senior. The best thing you can do is to tell her how you feel, as soon as you can."

"Thank you," Albert replied.

A local talent had just finished his song on the outdoor pavilion patio stage. Polite applause followed a few catcalls and boos from the back tables. Albert looked around and located the disturbance. Four young locals had staked out a table near the carousel and were banging on it with what looked like unlabeled bottles of an unknown beverage.

Albert looked at the rowdy table. "I hope those asses don't disrupt Ariadne's performance."

"Don't worry, my young man, I have things under control," Pompey said with a smile, as the orchestra's leader announced his daughter.

When Ariadne walked out, whistles and jeers were heard from the gang at the table. The terms "sweetheart," "babe," and "blondie" could be discerned. Suddenly there were moans, yelps, and the scrapping of chairs on the stone patio. Albert turned to see five very large men drag the young hooligans away.

Without looking from the stage, Pompey stated, "I told you I had things under control. The first item on my to-do list for our enterprise was security, and there are at least twenty plain-clothed officers stationed around the carnival. Years of touring with my company taught me that was priority number one when dealing with any group of people. There is always someone who wants to cause a disturbance, so it is best to remove them quickly so the rest of us can enjoy ourselves."

Ariadne thanked the crowd and announced her song. "For my first selection, I will sing a piece by my favorite French soprano, Ninon Vallin. It is Rachmaninoff's *Chanson Géorgienne.*"

Albert gazed intently as she sang. He had never heard Ariadne sing before, except in very short little phrases when she was being silly. She was so beautiful. Her long blonde hair was lightly curled, but still looked modern, even though it was not the fashion. Her dress was a pale blue cotton chemise with a delicate floral print that was barely discernible. Albert couldn't take his eyes off her and Pompey smiled as he watched him through the corner of his eye.

Ariadne's second song was Victor Hubert's *Sweethearts*. She surprised everyone with her third and final selection of a current favorite — *Yes Sir, That's My Baby* sung in a light operatic style. When she finished, there was a good level of applause from the people sitting on the patio and from customers passing by on their way to other attractions.

Albert and Pompey stood after her performance and clapped until she walked off the stage. When the applause calmed down, the orchestra leader announced that you could see Ariadne Wright sing again in the pavilion theater show that night and also at the fireworks. He then stated that they were taking a brief pause and that a local act, obviously known to the crowd, given their reaction, would appear in ten minutes.

Pompey sat, but Albert, still in a bit of a daze, stood until Ariadne came to their table.

She kissed her father and then Albert. "Did you both like it? I think the audience did."

Pompey hugged her. "You were superb as always, my dear."

"Yes, wonderful!" Albert added.

Pompey sensed it was a good time to leave the young couple alone. "Well, my dears, I need to do some more greeting and also find your father. Albert, have you seen him this afternoon?"

"No, I haven't seen him since he left the house early this morning."

"I think he is in the theater," Ariadne said. "I saw Mr. Guillory with Aunt Cleo when I was warming up."

"I'll check," Pompey said, walking away from them. "You two

have a lovely afternoon and I'll see you tonight."

Albert took Ariadne's hand. "Can we walk over to the beach? I have a surprise for you."

"I'd love to. I don't have to sing again until later."

Toward the beach, opposite the pavilion, were the picnic and refreshment areas. Simple tables and benches were broken up by the occasional sea creature sculpture. Food and drink stands lined both sides of the north and south perimeters of the walkway. Like the booths outside the gate, contractors brought in by Pompey ran these too. The concessions were positioned to allow customers an unobstructed view of the pavilion and the water. Two stone paths led from the picnic benches to the beach and the ocean.

Albert and Ariadne walked to the outer perimeter and sat at the last table. She noticed he was carrying an ornate box with a ribbon tied around it, but she decided to wait until he was ready to bring it up.

"Your singing was so amazing. I always knew you would be good, but that performance was beyond anything I ever expected. You should be singing in a big show or at the opera in New York or any big city. Something better than a carnival."

"Thank you so much, but I love singing here. I have already performed on the stage in several cities in Europe."

"Here is a little thank-you for the plaques, all the support, and your beautiful singing."

Ariadne took the gift from him and untied the ribbon. "Thank you so much. What an exquisite box. Did you carve it?"

"Yes, but look inside."

She opened it. Inside was a small wooden sculpture of a carousel horse. "It's Guinevere. You made me a model of my favorite horse. When did you have the time?"

She kissed him.

"We carved models of all the figures before we executed the full scale ones. I added this stand and put Guinevere's name on the side and an inscription on the bottom of the base."

Ariadne turned the model over and read the inscription.

To my Ariadne,
Here is your Guinevere,
To cherish forever.
Love, Albert

She put her arms around him and they kissed again, but this time he held her tightly and the kiss lasted long enough for a passerby to comment.

"He really liked that girl's singing."

*　　*　　*

Pompey arrived at the theater and Cleo was on stage talking to William. Then they both exited in different directions. William was gone before Pompey had a chance to get his attention. He walked toward his sister as he looked around his new performance space.

The auditorium was small, with only about two hundred seats. Twenty of them were situated on a small semi-circular balcony on the second level. Even though the color palette of the carnival was that of the sea, his theater was Pompey's signature burgundy red and gold. The walls were decorated in stylized motifs of coral, marine plants, and creatures, all in dark red with highlights of metallic gold. The seats and carpeting followed the same color scheme. The space had an intimate feel until you looked up at the open ceiling and saw Enrico's sculpture of glass and light.

The chandelier was more than half the diameter of the theater. The huge sculpture was made of metal and glass tentacles that rotated at different speeds depending on the theatrical illusion. It looked like a giant hydrozoa floating over its prey. The roof of the theater was open, with only a metal grid structure to support the proscenium curtains, lights, and flying effects like Carla's ascent in the magician's act.

Patterns of light from the piece poured over the stage and the audience. Spotlights covered with color gels and gobos were pointed at the glass artwork to create moving motifs. When the theater was dark, light reflected from the large windows at the top of the tower over the space below. Shapes of light moved throughout the theater as the sun changed its position or a cloud filtered its rays.

Wright approached his sister, who was sitting at her dressing room table. She looked upset and not herself.

She jumped slightly when he touched her shoulder. "My dear Cleo, what's wrong? I have never seen you so tense. In all our years together, nothing has ever startled you. Are we getting shaky and developing stage fright in our advancing years?"

This made her laugh. "No, not stage fright, just life and its complications. William just left. I thought we were bonding after last night, but I was wrong."

"I frankly thought the same. I have to confess, I saw more than I admitted to last night. I was sure he was beginning to really care for you." Pompey paused. "As you know, he has been a widower for over five years. Have you heard the story of how his wife and children died?"

"I know they drowned, but not much else. He never brought it up and I really didn't think it was right to ask."

"A workman who knows the family shared the story of what had happened. William's wife suffered deeply after the loss of their youngest son when he drowned during a storm that hit the island. The family moved back to Ridgewater because William's wife Emily became unhinged. She thought the boy lived in the sea and visited her. William had to pull her from the water when she tried to walk into the ocean to pursue what she thought was the child calling to her. The woman's illness lasted for a quite a while but she became better."

Pompey rubbed Cleo's shoulders and continued his story while she stared into her mirror.

"They had another baby, a little girl, and then moved back to the island. All was fine for a brief period. Then one day, William and a close friend came back to his house to discover both his wife and the baby were gone. It was presumed that she had killed herself and the child in a sudden fit of madness. There was never any proof so it was judged an accident."

Cleo squeezed her brother's hand tightly. "I didn't know. I think I now understand why he acted the way he did today."

"What happened just before I entered?"

"William apologized for kissing me last night. I laughed and said that I liked what happened. It was only a kiss and the dancing was fun. He repeated the apology and said it can never happen again. He still thinks of his wife and there's only room for her in his heart."

"I have been with William every day and he always acts so positive. He talks of the carnival, all his projects and of you. Something has happened since last night. Maybe a sense of betrayal and guilt came over him because he has become fond of another woman, even after all these years. They never found their remains, so William could never really bury or say goodbye to them. This lack of closure may be what is haunting the dear man. His feelings for you could be bringing it all back again. Give him time and room for now."

Pompey took his sister's hands in his. "Cleo we've both lost people we love, but we were able to say goodbye. I'm lucky to have my Ariadne. William, although he's had Albert by his side all these years, lost two children and a wife. I can only imagine his agony. I think that is why he works so hard."

Pompey took his sister in his arms and held her for a moment.

Above them on the catwalk, William stood in the darkness against the wall listening to what was being said. He felt guilty eavesdropping, but he needed to see Cleo's reaction to their earlier conversation. He wished he could tell her the truth, but he feared she wouldn't believe him.

Everyone thought his poor Emily was mad. Wouldn't they think the same of him? The sea had cursed him with a secret that he had to keep. William was concerned for Cleo. Emily had seen them together and she talked of her in a tone that made him afraid for Cleo's safety. Her statement was as much a threat as permission. Were these exquisite, frightening creatures that were his family a danger to the ones he loved and his kind?

CHAPTER NINETEEN

Fireworks and Phantoms

Pompey met Enrico Foscari at the pavilion patio at about six o'clock, an hour before the inner theater show was about to start. The performances were only about thirty minutes long, not the usual two-hour programs they did on tour. Enrico was with two friends he'd brought with him from New York City. The man was tall and handsome and the woman was the most gorgeous being Pompey had ever seen. Neither said a word when he greeted them. They just smiled and nodded.

Pompey embraced him. "Enrico, my dearest friend, have you and your guests been having a good time at our carnival? Did you show them your fabulous creations?"

"Oh yes, my friend, we have been to the pavilion, the carousel and the crazy but wonderful mirror maze. I even convinced Ty and Lana to go on the Ferris wheel. They both hate heights, but they loved it."

Ty and Lana just nodded a yes and smiled but still didn't utter a word.

"What do you two beautiful people do? Are you actors, models, or artists?" Pompey asked directly hoping to get them to say something.

They just smiled quietly as Enrico answered for them. "My friends do model for artists occasionally, but mainly they both are silent poets. Ty and Lana feel that if they don't speak, people will eventually hear their poems through the inevitable sharing of the minds."

"That is interesting," Pompey answered. "If we all sit quietly for a while maybe I can hear a poem."

Enrico explained, "It is chaotic here with too much noise and thoughts filling the air. A nice quiet place would be much better and more appropriate."

Pompey smiled and spoke softly as he looked at Lana. "Maybe after the last show and the carnival crowds have gone home, we four could go to my trailer and be very close and quiet over a bottle of wine."

Enrico smiled at Pompey. "That would be the perfect setting for the exchange of intimate thoughts and poetic expression between us all."

He looked at his two companions as they smiled and nodded their approval.

Pompey touched Enrico's shoulder and bowed his head to the two silent guests. "I must say goodbye for now, so enjoy our show and your evening. To the sharing of thoughts and art later tonight, my friends."

Pompey exited backwards gazing at Lana until he turned and entered the tower that housed the inner theater.

He went to his dressing room table backstage. The wardrobe rooms and living quarters were still under construction on the second floor of the pavilion over the arcade. Temporary screens were set up around the tables for the privacy of the performers when they had to dress or make a costume change. Sitting next to Pompey's dressing area was Cleo's space. She sat at her dressing table in her tango costume. He stood behind her and put his hands on her shoulders.

"Let us frighten and entertain them tonight, my lovely Cleo, as we always do."

Cleo smiled. "Yes, let's do that, my crazy perfect brother."

*　*　*

The inner theater's first show was a great success. Pompey's troupe performed five acts in an economical thirty minutes. It started with a comical magic routine featuring John the Magician and Carla. Then Pompey told a frightening vampire tale, followed by a tango act with Cleo and himself. She danced again with choreography that was tribute to her teacher, the famous Loie Fuller, who she met in Paris years before. Madame Regina performed her fortunetelling routine after Cleo.

The final section featured Ariadne as a mermaid siren singing an atonal modern piece. The song concluded with the theater filling up with sea creatures similar to the great balloons and kites floating over the audience's heads. Projections of color and shapes enhanced the total effect.

By eight-thirty, Ariadne was singing on the pavilion patio stage. The repertoire was completely patriotic. She sang *Yankee Doodle*, followed by *The Battle Hymn of The Republic*. The orchestra then did some more good ol' American tunes until it was nine o'clock and time for the fireworks. The pavilion patio tables were packed with patrons and so were the surrounding walkways, benches, and picnic tables all the way down to the beach. Even the Ferris wheel was full of customers waiting to see the presentation. The operator had an extra person on hand to ensure that no one fell out of a gondola while the show was in progress.

Pompey reserved some VIP tables on the patio for dignitaries like the mayor and his wife. He sat with Cleo, Enrico, and his friends. They saved a seat for William, but he hadn't shown up yet. Albert couldn't be with them because he was working at the carousel.

Everyone was drinking lemonade spiked with good Russian vodka that was passed around under the table by Enrico. Even the mayor and his wife had their lemonades touched up. When

Pompey asked the mayor's wife if she liked his earlier performance, she just giggled. The lady had already finished her first drink and was starting on her second.

As Pompey looked around the patio William suddenly appeared. "Is everything ready?"

"Yes," William whispered, "everything is fine. They're waiting for their cue. It's still the same?"

Pompey nodded yes. Then he stood and gave a hand signal to Albert at the carousel. The calliope started playing *The Star Spangled Banner*. The orchestra followed suit and both chandeliers began to rise together from the top of the pavilion towers. The two glass wonders were lit in red, white, and blue. The crowd clapped and cheered.

The first pyrotechnics exploded in the sky from behind the pavilion, then from the opposite beach, and then from the top of the island near the sandbar. Everyone stood in honor of the national anthem; then *America The Beautiful* began as the night sky was charged with eruptions of light and color. The chandeliers stopped at their full height and rotated like beacons. All the balloons and kites floating over the crowd and the island looked even more fantastic and amazing framed by the fireworks display.

Near the end of the show, customers on the Ferris wheel and next to the beach pointed to the sea and yelled, "Look at the lights! Look at the lights in the ocean!"

Green, white, and blue pools of light and strange forms glowed and rotated along the shore for at least a half-mile out to sea. Even the crowd at the pavilion could see this extraordinary event. Everyone at the VIP tables looked at Pompey and cheered.

"Magnifico, favoloso!" shouted Enrico. "How did you light up the sea?"

Pompey bowed and waved. With a huge smile on his face, he turned and spoke to William in a whisper. "How did you do that?"

William knew the source but obviously couldn't reveal it. "I guess everything likes the Fourth."

"Please tell me how you were able to light up the water?" Pompey whispered again.

"It's a secret." William answered, jokingly. The fact that he could make light of this made him feel better for the moment.

"I'll get you to tell how you did it. It must become part of the show. Let's talk tomorrow."

When the presentation was over, the lights in the sea disappeared as mysteriously as they had appeared. Everyone asked about the wonderful event. It was either explained as a reflection of the fireworks or as a secret new effect that you would just have to come back to the carnival to see again. The festivities continued until almost eleven o'clock, when the ferries started taking people back to the mainland. It was well after one o'clock when the last ferry finally left.

Pompey retired to his luxury caravan with Enrico and the two silent poets. Albert and Ariadne stayed at the carousel until one-thirty, then he walked her back to her trailer. Cleo was already in bed, having left as soon as the fireworks were over. She heard the young couple talking quietly outside the door.

"You were wonderful tonight. I wish I could have seen your other show. I heard you were magical," Albert said softly.

Ariadne said nothing. She pulled him close, kissed him, and he kissed her back.

"Ariadne, I have to go. Will you be at the pavilion in the morning? We can have breakfast together. There is a vendor I am friendly with that makes the best omelets. Nine o'clock by the stage?"

"Yes, nine o'clock by the stage. Good night, Albert."

"Good night." He kissed her one more time and then walked slowly away.

Ariadne stood there until he was out of sight. "Good night, my beautiful Albert."

She climbed up into the caravan, not knowing whether her

aunt was asleep or not. Cleo had heard everything that was said by the young couple. She was happy for her niece and knew that the two were a good match. She remembered when she felt like that when she was Ariadne's age.

Cleo thought of William and wished he wasn't so haunted by the death of his wife and children. She knew she was attracted to him from the day she walked up the beach with her brother to William's house. Cleo thought about that day until she fell asleep.

William walked home and looked out to sea. He still hadn't decided how to deal with his secret. He almost hoped to see Emily tonight. The lights in the sea earlier at the presentation made him nervous and also made him laugh. These beings had a sense of humor and they were more like us than they knew.

Their existence had to stay a secret more for their benefit than for anyone else. If everyone became aware that they were real, the mermen wouldn't last very long. Man didn't deal well with things they couldn't understand or didn't conform to what they believed in. The mermen would be hunted, killed, and put on display. These beings had to be a secret he could never reveal. William sat on his porch and pondered these thoughts until the early hours of the morning.

CHAPTER TWENTY

Mike's Turn

Mike awoke on the couch and immediately sat upright when he realized it was dawn. He rubbed his eyes and went to the bedroom to check on his mother and froze in the doorway. She was gone. He ran first to the bathroom, then to the kitchen, then checked every other corner of the house. In his panic he didn't notice that the front door was open. A squirrel poked his head in and Mike chased it away as he walked out onto the porch. He looked around and finally spotted Poo sitting on the beach at the edge of the surf.

Mike hurried down the steps and to the little dog's side. "Poo, where's our mom? Where did she go?"

Poo turned and looked into his eyes. *Our Lovey Grace walked into the sea. She told me to stay. She loves us all and we'll be together soon.*

"She walked into the sea? She loves us?" he repeated.

Did Poo just talk to him? Was he going crazy? He looked around and saw footprints that led into the water. The impressions in the wet sand were the size of his mother's small feet.

"Mom where are you?" Mike screamed until he heard Claire's voice.

"Mike, what's wrong?" she shouted from their house. "What happened?"

Claire ran to the beach, embraced Mike and held him tightly as they both looked out at the water. "Mom's gone. The sea took her. She's gone."

He held his wife and cried on her shoulder. They stayed that way for several minutes then slowly walked back to the house. Brian was standing in the doorway with Travis, but he didn't utter a word. He knew something bad had happened. The big dog also felt something was wrong when he looked toward the beach and saw his friend Poo. He wanted to go to him, but sensed it was best to leave his little friend alone for now.

Back in the house, Mike sat silently on the couch. Claire took Brian aside and explained to him what had happened. She held him in her arms as the boy began to cry.

Travis sat next to Mike and the big dog leaned his large body against the man's leg. Mike eventually stroked Travis' head and hugged the dog's face against thigh.

An hour had passed and Mike was still on the couch looking at the floor. Claire and Brian had gone to his room after the boy had finally calmed down. Travis went to the beach and found Poo still sitting motionless, staring out to sea. Travis sat close beside his friend and nudged him with his nose.

Are you okay, Poo?

My Lovey Grace is gone. My mother is gone. She walked into the sea. Things I've never seen before came and took her. One joined with my mother before she disappeared. When I tried to help, they touched me and Lovey Grace talked to me through their long fingers. She told me to stay. My mother said she loved us and we will all be together soon. I wanted to stop our Lovey Grace but couldn't.

I wish I could have helped you, Travis said.

There was nothing you or anyone could have done. Since the storm, everything is different. We are all different and everything has changed.

They both sat quietly for a while and then the big dog looked down at his friend. *Come home when you are ready.*

Travis nudged Poo gently with his head and went back to the house.

* * *

It was almost noon when Mike finally stood up and declared in a calm voice, "We're getting off the island. Let's pack what we need, load up the boat, and leave."

Claire looked at her son. "Brian put some clothes and basic stuff like your toothbrush, extra shoes and anything you know you will need but make sure it all fits into your backpack. The boat is only so big."

"Okay, Mom."

Mike and Claire quickly pulled together what they needed and put it by the front door. Mike started to cough. He tried to conceal it by clearing his throat every time it happened.

When everyone was ready they gathered in the living room.

"I have the phone, flashlight, and a hunting knife just in case." Mike said. "Uncle Ned has a gun. I should go get it."

He coughed and, without realizing it, grabbed his chest tightly.

"How long have you been coughing? Are you in pain?" Claire asked.

"I'm fine. The air is so heavy and thick it's affected my breathing. Also, getting wet the other night made me a little congested." Mike breathed in and controlled his cough. "It may take a few minutes to find where he keeps his gun. I don't want Brian, the dogs, and you to be waiting outside on his porch while I look. With all the crazy animal attacks, birds dive-bombing and that goo on the ground turning to God-knows-what, you are safer here until I get back."

"Honey, we'll be ready. Do you want to take Travis with you just in case?"

"Good idea." He looked at the Rottweiler. "Come on boy, let's go to Uncle Ned's."

Mike kissed his wife and headed for the front door with Travis. When he opened it, Poo was sitting calmly at the entrance. The little dog walked into the house and up to Claire. She hugged him and he sat by her side.

Mike and Travis closed the door tightly behind them. They walked to Uncle Ned's, avoiding the new cabbage-like foliage and its tendrils.

When they reached the house, Mike's cough came back and so did the pain, but in a more acute way. He composed himself, pulled out his key, and opened the front door. He checked that the house was free of any intruders. Fortunately, nothing had gotten in since he was there yesterday.

Mike searched the old man's office and then his bedroom for the weapon. Travis helped by sniffing around the two rooms. He knew Uncle Ned probably kept it in a locked box because Brian spent so much time there. He finally found the tin container under the bed. It was on a small shelf Uncle Ned had built below the mattress. The box was locked so Mike found a hammer and broke it open.

He slipped the gun and some extra bullets into his jacket pocket. The cough came back and his body began to ache all over, just the way his mother had described. Mike stopped a second to compose himself. Travis saw Mike's discomfort, so he brushed his leg and licked his master's free hand.

"I'm fine, boy," Mike assured the dog. "Let's go."

By the time they reached his house, Mike became nauseated and threw up at the side of the porch. The pain was so intense, he could barely stand.

When Mike entered the house, he collapsed near the doorway and Claire ran to him. The sickness clouded Mike's mind and blurred his vision so much that he barely sensed his wife and child standing over him, or Travis nudging his body.

The next thing Mike knew, he was in his bed. He looked at the clock on the side table; it was one o'clock in the morning. He sat up in bed, looked around, and noticed Travis in the doorway like a guard, watching his every move. When the big dog saw Mike stir, he ran to the bedside, jumped up and rested his front paws on his master's forearm. Mike tried to get out of bed, but the dog climbed up onto him.

Claire said to keep you in bed.

"Travis down. Let me up. We need to leave the island."

You're sick and cannot leave your bed. Claire said to keep you here.

Mike, delirious, gave in to the big dog's demands and lay back down. He knew he needed to get his family to the mainland, but he also realized that he was too weak and in too much pain to do so. He had been out for hours and their opportunity to leave was lost until the morning. Mike didn't even know if he would be able to walk if the pain was still surging through his body like it was now.

Claire entered the room and walked to his side. "Honey, are you feeling any better? I went to Lovey's and got a few of her Percocet in case you need them. There's also another whole bottle in her nightstand. I also brought the ham radio so we can check it for any new signals." She touched her husband's forehead. "Do you still have pain?"

"I can't begin to describe what I'm feeling. If this is what Mom was going through, I can understand what she did."

"Don't talk like that. We'll leave in the morning. Everything is ready to go. Take one of these and get some sleep."

She kissed his forehead and handed him a pill with a glass of water. He took it and lay back down.

"I heard Travis talk to me and he said I should stay in bed because you told him so," he laughed. "Am I crazy as well as sick? I heard Poo talk to me this morning too."

"I haven't heard either of the two boys give any opinions," she said half-laughing. "It's probably a fever. You will be fine in the morning and then we can leave."

He took her hand and they were silent for a moment. Mike adjusted his position in bed while Claire fixed his pillows.

She kissed him again and gave Mike a gentle hug. "Go to sleep. Love you."

Shortly after she left the room, Mike could hear the sound of the ham radio in the living room. The pain was still intense but he tried his best not to move and let the pill do its work.

CHAPTER TWENTY-ONE

Season's End

When the carnival closed at the end of September, Pompey held a party at the pavilion patio for everyone who had helped the amusement park be a success that first year. The vendors supplied the food and drink while his troupe contributed the entertainment. The only one missing that evening was Enrico, who was in Paris exhibiting his glass. The mayor of Ridgewater was there with his lemonade-loving wife and every other person from the town who had any part in the creation and operation of the carnival.

Pompey made an announcement to the crowd gathered at the pavilion patio.

"My dearest friends and fellow colleagues, I want to thank you again for such a successful first summer. It was the most work I have ever put into an enterprise and it also gave me the most pleasure of anything I had ever done before. I hope all of you lovely people feel as I do and will return to help our group do the same next spring. I have employed a small crew to secure and maintain the carnival over the winter months. Even though we closed last weekend, we will open for one more time at the end of October, Halloween, to celebrate a wonderful day and night of thrills and enjoyment for everyone."

Pompey gestured to his left. "Your gracious mayor has made an offer, in the name of the town of Ridgewater, to sponsor the children of the state orphan's home, so they can attend our carnival free of charge that day. The town will cover all their transportation and the ferry ride to Plover's Island. I will personally pay for the little dears' amusements and refreshments."

He gazed out at the crowd. "That night, in addition to all the usual activities, we will have a costume parade and contest right here at our lovely pavilion patio. The winner will receive the sum of one hundred dollars. Everyone will be eligible to enter, so start thinking about your costumes now."

The partygoers applauded. "Lastly, I also want to announce the engagement of my beautiful and talented daughter, Ariadne, to Albert, son of William Guillory, my partner in crime and the carnival."

Everyone applauded.

"Our little troupe will be leaving after Halloween to go on a European tour and we will be taking my soon-to-be son-in-law with us. Albert will be working as our stage manager on the tour. I hope this experience will give his already creative mind even more ideas and inspiration to bring back to our carnival next spring."

Pompey asked everyone to stand and toast. "To my daughter, to Albert, and to the future of Wright's Carnival of Curiosities."

After the party, William, Pompey, and Ned walked around the carnival checking for any stragglers left behind before the last ferry departed. They found one man asleep in a gondola on the Ferris wheel, two more in the Undersea Maze of Mirrors trying to find their way out, and a half-dressed couple in a deep embrace in a car on the octopus ride.

When everyone was gathered up and on their way, Ned bid the two men good night. "Well, time for me to go to dreamland, fellows. Carla is waiting up for me and I have to meet the cleanup crew first thing tomorrow. Take care and see you in the morning."

He headed in the direction of his trailer and Pompey walked with William on the beach toward his house.

"It was a grand party, wasn't it my dear, William? Did you have fun?"

"Yes, it was. I never thought we could pull it off, never mind do it so well. I have to say you really made our carnival a success. I think we may have at least broke even."

"We did better than that. We actually made a tidy profit."

Pompey moved closer to William and put his arm around him. "Let's not talk about business. Now that I have you to myself for the first time in months, how are you? You've been distant all summer and I've noticed it with my sister Cleo, too. You must know how she feels about you."

William didn't look at Pompey as he talked. "I'm sorry for the way I have avoided everyone. What made me act that way had nothing to do with you, the carnival or Cleo. I found out just before we opened that certain situations in my life had changed."

"What is it, my dear friend? Is it money, are you ill? Let me help you any way I can."

William contemplated telling Pompey the truth about Emily and his family from the sea. He thought of his overwhelming need to share this secret with someone who might understand. Pompey had witnessed plenty of strange events and the concept of his whole enterprise was about the unknown.

William was about to tell him everything, but all he said was, "I found my Emily." He paused. "My wife Emily is ... still alive."

"What wonderful news! Why didn't you tell us? Why haven't we seen her?"

"It is good news, but it's also complicated."

William wanted to be honest about what Emily had become, but before he knew it, he was telling something else.

"She is alive, but she is ill. My Emily is in a sanitarium. She was found on a beach north of here, but her mind was gone. It took them this long to discover her identity. The authorities notified me just before the carnival opened. I said nothing of this news because I didn't want Albert to know."

Pompey and William walked along the shore. "My poor man, I am so sorry. Is there anything I can do?"

William started this lie and now he had to complete the story that went with it. "Thank you, but nothing can be done. Remember when I went away for a few days to see a vendor?"

Pompey nodded, "Yes."

"I did go to the vendor but I also went to see my wife. She is gone from us and she will never be the same again. Emily can never leave where she is now and I have to let her live her life there." He told the truth, but left out the details that also made it a lie.

"What about your daughter? Didn't she disappear at the same time?" Pompey regretted asking this question as soon as he uttered it.

"They never found her, just my Emily. I know she is happy wherever she is," William answered. This was another truth with omitted facts that made it another lie.

"My friend, I am so sorry I brought up your daughter."

"I know you meant well and are only being a kind friend. Meeting you and everyone else has been wonderful for me and also for Albert. He has found his vocation, a trip to Europe, and most importantly the love of your daughter. You gave this little island life again."

"Thank you for saying that. The two of you mean a great deal to us." Pompey paused. "But you should tell Albert about his mother. The boy needs to know the truth."

"I am afraid to tell anyone else, especially my son. His life is going forward and I know he wouldn't leave with you if he knew. Promise me you will keep my confidence."

Pompey agreed.

They walked quietly for a while until Pompey stopped William and looked at him. "You have to tell Cleo your situation.

She would fully understand. Right now she thinks she is at fault in some way and it's making her very unhappy. I would never tell her your circumstances, but I cannot bear to see her this way."

"I'll talk to her before you leave on your tour," William assured him.

"Please talk to my sister sooner and tell her you're still grieving. And even though you care for her, it wouldn't be fair to start a relationship. It is half the truth and you wouldn't be revealing your secret."

William was hesitant to tell another lie, but he knew Pompey was only thinking of his sister. It did give this situation some resolution.

"I will tell you what I decide to do, tomorrow."

"Thank you, my dear William."

They continued their walk on the beach.

*   *   *

"You're going to love Paris," Ariadne assured Albert. "I'll show you all of it. The first thing we will do is ride on my favorite carousel in the Luxembourg Gardens. It's not as grand as ours, but it is the oldest one in the city and I've always loved it. You know, Paris is the City of Carousels and they're everywhere. We will be there at least two weeks and I'll take you to every carousel and we can ride them all."

"Every one of them?" he replied.

"Yes, all of them."

Ariadne cuddled up to Albert in the seashell gondola next to her favorite horse, Guinevere. The carousel was dark except for the light from a lantern hanging off one of the ornate brass supporting poles.

"You'll also be an expert on Europe by the time we get back. We are playing in all of the most beautiful countries. After France we go to Austria, then Switzerland, Germany, Hungary, Italy,

Spain, and Portugal. Our last stop will be London just before we return home."

Albert teased her. "Is that all? What about the rest of Europe?"

Ariadne poked him. "That's a really grand tour for someone who told me he's never left the state he was born in."

"Well I guess that will have to do." Albert poked her back and began to tickle her. After a few minutes they settled into each other's arms. "I do love that you call this island home." He kissed her. "We can build a house like my father did next spring."

"Can we have a garden like yours? I've never had one. We always lived in hotels, apartments and those cramped caravans. A house of my own with a garden will be perfect."

"On tour do I get to share a caravan with you?" Albert asked with a sly smile.

"My aunt will still be my roommate. You can share with John," she laughed. "Besides we will be in hotels."

"So it will be John, Madame Regina, and myself in the same hotel room?"

Ariadne said, "I forgot about her. You can share with father's company accountant until we get married."

"We haven't talked about a date. How about tomorrow? We can go to Ridgewater and see the mayor in the morning."

"No I want it to be special because I hope to only do it once."

"I hope to only do it once, too. How about in Paris, next to your carousel?"

"Paris it is, but let's keep it secret. I don't want a big wedding with all the formal trimmings. Father will want to spend a lot of money and have it all be very lavish." Ariadne looked into his eyes. "The Luxembourg Gardens will be ideal and romantic. Just us, and afterward we can invite father and the others to dinner and tell them." She paused again. "Your father won't be there. Will he be upset?"

"We can get married again in the spring for my father and our friends when we get back. I know he will be okay with that." He kissed her and they stayed in a long embrace.

Outside the carousel pavilion tower, Thomas quietly looked through one of the glass windows and had been watching the couple for some time. He had come ashore on the inland side of the island to watch the party as he did the night of the fireworks. Since his first trip on land to bring his mother and sister to his home, he was curious about the world he had left that day the storm took him. Thomas felt a connection to these beings who were once his people. In his home, everything was determined. You had your part to play and all was in harmony. Here, there was a chaotic order to the way these humans thought, acted and lived, which he liked but didn't understand.

He watched his brother with the female with the golden hair. He studied the way she moved and felt the vibrations of her voice. The tones she made, especially when she sang, affected Thomas more than anyone else. Females in his world created sounds that were beautiful, but this girl generated tones stronger than anything he had ever experienced. Thomas wanted to have a female like this. He could take Ariadne, but she was his brother's. He knew that abducting a being from the land was dangerous, but to have someone who created perfect tonal vibrations like she did was worth the risk.

Thomas took the chance once before when he brought his sister and his mother to the city. He decided to wait until he could find someone like this female with her beautiful tones.

"Sing that song you sang at the pavilion on the Fourth of July," Albert whispered to her.

"Which one? I sang so many that day."

He awkwardly hummed some if it and she knew he meant Rachmaninoff's *Chanson Géorgienne*. She began to sing it softly.

"That's it." Albert sat up to listen.

Thomas was about to leave when Ariadne started to sing. She created sounds like the exquisite tonalities he'd heard the night of the explosions and lights in the sky.

Even sung quietly, the vibrations went into his head and throughout his body. For those few moments he felt the warmth of the invisible waves she created. The translucent sections on the shell helmet that covered his head and spine glowed from the pulsation of her elegant vibrations. These pulses from his body created ripples that made the small window he was looking through crack and suddenly shatter.

Startled, Ariadne stopped singing when she heard the noise. "God, what was that?"

Albert leaped up. "Sounded like one of the windows broke. Who's out there?" he shouted.

He ran to the front entrance, looked around and then at the broken window. "Who's out here?" he shouted again.

Ariadne ran to his side. They waited, then looked around the area where glass was scattered on the ground.

He took her hand. "Everyone has gone. Maybe a bird hit the window in the dark."

"Wouldn't the poor thing be on the ground?"

"Sometimes they just get stunned and fly away."

The couple searched the area again, finding only broken glass and a strange sandy depression in the grass that led to the walkway, toward the inland bay.

CHAPTER TWENTY-TWO

Lolly and Lynette

Lolly and Lynette hated to take the bus that went through the small town they lived in. It only stopped twice a day, you had to wait on the main road, and it was never on time. The girls had no choice because the train was too expensive.

"When the hell is this bus going to show up? My bag with my costume in it weighs a ton," Lolly Campbell complained. "I'm already covered in dirt and we haven't even left town yet."

"Wait until we get to be big Broadway stars. We will never have to ride a bus again," Lynette Jones replied as she gazed up into the air. This was her usual gesture when she mentioned anything about their future plans.

"There better be some rich New York types at this party," Lolly said. "I'm gonna have to take a bath and put on a new kisser at the bus station in Ridgewater when we get there. We'll come off like a couple of orphans instead of lookers when we show up."

"I hear the bus station in that town is spiffy and brand-spanking new. I bet the bathrooms are better than at home."

"All bathrooms are better than at home," Lolly replied.

Both girls laughed.

A car sped by, raising a cloud of dust that rained on the two already dirt-covered girls. Lolly gave the vehicle the finger and they both laughed even harder.

The bus arrived and the two boarded. After perusing the passengers, they settled into two spots in the back. Three rows ahead of them was an elderly couple. The woman stared at them with contempt.

Another two rows in front of the couple, on the opposite side, were three young men. One was tall and muscular, the second was skinny with spiky hair, and the third was overweight. The stout lad must have been the leader of the trio because as soon as Lolly and Lynette were settled in their seats, he worked his way back to them.

"Hey, ladies, where are you two dolls heading?" he asked with an almost obscene smile on his evil "man in the moon" face.

"Where are you heading, Roscoe?" Lolly replied, nicknaming this large boy after the infamous Fatty Arbuckle.

He didn't get the insult. "Oh, my name is Carl. And my two friends are Jimmy and Billy. We're all headed to Lambton. There's a big Halloween dance there tonight. Might you ladies be going there too?"

Lynette was about to innocently reveal their destination, but Lolly poked her before she could get a word out. "No, we're going to Watertown to see my friend's sick grandmother."

Carl leaned over, whispered to them and pointed to the breast pocket of his oversized jacket. "We got some good hooch if you two ladies would like a swig."

"No thanks, we are good Christian girls and we never partake of the devil's spirits," Lolly answered in a pious voice that made Lynette giggle.

The fat, moon-faced lad grinned, slowly looked at his friends, and then turned his attention back at Lolly and Lynette. "Also, my good looking buddies are goofy over you two dolls."

Lolly smiled back at Carl and looked up to the roof of the bus. "We are both spoken for by the Lord."

Lynette started to really laugh and Lolly elbowed her in the ribs.

"Okay, ladies, but we are sitting right up there until Lambton if you change your beautiful little minds," Carl replied.

The chubby boy walked back to his seat, bumping into the old woman on his return. Her husband grumbled something inaudible and his wife looked back at the two girls with a stare of distain. Lolly promptly stuck her tongue out at the woman. The rest of the ride to Ridgewater was quiet, especially after the three young men exited at their stop.

Eventually, the elderly woman gave up on her judgmental looks except when the girls got off the bus. Lolly made a point of bumping into the old lady's shoulder with her bag as they worked their way to the front.

Lolly and Lynette were exhausted by the time they arrived at Ridgewater. They dragged their bags into the bus station and found the ladies room. It was small and didn't have enough space for both of them to be in there at the same time, so Lynette let Lolly get ready first. She knew her friend would be in a foul mood until she had pulled herself together.

"You go first and I'll wait here. I have a sandwich I packed and really need to eat something before I pass out from hunger," Lynette said.

"You're a swell friend, Lynette. I'll get my glad rags on in a jiffy."

Lolly went into the washroom while Lynette ate her sandwich and looked at the posters and advertisements on the bus station walls. There was one for the carnival that was burgundy red and gold.

The sign read: *Pompey Wright Presents Wright's Carnival of Curiosities*. The central artwork showed the balloon creatures, the Ferris wheel, and the pavilion. The large sign was filled with descriptive words over the artwork like: Thrills, Chills, Magic, Mystery, and Macabre. On the left and right sides were small gold-framed photos of Cleo and Pompey in costume, John the Magician, Madame Regina, and Ariadne singing.

The sign gave Lynette a chill. She looked to the ceiling, eyes half-closed and dreamed of being a dancer in a Broadway musical revue. She wondered if they would really meet anyone at this big Halloween party who could give them a break in show business. Her daydreaming helped pass the time until her friend was out of the ladies room and in costume.

Lolly looked delightful and even sexy in an amusing way. Her outfit was a showgirl-inspired mermaid costume based on a picture of a follies dancer she saw in the paper. There wasn't the usual fishtail and long wavy wig. Her homemade creation consisted of a short improvised eighteenth century bustle with gilded goldfish on each hip. Dangling from them were strips of metallic fabric, beads, and ribbons that gave her a jellyfish-inspired skirt.

She wore pale green stockings secured by garters. The corset covering her upper torso, decorated with more bows, ribbons, and beads, was too short and gave Lolly a very bare midriff. Completing the ensemble were two fin-shaped gauntlets and a Marie Antoinette-style wig made of glittered cotton batting, embellished with a real starfish painted gold, plus more bows and beads.

The sight of her friend snapped Lynette out of her daydream. "Gosh, you look swanky."

"Do you think the armbands are too long?" Lolly asked as she extended her arms to her sides in a showgirl pose.

"No, not at all. You look just like the picture from the *Daily Mirror*. I hope you get to sing tonight. With that outfit and your voice, you will knock their socks off."

"Thanks, sweetie. Now you better hurry and get that hotsy-totsy Queen of Sheba costume on. We have a party to go to and some swells to meet." Lolly urged her friend, with a gentle slap on her bottom.

*   *   *

Cleo sat at her dressing room table in the theater. She wasn't up for a silly night of costumes and partying, but she had to do this for her brother and the carnival. Her other responsibility, besides the entertaining, was helping Pompey promote his enterprise any way she could. Cleo had to force herself to focus on getting ready for the evening, but her thoughts kept going back to what William confessed three weeks before.

"I have wanted to tell you this for a long time, Cleo," William stated in a soft voice. "I have cared for you since the day we met, but I now need to be honest and tell you ... I'm still mourning my wife, even after all these years. The loss is with me every day and I was resigned to live with these feelings until I met you. Since that morning you walked up the beach, I have been so conflicted. But I know now that I can't be in any relationship until I can come to terms with the past. These ghosts would always be between us until I get closure. We barely know each other, so I wanted to tell you this before more time went by. Cleo, I would never want to hurt you."

He was right. They had only known each other for a short time, but it still wounded her. They had never been intimate and only shared a kiss once or twice in the last few months. Most of their contact was because of work or business. She felt like a foolish schoolgirl, letting a man affect her so much without even doing anything. What was it about William that made her feel so strongly towards him?

She laughed to herself, *Was this what being close to forty meant?*

There was an attraction the minute she looked into his eyes. Most of her lovers had baggage, but she saw a pain, a longing to be needed in William that she'd never experienced before. After they talked, she knew she wanted him even more. There was nothing to do but wait and see if time could sort everything out. She laughed again. *Yes, this must be what getting older was like.*

The tour started the following week and she'd be gone until spring. The work, new locations, and new faces might help. Distraction was what she needed right now, and to get through the party and the rest of the week. Later, she hoped things might change with William. Next year, everything could be different. She looked into the mirror. That night she was going to have fun or at least act like she was.

Pompey entered and kissed his sister on the cheek. "My lovely Cleo, are you almost ready? The sweet orphans from the home left on the six o'clock boat and I think they had a marvelous time. Thanks for entertaining them this afternoon. One little tyke said he would be back as soon as he had a job and then ask you to marry him. The boy may be a poor little waif, but he has a gentleman's taste."

This made Cleo laugh. "My best offer this month. All I need to do is wait until he grows another three feet." She checked her make-up in the mirror. "I'll be ready in a few minutes. I just need to put on my jacket and this crazy headdress you ordered for me."

"Enrico found it in New York at one of his friend's studios. I love the bat-like winged lace panels. Also, the black and purple birds of paradise feathers are exquisite. It is so you and so Halloween," Pompey said. "I'm also happy you're wearing the new outfit for the tour with it."

"I love it too, and the headdress really does match it perfectly."

"Enrico should be here soon. He is bringing a couple of friends with him."

"Is it the silent poets again?" she joked.

"Oh yes, the beauty of silence," Pompey proclaimed. "I think these are new friends he met at some club. They should be delightful and interesting like all his friends are."

Pompey kissed her and left. She was so lucky to have a brother like him, with his positive spirit to boost her in this negative world. His little visit was the right distracting note she needed to get her through the night.

*   *   *

Lolly and Lynette reached the Ridgewater ferry to Plover's Island just ten minutes before its departure. They stuffed their bags with their regular clothes into lockers at the bus station. It was cooler since the sun went down, so they kept their coats on over their costumes. The walk from the station was longer than they expected and a Marie Antoinette mermaid and the Queen of Sheba walking down the main street of town even covered by coats drew plenty of attention.

They went up to the ticket taker at the entrance to the ferry to buy their tickets.

"Can I see your invitations please?" the man asked.

"What invitations? The newspaper said this was a public party," Lolly replied.

"Oh that was for this afternoon's event for the state orphans home. Tonight is only for the people who worked at the carnival and their guests."

"Can't you please let us on the ferry? We have been on a bus all day and were all spiffed up," Lynette pleaded.

"I'm so sorry, I can see you two young ladies are indeed dressed and ready for a party, but without an invitation it can't be this one," the ticket taker replied.

Lolly was just about to say something to the man that Lynette knew they both would regret. She grabbed her friend by the arm and pulled her out of the line. They walked to the edge of the ferry station and sat on a bench next to the entrance.

Lynette looked at her friend. "Why don't we go back to the station and catch the train to Lambton? Those guys on the bus said there was a big party there."

"Those rubes? I'd rather die. I have a better idea, let's go get drunk. I saw something that looked like a speakeasy on our way here."

"They wouldn't let us in. We are too young and in these costumes they will think we are either hookers or crazy."

Lolly laughed. "Maybe not hookers, but definitely crazy." She stood up and in a fancy voice proclaimed, "Can we get two whiskeys? My friend, the Queen of Sheba, has had an extremely hard day and is quite thirsty."

The two girls started laughing so hard they dropped their coats on the ground just as Enrico and his two friends arrived.

The Italian was wearing a black-and-white Pierrot costume in the Caruso Pagliacci style, adorned with big buttons and long sleeves that covered his hands. His companions were both tall men who towered over the little Italian clown. One was a handsome African-American with green eyes who was dressed like a bullfighter. The other was overly muscular and in a Roman soldier's costume. They stopped in front of the two laughing girls, glanced at their outfits and smiled to each other.

Enrico spoke first. "My beautiful ladies, what charming costumes! Let me introduce *mi amici* and myself. I am the sad clown, Pagliacci, and these are my two companions, Don Petro the Bullfighter and Maximus Max, a true soldier of Rome."

The three men bowed to the surprised and confused girls, who quickly realized this could be their ticket to the party.

Lolly returned the introduction. "I am Marie the Mermaid and this is my friend, the Queen of Sheba herself."

Then they both did little curtsies and finished with silent film star exaggerated poses.

Enrico applauded. "*Bravo!* I assume you two angels are going to the party tonight on the island."

Lolly bowed her head and in a sad voice said, "We were, but we forgot our invitations and the ticket taker doesn't have our names on the list. I guess this means we'll have to go home."

Enrico smiled and made a proposal. "Well, I have done a lot of work for the carnival and Pompey Wright is my best friend. I am positive he would want me to make sure two such beautiful ladies should never miss any party, so you shall be our guests. Get your coats and we will be on that ferry or my name is not Pagliacci."

"Thank you so much, but we don't even know each other's real names. This is Lolly and I, the Queen of Sheba, am Lynette."

"It is so nice to meet you, my *belle signorine*. I am Enrico and this is Élan." He gestured to the bullfighter. "And this gentleman in all the armor and muscles is actually Max."

Lolly looked at Max and grabbed his arm. "I'm with you, handsome. Let's go to a party."

CHAPTER TWENTY-THREE

Two Pierrots

When Albert arrived at Enrico's table, he was surprised to see that they both had on almost the same costume. The Italian was dressed in white, trimmed with big black buttons and rickrack on his oversized collar. Albert was in the reverse, all black accented by white and his costume was more tailored and less comical.

The young man had never dressed this elaborately for Halloween before. When Albert wore a costume for the holiday, when he was a boy, he was usually a tramp or burglar.

Ariadne talked him into dressing this way to go with her Columbine costume. Even though he wanted to please her, he still felt a little foolish in the uncomfortable collar, black beanie, and painted face.

"My Albert, you make such a handsome Pierrot," Enrico complimented him. "I assume our beautiful Ariadne will be your Columbine."

"Yes, it was her idea."

"How sweet, *mi amici*. I also want to congratulate you on your engagement to Ariadne." Then the Italian asked, "When will the wedding be?"

"Nothing is scheduled yet," he answered with a little white lie, knowing their plans for Paris.

Lolly's smile diminished at the knowledge of Albert's

engagement. She hadn't even been introduced to him yet and was disappointed to know this handsome clown was not in play for her.

She looked around at the other tables and evaluated the costumed frolickers. Most of the people looked like they may be locals who worked for the carnival. She thought this because of all of the homemade outfits as compared to the elaborate, rented fancy-dress outfits of her male companions. She didn't see anyone she felt was rich, sophisticated, or from the big city except for the three men with her and Lynette and the group at the mayor's table.

It didn't take long, even for a small town girl just out of school, to see that Max was "with" Élan. She found out from the conversation that they were just a bartender and a bouncer in the same club in the city. They were swell guys to be friends and party with, but there was no ticket to Broadway there. Enrico was the closest thing to a celebrity she had met at the Halloween party so far. She glanced at Lynette and could see the little Queen of Sheba was also looking around and coming to the same conclusion.

Lolly whispered in her friend's ear. "We should take a walk soon and check out the crowd."

Lynette nodded.

Enrico turned to Albert. "Let me introduce you to my friends." He did so and then asked, "And where is your handsome father tonight? I looked for him when we arrived."

"He volunteered to run the carousel so I could be with Ariadne."

"What a nice gesture. He is such a kind man," Enrico said. "Now you must sit with us for a while."

"I wish I could, but Ariadne is going to sing any minute and I promised to stand with her during the performance," he said, tugging at his collar.

"Are going to sing too?" asked Enrico.

"No!" Albert laughed, still fiddling with his collar. "Ariadne is the singer. I'm just the carpenter."

"Let me fix that for you." Lynette jumped up and stood behind Albert. She loosened the button in the back and pinned it with a tiny safety pin that was tucked into her bodice. "I always bring a few of these. You never know when you might need one."

"Thanks. Is it Lynette?" Albert asked.

"Yes. I'm a dancer and my friend, Lolly, is the best singer."

Lolly rolled her eyes as Enrico spoke up. "Wonderful, my dear. Maybe we can see you both perform. I am sure Pompey would insist if I suggested it."

Lolly's eyes went from a roll to a pop at the offer. "We sure can!"

"It's time for me to perform with Ariadne." Albert looked up at the stage and then turned to Lynette. "Thanks again and I hope you get to perform."

Lynette smiled back as she took her seat.

The pavilion orchestra leader announced Ariadne. Albert joined her and took her hand. Lynette recognized her from the poster in the bus station and whispered in Lolly's ear.

Marie the Mermaid was not impressed until Ariadne began to sing. Albert hugged her as she started *I'm Falling In Love With Someone* from Victor Herbert's *Naughty Marietta*. Her voice was even more beautiful tonight than it was all summer.

Lolly's mouth dropped opened when she heard this girl sing. She wished now she hadn't agreed to perform. She knew she had a good voice, but nothing like Ariadne's.

The performance turned into a medley, ending with *Ah! Sweet Mystery of Life*. She bowed with Albert next to her. Pompey entered from the pavilion theater and crossed the small stage, clapping for his daughter as he walked to the center.

"Wasn't that lovely? Aren't they lovely?" he announced over the applause. "Is everyone having a good time?"

The crowd clapped and shouted a loud "Yes!"

Pompey continued. "It is now time for the costume contest. We will have four winners. The categories are: Most Comical, Most Frightening, Most Original, and Best Costume. Will everyone who wants to enter please line up in front of the pavilion arcade? Remember, the prizes are fifty dollars for each of the three categories and one hundred dollars for the best costume."

Pompey clasped his hands together. "In addition to your costume, we want everyone in the competition to do a little performance. You can do anything: sing, dance, play a musical instrument, juggle, do magic, recite a poem, or stand on your head. It is up to you. Helping me on the stage tonight as our judges are my delightful sister, Cleopatra Wright, our little ballerina, Carla Baldwin, our own Madame Regina, and my good friend, John the Magician."

Cleo entered, wearing the lace bat headdress. The others wore their costumes from the show.

Lynette, recognizing her from the poster as well, whispered to Lolly in a sad voice, "Boy, the real Queen of Sheba, and her name is Cleopatra. Plus, she's a hoofer like me, but a ritzy one." Her eyes filled with tears. "That's what you have to look like to get on Broadway?"

Lolly poked Lynette hard in the side. "Let's get in line."

Lolly turned to her three companions. "Are you gents joining us for the contest? Everyone can use a hundred bucks."

Enrico and his two friends stood up when the girls did. "No, my darlings, we will just watch. Would either of you like a little courage booster before you go?" He pulled out a velvet bag with a gold stopper peeking out of the top.

Lolly accepted, took a swig and then offered it to Lynette who declined. Lolly gave her a stare. "You're gonna need this."

Lynette took a large gulp that made her eyes water. Lolly turned to the three men, "Well boys, wish us luck."

They bowed and blew kisses as the girls headed for the line.

There were at least two hundred guests at the party, but only two dozen were brave enough to enter the contest. The performing aspect must have discouraged many of them. Also, by this time in the evening, many of the costumed revelers were a little too drunk to stand in any line. It may have been illegal to drink, but Prohibition didn't exist at the party. Even at the mayor's table, bottles were visible. No one was feeling any pain, especially his honor's wife.

One by one, the contestants braved the stage and either passed the first cut or didn't, but were applauded for their courage to get up there in the first place. After another round, the final four were picked. All of them were winners, but now it was time to perform and see who would get the big prize. In this group was a two-man cow, a jellyfish, a very bloody headless man, and Lolly, the mermaid. Lynette was cut after the second round of eliminations. She was greeted with hugs and kisses by her three table companions and Enrico gave her another little swig from his velvet bag.

First to perform was the cow. The two-man bovine did the Charleston and had the crowd roaring, especially when the back end almost fell off the stage.

Second up was the jellyfish. The wearer worked at the shop that made the kites and balloons, and the costume was an exact recreation of the biggest floating creature. His talent was playing the clarinet. The reed instrument magically appeared from the jellyfish's stomach. He did a rousing rendition of *Swanee* that the audience loved.

The bloody headless man tap-danced while juggling three large, scary butcher knives — one of which he dropped that almost pinned his left shoe to the stage floor. Again, there was a big applause.

Lolly walked over to the orchestra leader and whispered into his ear. He nodded in approval and she positioned herself center stage. The orchestra began Gershwin's *I'll Build a Stairway to Paradise*. Lolly started softly, but as the song and tempo built, she sang louder and stronger.

Lynette, with several swigs in her by then, jumped up and shouted, "All right, Lolly!" and began to dance at the table and sing along with her.

Her three companions joined and also began to sing. Table by table, people, in the crowd did the same, and by the end of the song, Lolly was leading the entire audience. When she finished, everyone shouted for an encore and the girl in the mermaid costume started singing again. When the song finally ended, she was greeted with the loudest response of any of the finalists.

Everyone loved her and her performance. Even the two figures in the shadows behind the trees near the carousel pavilion tower. Thomas and his companion had been watching the show from their dark corner. He felt her tones. They weren't as powerful as Ariadne's, but they were still strong enough to resonate deep within his body. Thomas knew he couldn't take his bother's mate, but this new one would be more than adequate to fulfill his needs.

Pompey walked on stage after Lolly's performance and Cleo and the other judges joined him. "Weren't those enchanting people marvelous? Our judges, along with your applause, have given us our winners in all the categories. First, Most Comical goes to our two friends, the dancing cow. Second, Most Original has to go to the clarinet solo by the wonderfully crafted jellyfish. Third, Most Frightening goes of course to our headless and beautifully bloody tap-dancer, which means that our big winner for Best Costume, and truly the best performance, goes to our beguiling singing mermaid."

The crowd applauded loudly and Lynette jumped up again, waving her arms so wildly she fell back into her seat and almost lost her crown.

Each winner was given a cash prize in an envelope and a small bouquet of flowers. When Lolly received her one hundred dollars she started to cry. Pompey hugged her and whispered in her ear.

Lolly approached her table and was greeted by more hugs and

kisses. She opened the envelope and looked inside. She never had this much money. Everyone was telling her how wonderful she was, but Lolly, in shock, didn't hear a word. This was the first time she had sung in front of a big crowd and the first time she had ever won anything.

She hugged Lynette and whispered, "We have enough dough to get us to Broadway now. And Mr. Wright told me to come back next spring to work at the carnival singing. It's so swell and we did it."

"It's more than swell, it's the cat's pajamas," Lynette replied, tipsy.

"You look like you need a trip to the little girl's room," Lolly said. She turned to Enrico. "How many of those velvet bag swigs did my friend have?"

"*Due o tre?*" Enrico confessed.

"Two or three. Or maybe more?" Élan admitted. He and Max held up their own velvet bags.

Lolly turned to Enrico. "We are going to find the John and take a walk to get my friend back on her feet. Can you and your friends watch our stuff and hold my prize money? I don't want to get mugged after all my hard work."

"*Naturalmente*, my pretty, talented Marie. We will be here until you get back. Then we can dance and get some food before the party ends."

The girls walked toward the octopus ride and found a restroom near the entrance. Lolly had to support her friend most of the way. She waited outside until Lynette came out. The little Queen of Sheba was not smiling. She looked like she had just been sick, with her crown and wig askew.

Lolly straightened her headdress. "I think we need to hit the beach. You could use some good old sea air."

As they walked toward the water, Lolly discussed their future. "With the hundred bucks we can get a room in Ridgewater tonight and take the train to New York City in the morning."

Lynette interrupted, "In the afternoon."

"Whatever, my drunken pal. I bet we can ask any one of our three new friends to put us up awhile until we get jobs. I think we can trust them not to jump us," she laughed.

Behind them in the dark shadows of the trees and the amusements, Thomas and his companion pursued the girls. The merman with him was younger and very nervous. Thomas nicknamed his friend 'Jake' because the language of the mermen was just sounds that didn't translate into human words. This was Jake's first time on land. He had always stayed in the safety of the deep surf. Thomas had talked him into going on this expedition to find mates and the boy looked to him for instruction.

Thomas signaled to Jake to grab Lynette before they reached the beach and while no one was around. The two mermen moved with the speed of slithering cobras. The assault was so sudden, Lolly and Lynette didn't have time to run from their attackers. Jake grabbed a shocked Lynette, lifted her off the ground by her waist, and covered her mouth with his large claw-like hand.

Thomas had a hold of Lolly. Being stronger and not intoxicated, she put up a fight, but Thomas was much too powerful. He covered her mouth before she was able to scream. Both girls fought, but could not break free of their captors. In the struggle, the girl's headdresses and wigs fell off and were left behind with one of Lynette's golden sandals.

As they approached the water, Lynette tried to scream again, but Jake jerked her head sharply. Her body went limp and stopped moving. The boy looked at Thomas with fear in his dark eyes. Thomas just gestured to him to move quickly.

They dragged the girls to the water's edge beyond William's house. Lynette was still not moving. Lolly knew something was wrong with her friend as she continued to struggle to get free from Thomas' grip.

Jake removed his hand from Lynette's mouth and her head dropped. He lifted it with his large, claw-like hand but it dropped again. The girl was lifeless in his arms. He looked at Thomas for any sign of what to do next, but all William's son did was motion to him to get into the water. Thomas took Lolly under the surf and his companion followed with his lifeless captive.

CHAPTER TWENTY-FOUR

Rescue for Some

Claire sat at the table and stared into space. She had given up on the radio and watched Brian asleep on the couch. The boy didn't want to be alone in his bedroom because it was too far away from her and his dad. She looked at him and thought how brave her boy had been during this craziness.

Brian was really holding his own, considering what had happened. Their home was turned upside-down, his grandmother was dead and his father was sick, and all in just a few days. She felt so lucky to have a child like him.

Claire touched Brian's hair and kissed the boy lightly on the forehead. She pulled his blanket up around his shoulders, then walked to the entrance of the bedroom. She was glad the generator was still running and they could keep cool. The atmosphere was getting worse outside and she hoped the air conditioner would keep filtering out whatever was making it so humid and hard to breathe.

She gazed at her husband, the most important person in her life besides her son. What was going to happen? In the last few days, her world had fallen apart too. Everything was good and they had so much fun that night with the opera and the silly costumes. Then the storm ended all that and she wondered if her life was ever going back to what it was before.

Fear and sadness ran through her body and mind so strongly, she started to tremble and feel sick. Then she stopped herself. She knew she needed to be strong for her husband and son. After a deep breath, Claire summoned all her strength. They were going to get off the island and she was going to make sure it happened.

She double-checked her son's backpack. That morning had been so crazy and rushed, she forgot to look at what he had packed. When she opened the bag, all she could find was a framed photo of them all together on the beach. Her eyes filled with tears at the boy's beautiful gesture. She told him to only take what was important and that was what he had done. She looked at the picture and started to cry. Then she went to Brian's room and got the clothes and other items he would need.

We are going to leave the island in the morning, she pledged to herself.

When Claire returned to the living room, she heard a deep drone that vibrated the walls and floor. It was accompanied by a pale green light coming through the shutters. She looked in the bedroom and saw Mike standing at the window. The light illuminated his face and he didn't seem to be in any discomfort. In fact, he was smiling. Travis sat next to him and looked up at his master.

Claire ran to him. "Mike, get back into bed. You shouldn't be up, you're too sick."

She tried to guide him backward, but he wouldn't budge. Travis pulled on Mike's pant leg, then nudged him with his head.

Mike smiled at her and walked past his wife and out of the room, toward the front door. The sound and light grew stronger, urging him on. Claire and Travis tried to block his way, but he was too strong for them. Awakened by the commotion, Poo and Brian got off the couch and joined their effort.

By the time Mike had reached the door, the sight of both dogs pulling on his pant legs and Claire and Brian pushing him back would have been comical if it wasn't for the tragic urgency of the situation. He was going to die like his mother and walk into the sea if they didn't stop him.

Brian moved away from the struggle. Claire didn't notice her son had left until she heard a dull clang from behind Mike. Her husband stopped moving and fell to the ground. Claire saw Mike at her feet with the dogs sniffing around his body. She looked up and saw Brian crying, holding a frying pan in front of his chest.

"I had to do it, had to hit Dad. I hope I didn't kill him." He stared at his mother. "I'm sorry, Mom. I didn't know what else to do."

Brian dropped the pan on the floor.

"Honey, you did the right thing. Your dad will be fine," Claire assured him.

She felt his pulse and noticed the large bump on his head. Mike was alive. They dragged him to the bedroom, but instead of putting Mike in bed, Claire had the boy pull out the recliner from against the wall. It took a lot of effort, but they placed his body into the chair.

Claire asked Brian to get the rope from the pantry closet. They tied him to the chair and then wrapped Mike in a sheet from the bed. She ripped another sheet into strips and tied them like the rope.

She never noticed that the light and sound from outside had stopped as soon as Mike was subdued. She felt guilty treating him this way, but she couldn't take the chance that Mike wouldn't be called by whatever was outside waiting for him again.

Claire knelt by the large padded armchair. "I'm sorry honey, but I had to do this. I won't lose you. I promise we will get out of here in the morning."

She pulled over the floor lamp that was always next to the chair and turned it on. "Thank God for the generator, I hope it lasts until morning."

Claire looked at the bump on Mike's head and realized it was bleeding. She went into the bathroom and retrieved peroxide, a towel, and some bandages. After the wound was cleaned, she placed a bandage over it as Brian watched, weeping quietly.

"You saved your dad's life. You had to do it."

She hugged her son, shut the lamp off, and led him to the living room. They worked together to move a big wardrobe in front of the door to help block Mike if he tried to leave again. Brian rigged it with a rope so that they could close it against the door from the outside if they needed to.

Claire got what ice was left in the refrigerator and wrapped it in a towel. She held it to her husband's head until she fell asleep at his side.

Within the hour the intense sound and light came back again and woke Mike up. He struggled against the bonds and cried out in pain.

Claire held him down as much as she could and tried to calm him. Travis, by her side, stood up on his hind legs and pressed his strong paws and body weight against his master.

Brian stayed in the living room with Poo by his side and held his hands over his ears until the sound stopped. The deep tone and the light happened again the next hour and then again. Each time they kept Mike in the chair.

The next light that came into the room was the silent glow of dawn, not the pale green light with its companion sound. Claire went to turn on the lamp to check Mike's head, but it wouldn't work. She tried another lamp by the bed and the result was the same. The power was off and the generator finally died. It wouldn't be long before the air inside was hot and un-breathable.

It was time to get off the island. She went to the closet and after rummaging deep in the back, pulled out an old sleeping bag. This was how she was going to get him to the boat. They would put him inside it, tie the rope around him, and then she and Brian would drag him, like a Native American travois, to the boat. The sleeping bag would protect Mike from the nasty plants and the crazy animals.

She drugged him with the last of the Percocet and needed to pick up the rest of the pills at Lovey Grace's house. She didn't know how long it would be before they saw a doctor or found any help. Once Mike looked like he was unconscious, Claire started to unravel the top sheet.

A sound that they hadn't heard before was increasing from above the house. The resonance grew louder and more familiar, it was the noise a helicopter made. She stopped the untying process and secured her husband again.

Brian ran into the room with both dogs barking behind him. "Mom. It's a chopper! It's help!"

Claire dashed to the window and looked through the cracks of the shutters. She saw flashing lights and felt the vibrations and the strong wind from the vehicle's blades. Even though he was heavily sedated, the sound and light woke Mike and he began to cry out in pain, struggling against the ropes.

Claire went to the door with Brian. The two moved the big wardrobe they had pushed in front of the entrance.

When Claire opened the door, the hot air hit her like a wet towel. It was also not breathable. She choked and covered her mouth; the mist burned her eyes. The air conditioning must have filtered out whatever was in the mist that was causing her discomfort.

When she adjusted to the change, men in protective suits and gear greeted her. The first man spoke loudly though his helmet, over the sound of the helicopter, the wet wind, and blowing sand.

"You okay, lady? How many people here?"

She coughed and shouted back with tears in her eyes, "Three and two dogs."

"Anyone infected?" he yelled.

"My husband is sick but —"

She was cut off. "Sorry, can't take any infected. We have to go now."

She was about to speak again when another man in a protective suit man moved in front of the first.

"Claire, it's Uncle Ned. Who's sick? Is Lovey Grace okay?" he hugged her. "Is it Mike or Brian?"

"Ned, you're here!" Claire cried. "Mike is sick. We have to get him to a doctor."

Brian yelled from behind his mother, "Uncle Ned! Uncle Ned!" He ran up to the old man and hugged his hazmat suit.

"We have to hurry. They won't wait. They will only take people that were not infected by the storm." He paused a moment and asked again, "Where's Lovey Grace?"

Claire touched his arm. "Ned, she's gone."

He said nothing and went inside. When he saw Mike, he knew it was bad. He turned to Claire and whispered, "They will only take you and Brian. We have to go."

"You take Brian. I'm staying with Mike until he gets better and we can leave."

Uncle Ned looked at her with tears in his eyes. "He isn't going to get better. Think of your boy, he needs you more than ever. We have to hurry."

Claire kissed Mike. "I'll come back for you as soon as I can. I promise. I have to get Brian out of here. As soon as he is safe, I'll will get you to a doctor." She kissed him again and hugged Mike tightly. "I love you."

The kiss stopped his moaning and then he looked at her and smiled. Claire began to cry and hugged Mike again. She released her grip, walked toward the front door, and looked back at her husband for possibly the last time.

Suddenly she heard gunshots and the first man yelled, "We have to go, now!"

Uncle Ned grabbed Claire and the boy and led them out of the house. Brian was trying to go back to his dad, but another man in a protective suit took him by the waist and carried him to the helicopter.

"Travis, Poo, come on boys!" Brian screamed as the dogs ran to the doorway.

Claire knowing they couldn't go with them, turned to Travis and Poo. "Stay with Mike and protect him and block the door. We will come back for you. I love you both."

She motioned to the dogs to go inside. Ned closed the front door of the house and led Claire by the arm to the waiting rescue helicopter.

When she got inside the chopper, a man gave Claire and Brian portable breathing devices. Five other people huddled together with a look of terror on their faces.

She heard more gunshots and saw two suited men firing at something in the water. The sound from the sea could be heard just below the roar of the helicopter's propellers.

The last to get on board before they rose into the air were the men with the guns. One man pulled himself inside, but the other had something attached to his leg. It looked like a horseshoe crab, but larger, with translucent tentacles that wrapped around his thigh.

Claire could see blood gushing out of his suit as the man screamed. Before they reached a height of twenty feet he fell from the helicopter. She looked out the window but he had disappeared into the water.

She felt the helicopter struggle in the heavy, damp air until it ascended above the layer of greenish-gray clouds. The air became noticeably cooler and drier when they reached a leveling-off altitude.

Claire, with her arms around Brian, watched as their home disappeared from sight. All she could see through the heavy mist was the spiral of light off the shore of the island. As they traveled farther away, Claire made out more of these spiral lit shapes scattered along the coast. This was not just an event that was happening to them and their area. This was much bigger.

Uncle Ned took off his protective helmet and she asked, "What are those lights? What has happened?"

"We don't know for sure but it has affected all the coastlines. The storm hit everywhere except farther inland. The middle of the country has been spared, from Ohio to Nevada."

"When you say everywhere, you mean only us?" Claire asked in a trembling voice.

"Every coastline all over the world," he replied. "Millions of people were infected and were taken by the mist and the oceans. If they weren't infected by the storm, they became sick from the air. It's become heavy, wet, and toxic too. The center of the country is safe for now, but this haze or fog is expanding every day. Our emergency government has relocated to Lincoln, Nebraska. We are going to Ohio where there are temporary rescue camps for survivors being set up. This happened so quickly, it is a miracle we were able to save anyone."

He paused and looked at her and Brian.

"Bridget is waiting for us there and she's baked a lot of cookies." He thought some good news would help a little.

Claire looked at him, leaned in closer and asked in a whisper so Brian couldn't hear, "What caused this? Does anyone know? Can we stop it?"

He shook his head no. The old man looked at her then down at the boy. Uncle Ned was always honest and straightforward and she knew if he had nothing to say it was really bad.

*　　*　　*

When the sound of the helicopter faded above them, Travis pulled the rope that helped him move the large wardrobe in front of the door. He and Poo pushed it until the entrance was again secure and blocked. They walked into the bedroom and looked at Mike, who was moaning in pain and trying to get free. He struggled against the bonds and ropes, desperate to respond to the sound and light from the sea.

Poo, we have to protect Mike until they come back. He cannot walk into the sea and leave us like Lovey Grace. I promised Claire we would watch him until they returned.

What if they don't come back? Poo asked.

Travis didn't reply, he just turned and looked at his master. Mike was trying to break free from the chair he was tied to as the sound and light persisted.

CHAPTER TWENTY-FIVE

Little Girls Lost

Enrico, Max, and Élan waited for Lolly and Lynette for more than an hour. The party was almost over, the festivities were winding down, and people were beginning to leave. The Italian asked Max to go with him to look for the girls while Élan stayed at the table in case they came back. Enrico hoped they were partying with some new friends they'd met because of Lolly's contest win.

They searched the area around the octopus ride and the restrooms near that amusement. Both men called out the girls' names but got no response. After twenty minutes, they became very worried. The girls wouldn't just leave and get on the ferry, especially without their belongings and the prize money. Enrico found Pompey and told him the situation.

"Let me get the security men to look around," Pompey suggested. "I'll also ask William and Albert to check the area near their house and the northern part of the beach. I pray they didn't go swimming in the dark because I would hate to have our party end on a tragic note."

"It is my fault. I should never have given them anything to drink. I thought it was so safe here with everyone knowing each other. I just wanted those sweet girls to have a good time."

"My friend your intentions were good," Pompey said. "We have to think positively and check the whole island until we find them."

The search for Lolly and Lynette went on for a few more hours. The last ferry had left, so Enrico and his friends were invited by Pompey to stay for the night. The three men didn't want to leave until they knew what had happened to the girls.

The moonless night slowed the search and made it much more difficult, but one of the security men eventually discovered the girls' headdresses and wigs and Lynette's golden sandal. It was too dark to tell if there were any signs of a struggle. They searched the whole beach, but the girls weren't anywhere.

Pompey gathered everyone together. "Let's please search all night until we find these poor women. Look for any signs that indicate that they might have possibly gone swimming."

They searched until daylight with no result. The only clues of the girls were the items found earlier. There were no footprints in the sand that might have indicated they were in the water or near the beach. The only unusual looking impressions in the sand were near their items and on the northern end of the beach. William recognized these imprints but kept silent.

Pompey reported the missing women to the police that morning by phone and went to Ridgewater to meet with them. Around noon, Enrico and his two friends, along with Pompey and Cleo, described the girls and handed over their belongings along with Lolly's prize money. They mentioned that one of the girls had been drinking but not where she had gotten the liquor. Pompey suggested that Enrico and his friends go back to the city and he'd keep them informed of any progress. Cleo and Pompey accompanied the police back to the island.

The search lasted the rest of the day, but nothing more was found. The only information they had on the two women, beyond the costume pieces, were their first names. No one knew what town they were from or that their bags were still in the lockers at the bus station. Several people from the party recognized Lolly because of the contest and a few remembered seeing Lynette. One person took Lolly's picture when she was singing. The film hadn't been developed yet so they gave the roll to the police.

*   *   *

William sat on his porch and looked out toward the horizon. It was sunset now and everyone's day had been spent searching for the girls.

The police had gone back to Ridgewater and the Wright troupe discussed the tour they were about to embark upon in the next few days. Pompey decided that everyone should leave as scheduled, but he would stay until the situation concerning the disappearance was solved. He felt responsible for the tragedy and wanted to make sure that whatever the conclusion, he was there to deal with it. Afterward, he'd catch up with the troupe.

William left the porch and walked up the beach to the place where the tracks in the sand were found. The thought that his family from the sea had a part in what had happened to the missing girls plagued him. Even though it was getting colder as the sun went down, he sat cross-legged on the beach.

He closed his eyes and pictured the place where his family now lived. He still didn't know if he had ever really gone there, but he was positive Emily was real. Did he meet his son and daughter in the depths of their city or was that something that his wife had projected into his thoughts? He wasn't sure anymore.

William heard a splashing and sensed a presence behind him. It took him a few seconds before he could bring himself to open his eyes. There was Emily, silhouetted by the sunset. She was wearing the pale yellow cotton dress he had seen her in the first time she came to him. Whatever she was, his wife was still beautiful to him. He knew he loved her when he looked into her eyes.

He stood in front of Emily and could tell something was wrong. She had the same look on her face he hadn't seen since they lost Thomas, so many years ago.

Emily cast her gaze downward and began to speak to him through her thoughts. *William I need to tell you about Thomas.*

His fears surfaced when she mentioned his name.

Emily looked into his eyes. *He was on the island last night with another and they took two of your kind against their will and brought them to our home. One was dead when they arrived at the city and the other was secured in an air chamber like you were when you visited us. Thomas asked to convert her into one of us, just like January and myself. We had to let him do this because she could never leave after seeing the city. Her will was too strong and she fought the conversion.* She glanced down for an instant and then back into William's eyes. *The girl died. We tried to save her but we could not.*

William stood frozen in front of his wife. He said nothing but just looked at her with tears in his eyes.

I am so sorry, I didn't know he had done this until it was too late. All this is my fault. I should have never come back to you, but I couldn't stay away. Now two innocent girls are dead because of me.

William touched the wet sleeve of his wife's dress. He wanted to say it wasn't her fault but the words didn't come.

"What about Thomas? What has happened to our boy?"

Emily moved toward the water's edge and turned to him. *As their punishment he and the other were made part of one of the tower plants that guard our city. They will be one with this plant creature as long as they live and will stand guard to protect our kind. They put our world in jeopardy because of their actions and this is how they will have to redeem themselves.*

William remembered the great towering, plant-like monsters from his journey in the dream. He pictured in his mind the mermen inside the tall flower that waved in the currents on its slender stem and glowed a cool green, illuminating their way.

He looked at her and repeated, "For life?"

Emily nodded and then spoke with words as she slid into the surf. "I will never come back again because I caused this.

Goodbye, my William. I loved you as your wife and I love you still." She moved deeper into the water. "I am sorry."

Then Emily disappeared under the waves and was gone.

William walked toward her, into the water up to his knees, but stopped. He knew she was right and that they should never see each other again.

He closed his eyes and pictured her when they were married. "I loved you too." Then he opened his eyes and looked out to sea. "I love you still."

CHAPTER TWENTY-SIX

1926

Pompey Wright's company tour concluded at the end of April the following year. Everyone involved with the carnival when it originally opened came back and prepared for its second season, the summer of 1926.

A crew opened up the pavilion and other buildings to the brisk spring air. Everything was checked for repairs and for any damage the winter weather and sea air may have caused. The beach and picnic area tables, benches, and roof enclosures used for shade received a good repainting.

The octopus ride's metal supports had rusted and had to be replaced. They were never coated in weather proofing because of the rush to open on the previous Fourth of July. The gondola seats had to be recovered and the whole structure needed a good touchup of paint.

The pavilion held up well, only needing minor repairs, replaced lights, and the installation of a few new nickelodeon machines Pompey had ordered. They were special because the short movies were in the new two-strip color process. None of the ornate windows and doors had suffered any damage. William oversaw all this until Ned Baldwin arrived back from the tour. He came a week earlier than Pompey and the rest of the troupe because Carla was going to have a baby, which was due in late June.

Pompey and Ned ordered two house kits from Sears. Ned's was for Carla, the new baby, and himself, and Pompey's was a wedding gift for Albert and Ariadne.

The young couple married, as they had planned, in Paris in front of the famous carousel in the Luxembourg Gardens just before Christmas. Only an elderly couple, whom they just met and asked to stand up for them, were at the ceremony. The gardens were lit in tiny white lights covered in a blanket of light snow that fell that morning. It gave everything in the gardens the look of a holiday fairytale.

That night they announced their marriage and Pompey insisted on hosting an impromptu wedding dinner for the couple with the whole troupe in attendance. This was the first celebratory moment for everyone since they'd left the island and the incident with Lolly and Lynnette.

Pompey had stayed on Plover's Island for two weeks to help the police solve the disappearance. He took the hundred dollar prize money and increased it to one thousand as a reward for any information about the girls. No one was able to find out where the two came from. They had a picture of Lolly singing on stage during the contest that was given to the police by one of the carnival workers that attended the party. It was a distant shot and with the costume and wig. Lolly could have been any young girl.

All the efforts to learn more about them proved fruitless. The reward generated inquiries from parties trying to cash in on the misfortune of the young women, but no useful or valid information came forward. The police thanked Pompey for all his concern and generosity. They told him that the missing persons process could take a long time and that he should leave for Europe and connect with his tour.

When Pompey and the other members of his company arrived back on Plover's Island in mid-May, the carnival was almost ready to open.

He greeted William with a big hug. "My dear friend, I missed you so much. You know, we are relatives now as well as business partners?"

"Yes, I received Albert's letter right after the New Year. He told me we're going to have another ceremony on the island. I spent the winter building our two children a fence, trellis, and gate to enclose a garden. When they are ready I can set it up for them in front of the new house."

"Ned told you about the houses we ordered? One is for Ariadne and Albert and the other is for Carla and the new expectant father. We picked them out of a big fat catalog and they should arrive any day. I may need your help with the building crew to assemble them. They are quite modern for little houses that come as a kit. Everything is included — plumbing, electrical, et cetera, et cetera."

Pompey put his arm around William. "Let's take a walk, my friend. I have a nice bottle of wine in my bag. We can have a drink on your lovely porch and catch up. It is such a delightful spring day, much like the one when we first met."

"Yes, it is."

When they settled into chairs on William's porch, Pompey toasted. "To us, my dearest friend, to the new carnival season, and to our lovely children." Pompey leaned forward and touched William's arm. "Cleo stayed in Europe after we finished the tour and went back to Paris. She arranged a booking for herself at one of the clubs for the spring and summer."

William said nothing at first and then just smiled. "I will miss her. I hope she'll be happy with this new job. Who will take her place in the carnival?"

"I hired a another dancer. A French woman we met in London. She resembles my dear sister and is a wonderful artist. She should work out well for the time being." Pompey paused and took an envelope out of his pocket. "Here is Cleo's address in Paris. You should write to her if you have time. I wanted to give it to you now before I forgot." He smiled and studied him for a reaction.

"Pompey, I am not much of a letter writer, but thank you." He put the envelope on the white wicker table between their chairs.

Pompey's thoughts turned to the situation of the missing girls. "Were there any more developments in the disappearance of those poor young women? I never received any communication from the Ridgewater authorities. I wrote to them three times but never received a response."

"I'm sorry to say nothing has been resolved since you left. I checked with the police every time I went to the mainland this winter. All they could say was, there was a storm of false leads when you posted the reward, but nothing that checked out. I think they have just given up. They were two young girls who probably left bad homes for the big city and the party on the island was a stop along the way. Enrico said they wanted to be entertainers and go to New York. He wrote to me once and even called a few times. I think he still feels guilty about what happened to them since he and his friends brought the girls to the party."

Pompey shook his head. "Poor dears. I hope they are happy wherever they are. I always tried to think that they met new friends, left the island that night, and no harm ever came to them. It kept me from worrying about it on the tour. I hope that is what happened."

William repeated the same thoughts but couldn't look Pompey in the eye. "Why don't we have another glass of the wine you were so kind to bring?"

"Yes, let's do so." Pompey poured them both some more and they toasted to the coming summer again. The rest of the visit was filled with conservations about the next day's carnival business, the new houses, and the wedding.

* * *

The second wedding for Albert and Ariadne happened on a

cool night in late May just before the Decoration Day opening of the carnival. It was a small ceremony followed by a dinner for the troupe and close friends.

William set up a canvas-and-wood canopy on the beach in front of his house and the almost-finished frameworks of the two new bungalows. Chairs and tables were brought over from the pavilion patio and placed on the beach. Torch-topped poles strung with paper lanterns surrounded the seating area and canopy in a semicircle.

After the vows, Pompey made his traditional speech, with one exception. "I would like to wish my dear, beautiful daughter and my new son the best of health, great fortune, and ... babies."

Everyone laughed and applauded as Albert blushed.

"I also want to wish them a long and beautiful future together on this island or wherever they travel or live." He paused. "I wish the same for my troupe, my friends, and my lovely sister, Cleo, who could not be here with us. May all of them and she, find the love and happiness these two young members of our family have."

He lifted his glass, toasted and looked at William sitting at the end of the bridal party table.

The guests on the beach were not the only observers of the ceremony. Watching from the water, far out enough not to be noticed, Emily blended with the motion of the soft waves and rosy hues reflected by the sunset sky. She cried a happy tear for her son on his wedding day and another sad tear for her other boy, condemned to a place he could never leave. Emily also cried for a daughter who would never meet any of these members of her family and know their love. Her last tears were for William and herself.

This was the last time she would see him. She risked the fate of her son by even being there now. When it became dark, Emily thought of her love for her family celebrating on the beach, wished them well, dove beneath the surface, and swam back to her home.

*　*　*

That summer William wrote to Cleo and she answered his letter. When the troupe left for Europe in the late fall, after another successful carnival season, William went with them.

Ned and Carla Baldwin stayed to run the carnival's off-season affairs and take care of their new baby. The child was small, but not a little person like his parents. He was born a week earlier than expected, in mid-June.

The following spring everyone came back to Plover's Island, including William. He met Cleo in Paris, but the time apart hadn't changed things. His lie about his wife haunted him so much. Even though Emily had said goodbye, William felt he had hid so many things from Cleo that he couldn't reveal, it would be impossible to start their relationship again.

Cleo also realized that no matter what she was willing to accept, his wife's memory would still be an obstacle between them. She knew any relationship they tried to have now would never work. William said goodbye to her in Paris at the Luxembourg Gardens where Albert and Ariadne were married.

CHAPTER TWENTY-SEVEN

Lights in the Sky

In the fall of 1930, after five successful carnival seasons, the troupe left on another tour. The stock market crash the year before hadn't affected business as much as they had expected. People still wanted to have a good time, even if they didn't have the money to do it. The crowds were smaller, but the crew stayed the same. Pompey didn't want his carnival family to suffer, so he put all his profits into keeping them employed and the amusement going as long as he could afford it.

This time the group that left on tour had changed. Albert and Ariadne were expecting their first child, so Ned went to cover for him and Pompey hired a singer Enrico had recommended from New York to replace his daughter. Ned was reluctant to leave his family for so long but Carla talked him into going. She knew he loved being on tour and hadn't gone since before their baby, Ned junior, was born. Their boy was the first baby born on the island and also the first child that was part of the Wright troupe family since Ariadne.

"Are you sure our boy and you will be all right?" Ned asked. "There will be so much to do even without caring for the baby."

"I'll have plenty of company with Albert and Ariadne so close and I want to help with the birth when the child comes in January. We've seen Ariadne grow up and I feel like she is our little girl too. She will need a woman around she trusts when the time comes. As for the carnival, the season is over and the almanac says it's going to be a mild winter. Plus, Madame Regina's cards said so too."

He laughed. "I didn't know Regina predicted the weather now." He looked at his wife. "So you are sure you two will be okay?"

"I'm sure."

"I'll go over everything with Albert and the winter crew to make sure all is understood."

She laughed. "Did you forget Albert grew up on the island? Everything will be fine and there will be a new baby and friend for our little Ned when you get back. If you don't make up your mind soon, I'm going on tour and you will have to help with the delivery."

"I'm going, I'm going." He kissed her.

*   *   *

Albert and Ariadne's child, Michael James Guillory, was born the last week in December, 1930. A light snow fell, but it didn't keep the doctor from arriving on time to deliver the baby. Carla was there to assist as she promised. The couple loved having her around because she was always so positive and cheerful. Her laugh was contagious and even made her little boy, now three-and-a-half, laugh until he developed the hiccups.

She brought Ned junior over the next morning to see the baby and gave Ariadne a picture he drew for the child.

"Look, little Ned," Carla said as she pointed to the baby. "See how sweet little Michael is? He is so wee and mighty."

Little Ned repeated what his mother said. "Ah, wee and mighty."

"Little Michael will be your new friend as soon as he's big enough to play with you," she said, prompting him to give his gift.

"Here is a picture I drew of your house, Michael. It's your

birthday gift."

Little Ned placed the picture on top of the blanket in the baby's cradle.

Ariadne smiled and picked Ned up and kissed him. "Thank you so much for such a beautiful drawing of our house. I'll hang it on the wall in Michael's room, right over his crib so he can see it before he goes to sleep and when he wakes up in the morning."

She held the gift over the baby as the newest Guillory smiled and looked up wide-eyed at the picture and his mother.

"See the sweet picture Ned made for you? It's our house and your room is here," Ariadne pointed to a window in the drawing.

Little Ned smiled and repeated, "Every night and first thing in the morning. That will be very good."

*   *   *

Carla was right. Little Michael did grow fast. He was playing on the beach with Ned by the summer. The little lady took care of the children when she wasn't working at the carnival and Ariadne did the same for her.

The babies brought the two women closer together than they had ever been. Carla had watched Ariadne grow up and now they were both mothers and friends.

The boys also became close. Ned treated Michael like a brother, and even at four years old could be trusted to watch and care for him when they played on the beach. He made sure little Michael didn't go into the water or eat something he shouldn't. Albert referred to the boy as Uncle Ned around his son and then, eventually, all the time.

Carla and her little boy sat with Ariadne and the baby on her porch. It was the middle of March and they were expecting everyone to return from the tour of the southern states any day. Pompey had decided not to go to Europe this season and focused on an American tour. The evening was nice and warm, the first time since the fall.

Ariadne made some tea and all of them enjoyed Carla's Irish soda bread cookies, full of currants, caraway seeds, and her own personal addition to the recipe, chunks of chocolate. When they got together like this, which was almost daily, Ariadne sang a song for the children and Carla usually joined in. The little lady also told a story about fairies or funny animals. Her tales were always acted out so expressively, that she made everyone laugh.

"The mouse had the biggest ears," Carla put her hands on both sides of her head and wiggled them while she twitched her nose.

Everyone giggled, especially her little Ned who was on the verge of hiccups.

"And he walked with the smallest steps, tripping over his long fat tail." She mimed and then tripped. The inevitable hiccup now punctuated Ned's bursts of laughter. Everyone joined in, laughing even harder.

Baby Michael pointed to the sky over the water.

Ariadne glanced up at the heavens. "Sweetheart, those are shooting stars. Look how wonderful they are."

Carla looked up in amazement, stopping her story mid-sentence. The sky was filled with tiny shooting stars. They seemed to be in the distance, but soon the streaks of light appeared to be closer. First one, then another, burned brightly through the night toward the beach. They were tiny, but made a big splash when they hit the water. When the first one landed on the beach, a small streak of brilliant light exploded as it hit the sand. Then two more shot closer to the house and detonated in Carla's garden.

"This doesn't look good. I think we better get inside," she shouted.

The women grabbed their boys and retreated into the house. One piece of tiny rock broke through the edge of the porch roof and landed with a fiery explosion on the front steps. Carla saw this and ran out onto the porch. She emptied the contents of the teapot, dousing the small fire that the speck from heaven had started.

They held their boys close to them, looked out the front window, and watched as a few more fragments fell near their houses and in two of the three beachfront gardens. The largest concentration of the tiny fragments from space landed in the water. Within minutes it was over. The fires that broke out after impact were so small, most of them had gone out on their own.

By the time Carla and Ariadne felt safe enough to go outside, Ned had arrived in front of his house. He didn't go on the southern tour, letting Albert go in his place.

"Are you ladies okay? That was some show. About a dozen or more hit us but there wasn't any damage. They all thankfully landed in the sand."

"Except for the holes in my nice porch roof and steps," Carla said. "They could have gone right through us."

"Well, we are safe and sound now, my darling. I'll fix those little holes in the morning."

"You can also make me a steel-plated umbrella. I'll be wearing that old doughboy helmet when I am gardening from now on."

This made Ariadne laugh and then Ned joined in. "My darling Carla, gardening in an old army helmet — that will be a dandy picture for the family album."

Carla began to laugh too, which always made everyone laugh even harder.

CHAPTER TWENTY-EIGHT

In the Deep

The shooting star event was worldwide, not just restricted to one area like the usual fragments of exploded planets or dead stars that entered our atmosphere. The tiny, luminous crystals were part of a huge cloud that blanketed the earth in one night. It was not space debris, but an alien organism looking for a new place to call home. Only the larger particles were visible as they passed through our atmosphere as streaks of light. The bulk of this mass was small and unseen and their burning paths were only visible at very close range. Most of the crystals, as if by design, landed in the oceans and other large bodies of water. Any landmasses that were struck, only bordered on the coasts of the continents and the many island groups. All inland areas were spared the particles from the alien cloud.

The media had reported the phenomenon sporadically all over the world. Independent astronomers and observatories had detected the mass of particle crystals before it dispersed over the planet. They studied the cloud and their conclusions drew little if any discussion or alarm. It was dismissed as harmless space dust.

News agencies from around the world ran stories on the radio and in print featuring several detailed eyewitness accounts. Some were taken seriously as weather-related disasters and others were discussed lightheartedly or dismissed altogether.

One scientist expressed concern about this cloud of dust, or crystals from space as he referred to them, but his comments were only published in an article in one pulp science fiction magazine. The man also gave a radio interview at a station in the Midwest, but for the most part the event was forgotten in a week or two.

The more important and telling situations were in areas as remote as small Pacific islands, floating villages in Southeast Asia, and some towns bordering large bodies of water in Nordic countries. Reports of rivers and lakes filled with unexplained dead fish and plants that rose to the surface and washed onto their shores were investigated.

Unknown vegetation replaced the local flora along the banks of remote rivers. They created a stir among the native residents because of their unusual colors, shapes, and translucent tendrils. There were some accounts that these new species of plants grabbed fish and small animals then pulled them into their dark green leafy cores.

The same problem was chronicled sporadically in several coastal towns, including Ridgewater and Plover's Island. Many theories were presented, but few tied the death of the aquatic life and vegetation to the shooting stars that fell that night.

Ariadne and Carla had discovered the strange plants in small patches around their gardens. While weeding, they uncovered dark green and purple leaves with shriveled long brown fingers that had entangled themselves among the early spring flowers.

Carla found, to her horror, a tiny half-eaten bird and some fragile bones in the soil next to one of the dead plants. Scattered patches of the same flora were also discovered on the beach and hidden in the dune grass.

All the plants seemed to have developed and died as quickly as they had appeared. This same species and other similar varieties were found in most coastal areas. Since the new flora died so quickly, few were acquired for research.

That night, the shower of crystals from this unknown cloud did successfully penetrate the waters of the planet. The percentage of the particle cloud that had dispersed into the oceans was much greater than the amount that hit the land. It was no coincidence that they scattered into the seas of the earth in such great numbers. The chemical composition of the oceans was what the cloud entity had traveled so far to find.

If a fish was unfortunate enough to be in its path, it died instantly or was infected by the alien particles. The tiny micro-specs of matter made their journey to the deepest regions of earth's rivers and oceans.

Inside the millions of alien crystals was the basic structure of a life from another solar system. The alien organism settled into its new home, linked, then combined with the DNA of the life forms in the abyssopelagic depths of the ocean.

Water was the prime factor that made the organism activate, but the enormous pressure at these depths was what it needed to thrive. The great volumetric compression of the deepest zones in the ocean was the perfect climate for its evolution.

The night of the lights from the sky was also a turning point for Emily's world and their undersea city. These beings, existing in their hidden undersea world, didn't know the invasion was coming until it was too late.

As the crystals passed through the water on their way to the bottom, they cut through beautiful creatures like the angel-wing jellyfish as they danced in the lower depths. Their luminescence died as their delicate bodies were torn and punctured. All floating crustaceans and fish that were penetrated by the particles either died or developed lesions that ate away their gossamer forms.

When the light shower reached the mermen guard towers, like the one that imprisoned Thomas, the crystal organisms pierced and dissolved the tall stems mooring them in place. Their bubble domes were invaded, and eaten away. Thomas and his fellow inmates were torn from their collapsing prisons, split in half, and separated from the towering plant structures they were once joined to. Thomas' mutilated and lifeless body sank to the bottom of the ocean floor, along with the remains of his stricken kin, and drifted away in the powerful currents at the bottom of the sea.

The same fate befell the other mermen of the great hidden city. Emily watched helplessly as the speeding crystals threatened her little January, whom she thought would be safe inside the membrane barrier of the metropolis. The speeding fragments passed into the organic walls of the chamber where the child, along with others like her, resided. Within seconds, numerous tiny crystals penetrated their small helpless bodies. Most of the merchildren died quickly from the multiple wounds or were infected by the new life form.

January was lucky to break free of the dissolving chamber before the crystals caused the walls of the city to dissipate. As the child escaped she saw the exquisite green glow of her home dim, flicker, and then exist no more.

She swam into her mother's arms and away from the dying city. Emily took her to the safety of a small cave, where they watched the particle invasion demolish the rest of their world. She held her daughter close as they witnessed the giant plants and huge tubeworm towers that populated the surrounding stone cliffs become decimated. One by one they lost their light, broke from their foundations, then tumbled and slowly drifted to the bottom of the dark canyon.

When the shower of death and destruction was over, Emily and January left the safety of the cave to search for Thomas. The guard towers, with their beacon domes, were gone, except for their decayed and rotted roots. They looked, but the currents had taken any sign of him with it.

When the surviving mermen regrouped, they sought out any remains of life within the ruins of their city. Most of them had suffered wounds that were now infected by the invading life form. They banded together in small groups and left in search of the other cities that may have been spared. Their quest was futile because this new life form had invaded and occupied every part of the deepest depths of the sea.

Some of the victims of the shower of light existed in the upper zones of the oceans but didn't survive unless they relocated to the lower depths where the pressure and climate was ideal for the invading life form. Those creatures who did remain near the surface, later washed up on the shores of coastlines, dead from the wounds inflicted upon them that night.

* * *

Once the alien DNA conquered the deepest depths of the oceans, it combined with, mutated, and evolved the former residents into something new over the next decade. The process was slow and precise as each generation was slightly more transformed than the last.

The children of the small bands of mermen, like Emily's nomadic group, were less fishlike than their fathers and more humanoid, but also more of something else. Their elegant lower torsos with beautiful fantails became legs with powerful finned feet. The shell helmets changed little, except for the development of new patterns of colorization. The muscled athletic torsos were even more human, but the flesh-colored skin was now greenish and covered in tiny soft scales.

This new hybrid species was more attuned to the pressure of great depths than ever before. Unlike their earthly mermen ancestors, they didn't do well in the shallow waters where the pressure was less. None could travel on land like Emily and her kind had. The tremendous pressure and chemical composition of the lower regions was a necessary element they needed to survive. It was also what protected them from detection as they multiplied and built their new world. Humans hadn't yet explored the zones where these creatures lived, so no one could witness and record their progress.

The mermen cities ruined from the invasion were rebuilt

organically, but with a more intricate design and flexibility. Their source of energy was rooted in the core of the earth more strongly than ever before. The new life thrived on the more toxic gases and chemicals that the earth's core pumped into the deep water. The cities had become as much living organisms as they were metropolises and had the ability to uproot at will and relocate.

The developing cities were interconnected with their inhabitants and the surrounding sea life. The new species were not separate colonies or clans, but one interconnected unit in communion with each other.

The essence of this alien life became part of the core of the planet from which it derived its power and nourishment. Any life from the upper levels of the sea were quickly co-opted into the genetic plan if it entered the deeper levels of the new world. A great whale or giant squid that sometimes dove to these depths was seized and reimagined to fit the new scheme.

Slowly, this undersea world started its evolution. This was the beginning and it worked towards its ultimate goal, which would happen on another night, with another storm.

CHAPTER TWENTY-NINE

Before the War

The carnival survived the Depression and the 1930s with the help of Pompey Wright's money. Without his continued infusion of finances, the pavilion and the other attractions would have decayed over the years prior to World War II. The amusement park was now a strange curio that was only enjoyed by a few visitors, the small group of residents and workers that were the carnival family. Pompey never built a house on the island or took rooms in the pavilion for himself. He loved his little stylish caravan and staying in the Ridgewater hotel.

Letters from Cleo kept him up-to-date regarding the events in Europe on a much more intimate level than what he read in the papers. It was 1938 and he knew it was time to go back to Paris and bring his sister home to the island. She'd never seen her nephew or Carla's boy. Also, Pompey wanted Cleo safe with her family and away from the war that everyone feared was about to unfold.

Pompey called on William just after Thanksgiving. He was on his porch showing little Michael how to carve a tiny horse ornament for the Christmas tree they were going to put up in a few weeks.

"Hello, my dear friend. Teaching our grandson your craft? Is another carousel in his future, too?"

"Our Michael is just like his dad, a natural carver."

"Like his grandfather too. He is another Guillory apple that hasn't fallen too far from the tree. It's a little early to see if he is a showman too," Pompey laughed.

"Not true," Michael shouted out. "I can sing and dance. Momma showed me."

The boy put down his carving and did a short dance routine with a few lines of song.

Pompey smiled and applauded. "I guess I spoke too soon. I think there will be a place for you on our next tour."

The boy replied, "Let me know when, so I can pack my bag."

The two men had a hard time trying not to laugh.

Pompey bowed to him. "I most assuredly will."

The boy nodded in approval as Pompey turned to William. "Can I speak to you privately for a moment?"

"Sure, let me finish showing Michael what to do next and I will be right with you."

Pompey waited in front of the garden until William joined him and asked, "What is it?"

"I want to have a meeting this afternoon with Albert, Ned, and yourself. I am leaving on a boat for England in two days. Then on to Paris."

"Are you going because of Cleo? Is she all right?"

"She is fine as of the last letter I received, but I know that it's going to get worse and I need to get her back home."

William froze for a second. The idea of Cleo returning to the island stirred up emotions he hadn't felt for a long time. "That would be a good idea. There is a war in Asia already and the Germans are getting pretty bold. Who knows where it will all lead? It is important to bring Cleo back."

"I hope to be home before the spring. I wish I could go after the holidays but I am afraid to wait. My sister has close friends there and persuading her to leave may take some time. I must convince her that she needs to be with her family now."

"Yes, you have to bring her back as soon as possible," William said, with a silent hope in his heart.

*   *   *

Pompey left two days later and took an ocean liner to London and then the boat to Calais and the train to Paris. He reunited with Cleo, but they didn't return before spring, as planned. They got involved with helping friends leave areas that were becoming more dangerous as the German threat came closer. Their efforts took time. Circumstances changed as the war escalated.

Over the next few years, two wars were being fought simultaneously. One battle spread to all the continents. The other was a silent evolution of the new species, born of two worlds, in the unexplored depths of the oceans that comprised two thirds of the planet.

The struggle was one of a genetic reimagining of the former life forms into something different and more powerful. On the surface, the world was at war. Below, a new order was building and growing, waiting for the right moment to take its next step.

CHAPTER THIRTY

Cleo's Visit

April of 1946 was the first spring without a war in five years. Ariadne was still waiting for Albert to come home. She hadn't seen him in two years and he was only home on leave twice since he'd enlisted in the Navy when war was declared.

Ned and Carla hadn't received any word of their son since the winter before. Young Ned left two years into the conflict once he was old enough to enlist and they didn't know if he was dead or alive.

Albert was due home next month and the town was preparing a big welcome for him and other returning troops who lived in Ridgewater. Once everyone was back, they were going to open the carnival and have a party at the pavilion like they did in the early days.

No one had heard from Cleo and Pompey nor John and Regina. One or two letters made it to the island, but that was years ago. Once the war began, all four were stranded in France. One letter mentioned the French Resistance, but no details beyond that.

One spring day, Carla sat with Ariadne on her porch having their usual tea, while Michael was working with Ned at the pavilion. The two women discussed the show they were going to perform at the party when Carla noticed that a tall woman wearing a long coat and hat was walking toward them, along the edge of the grassy dunes.

Carla asked, "I wonder who that is?" She focused on the figure. "Oh, my God. It can't be." She stood up and Ariadne did the same. "Is that Cleo Wright?"

The two women ran from the porch and down to the beach. Wearing a man's black fedora, pulled down to shield her from the wind, they couldn't really see if it was indeed Cleo.

She looked up, and it was. Her face was thinner and gray wisps of hair peeked out from under her hat. She wore little makeup and what she had on was muted, except for her dark red lips. Cleo was fifty-nine now, but still as beautiful and exotic as ever.

Ariadne reached her first. Carla was out of wind, but not far behind. "Aunt Cleo, it is you! We never received a letter. We didn't know you were coming or we would have met your train in Ridgewater."

She hugged her aunt until Carla caught up and joined the embrace.

"I didn't know when I was leaving England, so I never sent a telegram until after I landed in New York. I am so sorry. You will probably get it today." She smiled and kissed her niece, then bent down to give Carla a peck on the cheek.

"We haven't had any word for so long," Ariadne exclaimed. "Is Father coming too?"

"Are John and Regina coming?" Carla asked.

"I'm the only one. I have a letter from Pompey for you."

Ariadne saw the smile leave her aunt's face and knew something was wrong. "Let's go up to the house."

The women walked along the beach to the bungalow, arm-in-arm. Cleo felt nostalgic when she saw the three little gardens lined up in front of each of their houses. Everything looked just like it did that first day she came to the island, except threefold.

Cleo asked if they could stay on the porch. She loved this part of the island, especially now, with how much prettier it was.

"Aunt Cleo," Ariadne said, "it's been so long. You haven't met

Michael, who is sixteen now. God, I haven't seen you since the last tour we went on."

"I'm so sorry," Cleo said. "Here's the letter from your father. He wanted me to give it to you."

When Cleo said "wanted" it triggered a fear in Ariadne. She hesitated, "Is Father all right? Why didn't he come with you?"

"Your father, my dear brother Pompey, died last year in France. I just found out a few months ago. He was in the resistance movement with John and Regina. They were helping refugees get out of the country when they were caught on a road near Orléans. I met John in Paris at the end of the war and he gave me this letter."

"Oh, Father," Ariadne cried as Carla took her hand.

Cleo handed Carla a letter also. "This is from John. He wanted me to give this to you."

"And Regina?" Carla asked.

"She is gone too," Cleo replied. "It happened the same time as our Pompey."

Everyone was quiet. They held hands and looked out to the sea. Neither Ariadne nor Carla could open their letters.

Michael and Ned approached the front of the house from the direction of the pavilion. Ned was in shock when he saw Cleo. He embraced her and was also told the sad news as Michael stood back.

The news of his grandfather was shared later when Ariadne read Pompey's letter to the boy. The first few paragraphs stated that he had left the carnival to his only daughter and her family; important papers were in a safety deposit box in Ridgewater with his will, financial instructions, and certain valuables.

Pompey gave the name of a lawyer on the mainland whom Ariadne should contact upon his death. The rest of the letter contained his thoughts about his family.

"My dearest Ariadne, I am so happy that you and my grandson are safe with Albert on our island. I wish Cleo and I were there too, but we need to be here to help our friends caught up in this madness. I hope this insane war is over soon and we all can be together. I am giving this letter to John. He is going back to Paris to find Cleo, give her the letter and keep her safe until I get there."

"At night I close my eyes and can see you on the pavilion stage singing. The memory of the sound of your beautiful voice drowns out all the sorrow around me. We will be together soon and in a better world than we have now. I love you so much, my Ariadne."

She had never heard her father speak this way before. He was always lighthearted and never melancholy or overly emotional. Ariadne knew he loved her, but it was never expressed in such a way. The mother and son read the letter again and sat quietly for the rest of the afternoon.

Later that day, Cleo took a walk with Ned to the carnival pavilion. No one had mentioned William in the hours she had been there. With all the sad news she had to deliver, Cleo was afraid to receive any herself.

Ned asked about his friend John the Magician, what it was like during the war, and more about Pompey as they looked around the pavilion and then entered the theater. They walked backstage and Cleo sat down at her old dressing table. It was still set up, almost the way it was when she left.

"It is good to be back after all these years," she sighed. "Are any of my old costumes still here?" She looked around the dark space.

"Yes, they are in trunks stored in the upper level. William built a locked room to keep all of the touring props and costumes."

She looked in the mirror and caught Ned's eyes. "How is William? Where is he today?"

Ned looked at her with a smile. "He's in town for the night. We're planning a big welcome home for Albert and all the others who were away, so he's meeting with the mayor and should be back in the morning."

"That is a wonderful thing to do. They deserve a big welcome home after all they have gone through." She paused. "Is he well?"

Ned sensed how the two felt about each other ever since the hotel dinner, the evening they celebrated starting the carnival. Everyone knew, even his dear friend John who wasn't the best judge of these things.

He smiled. "He's well for a man with no love in his life."

Cleo looked at him in shock. Had everyone realized that they were so close? "Can we go upstairs? I would like to see my old outfits again."

"Sure. I bet they'll still fit."

"I am glad you think that because I'm not that confident." She laughed and gave him a hug before they went upstairs to the storage room.

"What time is William back from town tomorrow?"

"I believe he will be on the nine o'clock ferry."

*　*　*

When the boat docked, Cleo was there to meet it in her long coat, tan slacks, and black fedora, looking much like she did the first day William saw her walking up the beach.

She smiled at William. "Can you buy a lady a ride on a carousel?"

He took her hand. "I know a beautiful carousel just waiting for someone like you."

William put his arm around her shoulder and they walked to the pavilion tower that housed the attraction. He turned on the lights.

William jumped up onto the ride's platform and extended his hand to Cleo. "Which one of these colorful creatures strikes your fancy?"

"I think I'll ride the black horse with the white mane and tail. I seem to remember a horse just like that on a much smaller carousel inside a gazebo years ago."

She took his hand and William guided her to the steed of her choosing. He then grabbed her around the waist and lifted her onto the beast.

William walked to the center of the carousel, pulled the lever, and the ride began. He worked his way to her side and climbed onto the creature next to the black horse.

"Is the ride to your liking?" William asked.

"Very much so," Cleo replied.

They enjoyed the rest of the morning together, then went to Albert's house to be with Ariadne and Michael. The latter part of the day was spent talking about the good times, the carnival, and the family.

After dinner, Cleo and William sat on his porch until late into the evening. She never went back to her niece's house that night or the next. The reunion of the two helped make all the sad news that day seem just a little less unhappy.

Cleo stayed on the island with William for the next few months. She even performed that summer at the pavilion theater, reviving a dance she had done at the club she worked at in Paris during the war. They did some redecorating in the old house and she also learned to tend the little garden.

In the fall, William and Cleo were married in Ridgewater and went back to Paris for their honeymoon. The first place they visited was the Luxembourg Gardens, where they had said goodbye so many years ago. Cleo sent her niece a photo of William and herself on the very same carousel that Albert and Ariadne, as a young couple, were married in front of just before Christmas in 1925.

CHAPTER THIRTY-ONE

Sweet Music

The small group of trees had grown closer to the house in the days since the Green Storm. Before the event, they were just scrub trees and small pines living around a gnarly oak situated on a hilly mount near the three bungalows. Their branches pulsed in the wind and spread out from their usual boundaries.

The little pines did the same. Their furry branches were an inhospitable place to hang any holiday ornament. The old oak had developed translucent varicose veins pushing through and illuminating its bark. The ancient tree was always a haunting image, especially at night when the moon was full. After the Green Storm, the oak mutated into something more frightening than just shadows could convey.

Near the old tree was the family cemetery started by William Guillory. His ashes rested below a simple stone next to the three weathered crosses he'd carved for Emily, Thomas, and January.

Also in the family resting place, with its white picket fence and gate, was his beloved wife Cleo's stone, next to his. On the other side were the Baldwins' stones: Ned and Carla, and beautiful Ariadne and her Albert. Michael Guillory, their son, was there too, next to his first wife, Tina.

There was also a place for Lovey Grace next to Michael that was never taken. The roots from the thick black scrub trees pressed against the faded picket fence posts, pushing them inward toward the graves. The vines and leaves grew over the stones, obscuring some of the names and tilting the simple crosses.

The squirrels headquartered in the oak tree were always mischievous and bold, but now they were calculating and just plain evil. The once-devilishly playful rodents sported matted coats instead of fluffy fur. They were greasy and knotted; their fleece resembled lethal spikes. The most unsettling transformation of these previously lovable residents of the island was their eyes. The dark orbs were larger and covered in cataract membranes that looked acid green in the light of day and glowed at night.

At dusk, the serpent-tailed rodents scratched at the windows and doors of the Guillory bungalow looking for any way in. They were smarter since the storm. They seemed to know how to open windows and doors. They constantly searched every inch of the house for entry. Some of them even had crude tools they made from branches, seashells, or pieces of the wood they found in the backyard.

Travis sometimes heard them conspiring in high grass. Since the storm, he could hear everything they said. Only deep concentration or the rare opportunity to sleep could quiet the chorus he heard outside. It was like having a construction crew of tiny workmen banging and probing the structure twenty-four-seven.

The power had been out since the men in the protective suits took Claire and Brian. Each of the three bungalows had its own backup generator, but encroaching new vines and plant life, evolved since the storm, strangled their internal parts. Without power for the air conditioners, the house became as unbearably hot and humid as the outside.

The two dogs sniffed at the cracks in the window shutters for any bit of breeze. The air tasted and smelled different. Travis had seen how Claire had trouble breathing when they came to take them away. The men in hazmat suits wore helmets so that they were protected. However, Travis and Poo liked the new, tasty air. Each day the flavor was better. But the dogs couldn't tell whether it affected their master. He was either in pain or unconscious most of the time, unless the light and sound called him to the sea.

Mike's condition had declined since the morning of the rescue. All he seemed to feel when he was conscious was pain — a torment Travis tried to comfort, but nothing helped except the music. The antique crank phonograph that belonged to Mike's grandmother, Ariadne, still worked, and the sounds from the old scratchy seventy-eights seemed to ease Mike. But it also sparked activity outside. The opera records awakened the light and sound that called to him.

It was a low, deep tone that seemed to travel through the ground as well as the air. When the music from the phonograph stopped, so did the sound and light. Travis knew the deep tone and its accompanying glow had something to do with the storm, the changes, and the sickness. The sound and light from the sea became the big dog's greatest fear.

Mike and Travis could still communicate through thoughts. If the Rottweiler needed Mike to do something, he just thought about it and the man seemed to understand. This was the closest to a sense of intelligence or awareness that Mike seemed to have left. The big dog loved his master and tried anything to protect him. Out there was dangerous but, inside was safe, for the moment.

Poo told Travis that Claire and Mike had given Lovey Grace big white pills from a small bottle. They kept them somewhere in the bedroom or maybe the bathroom. The pills stopped her pain and worked until the day she walked into the sea.

The two dogs searched the bedroom and found nothing. The Rottweiler climbed up and balanced on the sink in Mike's bathroom and nudged the mirror door with his powerful snout until it swung open. There were three or four bottles of pills on the middle shelf. He knocked them to the floor and together they sniffed and poked the different bottles and pills looking for the right ones.

Poo shook his head, *No big white pills. There are blue ones, red ones, and even little white ones, but no big white ones.*

Think hard. Where could they be?

The golden westiepoo paused and remembered. *They were next to Lovey Grace's bed on a table with a light. We need to go to my house.*

Both dogs started toward the door, but Travis stopped, looked back and thought of his master.

He gestured to Poo. *Only one of us should go because someone has to protect Mike.*

Poo started to leave, but Travis blocked him. *No, Poo. I'll go. It's too dangerous for a little dog.*

Poo, angered, looked hard at Travis. *I can kick any squirrel's ass out there and the big birds', too.*

We are outnumbered, the Rottweiler said. *Both of us should go. I need a brave friend like you to watch our backs. Mike will have to be okay for a few minutes on his own.*

Poo nodded. Travis unblocked the door by moving the wardrobe aside, then inched open the door. They darted out and closed the door behind them with the rope that had been tied to the door handle.

The air was hotter and heavier than it was when the men in the suits had come for Claire and Brian. It was also sweeter tasting too. The dogs breathed in the hot, wet air without discomfort.

Before they even reached the porch steps, the birds perched on the fence and the squirrels occupying the roof, moved from their positions. Travis signaled to Poo and they ran the short distance between the two bungalows, leaping and dodging the strange, illuminated groping fingers of the new plant life.

Two squirrels pursued them but one got his leg caught up in a vicious-looking cabbage flower's purple glowing center. A seagull swooped in, targeting Poo. The rest of the creatures on the fences and around the houses squawked, screamed, and cheered their confederates on.

When the dogs reached Lovey Grace's porch, Travis jumped up onto the door and pushed it open. Luckily, it was still left unlocked since Claire and Mike's visits.

The pursuing seagull latched on to Poo's tail just as he made it to the porch, causing him to stop dead and flip over. The bird's claws dug deep into Poo's side and the dog suffered a vicious peck above his right eye. Before the seabird had a chance to deliver another assault, Poo swung around with a speed that defied the capability of such a squat canine, jumped up, and grabbed the bird by the neck in mid air. They tumbled down Lovey Grace's steps to the stone pathway that led to the beach. Poo, with his teeth sunk deep into the white bird's neck, shook his head until the seagull's neck broke. The bird went limp in his small, powerful jaws. Poo, injured but triumphant, dropped the dead bird and limped up the porch steps.

With a slow and sinister grace, dark jade luminescent vines entwined the dead bird and pulled its body into the plant's center. The blossoms, with the assistance of its tentacles, pulled the carcass beneath the leaves and into the sandy soil.

The little dog snorted and went into the house as Travis pushed the door closed. He nuzzled up to Poo, licked the wound over his eye, and sniffed the one on his side.

Are you okay, my friend?

Poo nodded. *I told you I'd kick their ass!*

They went into the front bedroom. The space had three windows, but the only illumination came from a few cracks between the boards in the storm shutters. Their eyes quickly adjusted and they could see the hydrangea-print wallpaper surrounding them on every wall. It was always Poo's favorite.

Thinking back, the soft lavender colors, with just the right touches of green, quickly relaxed Poo when he and Lovey Grace took their afternoon naps together. She read to him from a magazine or the newspaper. As he listened, Poo looked at the pretty flowers and felt the softness of the cream comforter and fell into a deep sleep. Those afternoons, like his Lovey Grace, were gone now.

Travis snapped him out if his daydream. *Poo, is this the table with the lamp? There are two, and I don't see any big white pills.*

That's it. Sometimes Lovey Grace kept them in the drawer.

Travis grabbed the handle with his teeth and pulled hard until its contents spilled out onto the braided rug. A pill bottle fell out with some paperback novels, a hairbrush, three cassette tapes, and a Walkman tape player with the headphones still attached. The crash to the floor pushed the play button on and they could hear static sounds of music coming from the headset.

Poo sniffed the pill bottle and looked inside. *I see the big white ones, big white ones. These are Lovey Grace's pills.* His little body danced left and right from the wagging of his stubby tail.

Travis was distracted by the sounds from the headphones. He put his black-and-brown floppy ear next to them. *Sweet music! Sweet music! This box has sweet music for my Mike.*

He gathered up the headphones, cassettes, and Walkman with his nose and paw.

Poo, you bring the pills and I will get this sweet music for Mike.

The little dog with the pill bottle in his mouth and Travis with the Walkman, headphones, and tapes in his, headed for the front door. Poo looked back at the pretty wallpaper and his fond memories.

The bed was the first place he remembered sitting with his Lovey Grace. It's the place she'd given him a little red shirt and named him Poo, after the famous bear she said he looked like. That was a long time ago. The shirt only fit for a few weeks and when his coat became longer, he didn't look like the famous character anymore. Poo missed his Lovey Grace and wondered if they would be together again. She said so before she walked into the sea. The things that took her, said so too, with her words.

Travis and Poo headed down the porch steps to the short, dangerous path home. Nothing was waiting to attack or hinder them. Only the strange vines and plants were in their way, but those were easily avoided. They ran up onto the porch and pushed open the door. Travis tripped over the headphone cord and dropped two of the cassettes before entering. Safe inside with Poo, he put down what he was carrying and headed back outside to retrieve the tapes.

As Travis was about to pick them up, Trotter, hiding in the shadows, suddenly charged. When the bird reached the dog, the full force of Travis' powerful head greeted him. This defensive move knocked the fowl through the porch railing and onto his back into the scrub bushes that surrounded the base of the bungalow. The vicious bird quickly got to his feet, side stepping the snakelike vines trying to grab him, and ran off to his arcade lair.

Instead of pursuing the gobbler, Travis picked up the cassettes and headed inside. The two dogs used all their strength to push the wardrobe back in its place, securing the front door. They headed to the bedroom with their treasures for Mike.

In the corner of the darkened room, wrapped securely with bed sheets and lengths of rope, sat Mike in the recliner. His skin was pale and its surface seemed to be developing a scale-like rash. His hair was thinner and not its usual curly dark brown. Travis was thankful Claire had tied Mike to the chair so he wouldn't roam.

Poo opened the bottle with the big white pills and took two of them into his mouth, careful not to swallow them. Travis put his weight on Mike's chest and the little dog climbed up the man's body and got into position to give him the pills.

Open your mouth. Open it wide, Travis said to his master. *Let Poo drop the pills into your mouth. Eat the pills and they will help the pain go away, like they did for Lovey Grace.*

Mike understood and swallowed the pills.

Travis, with much difficultly, put the headphones over Mike's head, trying to cover each ear. The canine dropped the Walkman into Mike's lap and pushed the button with his nose.

Mike made a happy moan that signaled that he heard something he liked. Travis hoped the pills and the music would work for now. When they didn't help anymore, he would have to think of something else, until Claire or Uncle Ned came back for them.

I'm very hungry, Poo said. *Is there any food left in the kitchen cupboard? I could eat the whole bag of the fancy treats they bought.*

There is some left. Claire got more before the storm. All of it is in the cupboard by the table. I'll get the bag while you rest.

Travis sniffed his friend's wounds. They had already started to heal, but in a different way. The lacerations were covered in a clear membrane that stopped the bleeding and sealed it. Poo also looked more muscular with the slight appearance of a translucent skin beneath his golden fur in a few places on the side of his body.

On his way to the cupboard, Travis passed the big mirror and looked at himself. His face and body looked different, but he wasn't sure how. He realized they both were changing since the Green Storm, in more ways than one.

CHAPTER THIRTY-TWO

Belly Rubs and Lightning Bugs

"You like that belly rubbed, little guy?" Mike said to his new three-month-old Rottweiler puppy, Travis. He scratched and massaged the big pup's stomach while he sat on his porch.

"You're a tough guy on the beach chasing the seagulls and a those funny little plovers, but on your back getting that fat belly rubbed, you're just a pussy cat."

The young pup's oversized feet flopped above his wiggling body. His tail was so active, it constantly threw his torso on to its side. Mike played with him until the pup tired from all the attention. Travis sat on the porch beside his new master's chair and looked out at the beach of his new home. He was lucky to live in such a beautiful place where he could run, chase birds and squirrels, explore, swim, and roll in the warm sand. At that moment, all little Travis wanted to do was lie on the porch and take a short nap next to his friend and master, Mike.

While the Rottweiler slept, something poked him and bit his hind leg. The pup rolled onto his back, but the poking and biting continued until he woke up. Travis opened his eyes and saw Poo nudge his side with his paw. Then the westiepoo laughed and poked him again.

Travis woke to a darkened house, not a warm sunny day on the porch. He wasn't a happy pup but a grown dog, and it was nighttime and it was now. The reality of where he was and the loss of his happy dream made him sad.

Poo said, *You were dreaming and rolling on your back. Thank you for making me laugh, my friend.*

Travis sat up, poked Poo, and chased him into the other room. Poo stopped, challenged him, and took off into the kitchen. Travis continued the chase until they both slid into the wall near the wardrobe that blocked the door and they hit a table under the front window.

This caused a chain reaction, as the table tipped over and the lamp on top of it crashed into the window and broke a small section of a glass pane. The dogs were having so much fun, they didn't notice what had happened until the same lamp that broke the window almost fell on Poo, crashing right next to the little dog.

A moan of pain came from Mike that curtailed their fun. With this tormented cry, came the sound and light from outside.

The sound is calling Mike again. I wish it would stop, Poo cried.

I wish it would too, but all we can do is keep Mike from going. We can give him more pills to help. Get the bottle.

Poo retrieved the plastic pill bottle and dumped the contents on the floor.

Two pills left.

Is this all we have?

They repeated the ritual. Travis held Mike in place while Poo walked up his body and dropped the pills into his mouth. Travis also climbed up, used his large bodyweight and tilted his master's head to the side with his snout, and then poured the contents of a small bottle of water over Mike's face, hoping he would swallow some.

When Travis looked at his master closely, he could see that his face had really changed. It was only a few days since the sickness hit him and already he looked like someone Travis didn't know. His skin was greenish-gray and his eyes were more pronounced, with larger pupils.

This wasn't the robust face of his master, Mike Guillory. This illness was changing him into something else. Travis knew Poo and he were different too since they were covered in the green goo from the rain. Why they never became ill was a mystery, but also good fortune. If they were sick, who would protect Mike from the outside and the sea?

Mike eventually fell asleep from the effect of the pills, but the sound and light continued. Travis tried to stuff a small dishcloth into the hole in the broken window, but was only partially successful. He peered through the cracks in the shutter. A thick mist prevented the big dog from seeing beyond a few yards. It was like looking through a diffused pane of glass. There was color and light, but the view was distorted.

He saw specks of light, like fuzzy glowing stars, that seemed to move closer. When they reached the shutter, the particles squeezed right around the dishcloth and passed through the cracked window. The tiny organisms floated in the dense air and began to circulate inside the dark house.

Surrounded by a soft white glow, they floated gently in the air. When the creatures touched Travis' nose and mouth, he tasted them. Their flavor was agreeable. Poo jumped and snapped up several of the organisms and he liked them too.

The particles, whatever they were, filled the room. Some settled on Mike and glowed brighter when they touched his skin. Once absorbed, the man's flesh also illuminated for a second or two. The mist outside must have kept them alive because once inside the house, they died quickly.

Following the glowing organisms, slightly larger creatures came to the broken window. They pushed on the dishcloth until they squeezed around the fabric and traveled into the room. The things reminded Travis of the lightning bugs he chased on summer nights.

One landed on Travis' nose, but this time its touch was painful. He could see it was no firefly, but something that resembled a jellyfish. Its body was circular and had threadlike tentacles that pulsed with chaser lights outlining its transparent body.

Travis pulled back his nose and gobbled up the tiny predator. To his surprise, the stinging floater was tasty too. More of these life forms entered through the cracks and consumed the smaller particles. The two dogs kept busy devouring all of them.

The glowing bugs also gravitated toward Mike and landed on his body in great numbers. The big dog tried to brush them off his master, but they stuck fast. Mike didn't seem to feel their stinging touch. When their glow dissipated, they fell off and dissolved onto the floor. What Mike absorbed from these creatures made him stop moaning.

When the last rays of light from outside faded, the canines heard thumps on the shutters. Whatever made the noise had squeezed through a shutter crack and pushed the dishcloth out of the hole in the window. The new larger creatures brought more of the stinging jellyfish life forms and the delicious organisms with them.

This thing was more crustacean than coelenterate, but still ethereal in form. It seemed to have only one goal: to eat as many of the little glowing taste treats and stinging lighting bugs as possible. Then it focused upon Mike and the dogs. Both frightening and beautiful, this larger beast buzzed around Poo and Travis, making an evaluation. It decided to pass on them and turned its attention Mike.

When it landed on his sheet-covered chest, Travis ran to the rescue. Mike woke from his pill-induced sleep and looked down at the thing slowly crawling toward his head. They appeared to be communicating in some way the dog didn't understand. The thing reached Mike's face and two spear-like arms projected from both sides of its body and injected a glowing liquid into Mike's temples. As he took in the liquid his head vibrated and glowed. When the feeding was over, the creature levitated from Mike's chest and floated into another room.

Travis and Poo ran after the thing, but found it dead and dissolving on the floor like the other visitors. The loss of its fluids must have sealed its fate. The dogs weren't sure what these creatures were or where they were coming from, but what they did know was that these things of light were food for them and even more so for Mike. He seemed calmer than ever and in less pain.

Nothing else entered the house except some of the luscious tiny particles that first appeared. The larger ones must have communicated that the inside of the house was a terminal destination, because only a few more made the trip in. The last of the glowing things preferred Mike to the dogs as the recipient of their nutrients.

The two canines spent the rest of the night gazing through the cracked shutters and watching the show of light. They could see larger shapes approach the windows but all, thankfully, were too big to enter. Instead they busied themselves with the consumption of smaller animals, including birds, which were snatched mid-air and either sucked dry or devoured whole.

These were the new predators that came with the aftermath of the storm. Travis wondered how long it would be before monsters would appear that considered Poo, himself, and even Mike, as dinner.

They fell asleep by early morning and napped until noon. The air was still a fluid mist, but the parade of new glowing beasts ceased in the pale green hue of daylight.

Maybe Claire and Uncle Ned would come back and save them from this new world. Would help come before the expanding sea took over and it was too late for Mike and the dogs? Travis looked at his master and wondered what would become of the three of them.

CHAPTER THIRTY-THREE

Trotter

It seemed as though the sea and air had become one. The shutters and walls of the house strained from the unseen weight. The atmosphere inside the house had become so dense with moisture, Travis could see it. As the big dog moved, the air rippled with thickness. There was no circulation in the boarded up bungalow, only the liquid breeze from the broken window in the front room.

The dogs couldn't go outside for relief because of the unknown dangers out there. Travis and Poo had to use the small hallway that led to the back entrance to do their business. They closed the door that separated it from the kitchen, which helped at first. But now the stench was seeping through.

The lack of drinking water had also become a problem. They had had bottled water in the kitchen cupboard, but none were left. The normal supply from a tank that collected rainwater was contaminated and undrinkable. But as Poo and he changed, the air itself and the few glowing taste treats that wandered in through the window satisfied both their hunger and thirst. There were very few luminous visitors that night or the next day. Travis saw them floating outside as the long tendril fingers of the plants grabbed them up or larger beasts vacuumed them inside their clear bodies. Both dogs were hungry for their taste and wished more would venture inside.

Travis also noticed that the smaller birds were gone and that the larger ones, like the seagulls, were clearly more cautious of the new predators. But it was a losing battle. Also, since the new glowing creatures appeared, Travis didn't hear the constant banging of the crazy squirrels trying to get in anymore. The big dog knew that whatever Poo and he faced as adversaries, like the seagulls and the squirrels on the trip to get Lovey Grace's big white pills, were now either dead or the last ones left. There were new unknown enemies outside that they would have to deal with when they tried to leave the island.

Travis sat by Mike, observing him for hours as he slept. The man didn't need the music anymore, which the dog was thankful for, because the batteries for the Walkman were dead. His master had lost most of his hair, which was replaced by hard shell-like patches. His skin was paler and more translucent.

Mike's lower extremities had developed a scaled covering and the skin on his feet was thin and transparent. It revealed all the muscles and veins underneath. The toes had flattened out and a web of membrane had grown between them. Mike had developed feet that were more like swim fins that no shoe would ever fit.

Travis saw similar changes in Poo. The little canine had a thinner, sleeker coat. He was also leaner, not from lack of food, but due to the transition of his body into something more efficient. The sweet dog was not the cute rascal that scampered on the beach and cuddled in Lovey Grace's lap anymore. Poo had also developed a series of openings on both sides of his torso.

Like his Lovey Grace, Poo's least favorite thing was hot and humid weather. On scorching summer days he stayed indoors with his mistress in the comfort of the air-conditioned house. Now, the new Poo inhaled the dense wet atmosphere with ease and comfort. Even though he was physically different, Travis knew his friend was still the same Poo he had always known.

The little dog nudged Travis with his snout. *How long can we stay here?* He looked up at him. *We must leave.*

Travis knew Poo was right. It was only a matter of time before the shutters and walls gave into the pressure of the liquid mist and the new predators invaded the house. And he worried about Mike. They didn't know if he could walk, and if so, would they be able to prevent him from going into the sea.

Travis looked at Poo. *Let us see how Mike is tomorrow. Then we can decide. Claire always said things are better in the morning. Plus, the tide should be out and we might be able to cross the sandbar.*

He knew this was a risky plan but there didn't seem to be an alternative. They would just have to deal with whatever was outside and hope they could make it to the mainland.

We will decide tomorrow, Poo agreed.

That evening was calm and quiet, which allowed the two dogs to sleep through the night. This was something they hadn't done since the storm.

Travis was awakened first by a thud against the front door. A second thud woke Poo and made Mike stir. Over and over again, the banging continued until the force shook the wardrobe securing the entrance. Something was using all its strength to get in. Travis peeked through a space between the shutters and saw a small scaly head with large red eyes.

Trotter is trying to get in, Travis alerted Poo. *He's back for more. It's time to end this.*

Time to end this, Poo repeated, *I will do it this time. I will kill that bird.*

Travis looked at his little friend and knew that even in his new evolved state he was no match for the monster fowl on the porch.

The big dog looked into the eyes of his brave friend. *This is my fight and it ends today. Help me move the wardrobe enough to get out then watch the door and please protect Mike.*

Poo respected his friend's wishes as they pulled the rope and opened the door just enough to allow space for Travis to squeeze through it. Once the Rottweiler appeared outside, the large bird stepped back to the edge of the stairs. His tail spread open in a display of spiked plumes with clear tentacles interspersed between his tail feathers. Trotter had obviously changed, even more since their last encounter. He physically looked like the monster he had always been.

Everything was different since the two dogs went for the pills. The perimeter of the porch and the stone path leading to the beach was completely lined with ominous plants of all varieties. Floating above them in the liquid atmosphere were several of the crustaceans similar to the one that landed on Mike.

Travis looked up and saw larger versions of the stinger jellyfish suspended in the air, feeding on the flowers of tall translucent tubeworm plants or carrying away what was left of the birds or squirrels. Beyond these beasts were even larger creatures and plants either growing out of the mist or suspended in it. This was a totally different world than the island he had called home. The green haze also seemed to move with the action of the surf, contracting and expanding with a motion he could see as well as feel.

The big dog was overwhelmed and distracted by the transformation of his surroundings but he focused on the bird in front of him. Travis positioned himself on all fours and breathed in the thick liquid air filled with the tiny particles of light that were so tasty. This influx of nutrients gave him a rush of energy. He lowered his head and looked the evil bird directly in his dark, blood-red eyes.

Trotter made the first advance but was quickly thwarted by a powerful butt from the dog's big head. The gobbler tumbled backwards off the porch, but quickly got to his feet. He stomped around and made a chilling sound that was more roar than gobble. The bird retreated to the edge of the dunes and then waited.

Travis knew this move was to get him away from the house but the dog didn't take the bait at first. He froze in a pose that neither signaled an attack or a retreat.

Suddenly, Travis leaped off the porch at a speed he was never capable of before. The thick, liquid atmosphere passed over the dog, making his body sleek and slippery. This transformed Travis had a strength that even surprised him.

When he hit Trotter, the force knocked them both down the shallow slope to the sandy beach. The tentacles of the plants surrounding them reacted to the sudden motions, as did the creatures that floated above them. Tall, translucent tubeworms snapped their jellylike necks in the direction of the battle as the big dog sunk his teeth into Trotter's breast, hitting the bone.

The turkey then pecked into the dog's thick shoulder muscles with his sharp beak. Trotter used his long, powerful neck like a club, each stab deeper and more painful. Travis stood the pain for as long as he could and then released his grip and backed away from the evil bird. Sprays of blood were suspended in the thick haze of air before they landed on the sand. The blood pooled, then disappeared, feeding something under the surface. The spectators moved closer, positioning themselves for first pick of the victims of this battle.

The wound on Travis' left shoulder affected his ability to maintain his stance. He summoned all the strength he had and attacked again, leaping onto the turkey and knocking him to the ground. Each movement the two combatants made caused the thick air to ripple and undulate around them.

They rolled around until Trotter was on top, slamming his beak into the dog's wounded shoulder. The dog bit into the feathered monster's chest again, hoping to stop his repeated advances. He held onto his grip, when suddenly the bird was pulled from his perch atop of Travis.

Blood bathed the dog's face and blinded him. His vision was restored as the red liquid slowly floated into the liquid air. He saw the turkey, chest torn open from his bite, in the grip of a powerful scale covered arm.

Protruding from above the wrist of the arm was a long

translucent blade of bone that pierced the bird's skull, then retracted and disappeared. The hand lifted the bird up to a wide-open mouth filled with sharp teeth and it tore into Trotter's neck, separating the bird's head from its body.

The two pieces of the bird were thrown into the air and floated toward the spectators. Tentacles grabbed at the pieces of the now-dead turkey. His head was retrieved stealthily by one of the floating crustaceans. The big bird's body was fought over and torn apart by plant appendages, which transported the bloody pieces beneath the leaves, vines, and red soaked sand.

When Travis was able to bring himself to a standing position, he saw Poo nearby. Next to him was Mike, looking down at him with a blood-soaked smile. Naked, most of his body was covered with gleaming scales patterned in gradated sections down his torso and legs. The man's chest was stained with the old bird's blood, which caused him to faintly glow.

This was not the man Travis had seen the night before. He hadn't checked in on him that morning before the sudden call to battle. An evolution was completed overnight, one that had been going on since the Green Storm. This wasn't his master Mike who saved him from Trotter but someone else. This was a new Mike.

CHAPTER THIRTY-FOUR

New Mike

The blood-soaked chest of this new Mike attracted one of floating creatures. It caressed his scale-covered upper torso and sucked in Trotter's dark liquid. The stream of red traveled up its clear tentacles and toward the center of the crustacean's gelatinous head. As the blood coursed through the floating creature, the fluid glowed bright vermilion, then turned to a luminous green as it was assimilated.

During the process it attached narrower tubes to the back of Mike's skull and injected the processed nutrients into him. This caused Mike to glow as it traveled to every part of his body.

When the process was finished, he felt a burst of energy and spread his arms into the air, revealing fanned webbing that grew from the inner sides of his torso to his underarms and extended to his wrists. These translucent wings looked like aquatic fins and he resembled a large flying fish in humanoid form.

Mike dropped his arms to his sides and walked over to Travis, as Poo followed. He smiled and knelt down next to his wounded friend and gently wiped the blood off of his face. *Let me heal you, my friend.*

He ran his hands over the dog and caressed the wounds on his shoulder. From his fingers, tiny probing tubes injected glowing liquid into the dog's open cuts. This caused a luminescence that radiated throughout the canine's upper body, and Travis felt an ecstasy and warmth as the lacerated flesh was healed. The big dog rolled over onto his back, like he had as a pup.

Mike smiled and rubbed his friend's belly. *You love that, don't you boy?*

When he finished healing Travis, Mike walked to what was once the water's edge and inhaled deeply, filling his lungs with the mist and the food it contained. Slits in the sides of his chest opened and closed with each inhalation.

The sound and light from the sea started again, but this time it didn't induce fear. It filled the three friends with joy. Mike spread his wing-like arms up and out and created a tone of his own that came from deep inside his chest and vibrated his whole body. The two dogs stood at attention when they heard this. The floating beasts reacted to it also as they responded with their own vocalizations. At that moment, the small beach resonated with vibrations that visibly rippled in the liquid misty air.

Mike walked into the haze and water. His lower half was invisible beneath this thicker part of the gradient mist. The fantastical arthropods that had enveloped Lovey Grace when she walked into the sea returned and swam up into the thick, hazy air. One of them circled Mike like they had done with his mother and joined to the back of his head and spine. Two more of these creatures swam toward the dogs, still frozen at attention.

Mike called to them with thought and sound that danced in the misty atmosphere. *Come Travis. Come Poo. Join with us. Join with our kind who love you.*

Both canines walked into the watery fog. The two arthropods moved around both dogs until they chose the recipient of their union. Like the creatures had done with Mike and Lovey Grace, these things attached to Travis and Poo, then became part of them. The three friends were now in fellowship with the sounds and light from the sea that had once threatened their existence since the Green Storm.

Instead of walking into the waiting sea, Mike addressed his two friends. *Let's go home.*

They went back to the bungalow and he opened up the front door, the shutters, and the windows until the heavy mist washed throughout the house. Mike entered into the bedroom and looked in the full-length mirror on the closet door. He studied his body for a long time. He laughed and turned to Travis and Poo. *I'm naked. You can see my butt and my ...* He laughed again.

Travis puzzled, answered back. *What's wrong with being naked? I have always been that way.*

Mike looked into the closet and found a pair of khaki pants and put them on. He went over to the old phonograph, engaged the crank, and put on a record. The old machine and the muffled sound of the opera, *Turandot,* started to play. It was the same section in the third act they'd performed the night of the storm. The thick liquid air affected the vinyl disk until the needle arm flowed off. Mike moaned in dismay.

Some of the creatures from outside floated in and explored household items and pieces of furniture. When Mike saw one of them pick up a photo of Claire and his son, he grabbed the picture from its tentacles and then slammed the thing across the side of its body with so much force that it hit the living room wall. The chaser lights of pulsing fluids in the beast's body flashed, flickered, and darkened for a moment. The thing quickly left the house through the window and some of the others followed, fearing Mike's anger. Only the smaller creatures were brave enough to stay and continued to explore the rooms and hidden places around the bungalow.

Mike took the framed photo of his family, studied it and walked out of the house. He sat in his usual chair on the porch and put his fin feet up on the railing. He glared out into the fluid mist and toward the pulsing lights and tones that projected rippled waves through the green haze.

*   *   *

The dogs left Mike alone on the porch. They kept occupied by testing their new evolved state and exploring its benefits and disadvantages. When they moved, it was fluid and fast. They floated more than walked around the house. Eating was easy. No more waiting for someone to tear open a bag, fill a bowl, or find a bone to chew on. All the dogs had to do was inhale the infinite tasty creatures that floated like tiny lightning bugs in the wet mist. They took in this nourishment through their mouths and also through gill-like slits on the sides of their bodies. For a bigger meal, there were always the stinging beasts that competed for the snack-sized floating treats.

What the two canines did miss was the variety of scents, textures, and tastes they'd experienced as normal dogs. Now everything was delicious, but the same. All textures were smooth, wet and luminous. Scents and smells were now felt in the form of vibrations and through tentacles that graduated down their shell-encased spines. Their tongues and paws also sampled the liquid air continuously. Since their communion with the strange arthropods, they were in communication with everything around them.

This was not a completely pleasant experience for Travis and Poo. They heard and felt the vibrations, thoughts, and life forces of every creature in this new world. It was like what they had gone through with the crazy squirrels and birds when they were trapped in the house, but one hundredfold. All the beings, changed since the storm, originated from the same source that connected them all to each other. Focus was the only way to clear their heads of the onslaught of information coming in.

Travis sensed quickly that every creature in this new world was not equal. The dogs knew they were superior to the taste treats and stinging beasts that floated in the air, as well as to the carnivorous plants. But as before, they were not superior to the new Mike.

There was an order and Travis was glad he was nearer the top than he was before. In his old life, as a happy dog, he was one of the fortunate canines that happened to live with a good master. Now he was a top predator in the line of life forms he had met. There were probably larger and stronger beings than even Mike, but he wasn't going to worry about them until he had to.

When it became darker, the dogs left the house and sat next to Mike on the porch. He was still in his chair with his feet up, gazing intently at the picture of Claire and Brian. His body glowed softly and tiny throbbing points of light traveled up his spine to his shell-helmeted head.

I can't sense them. I can't feel any of their vibrations, he shouted through his thoughts.

I can't feel them either, Mike, Poo replied.

Mike looked down at him. *I can't feel Claire and my son. I don't know if anything else exists but us. Will I ever see them again?*

Mike's glow dimmed in the darkness. These thoughts made him feel unhappy for the first time since he became his new self.

The men in protective suits took Claire and Brian into the sky. They took them out of the wet mist, Travis reminded him.

Mike's glow brightened. *Into the sky and to a place where the land is like it was before?*

I don't know, Mike, Travis replied. *We just saw them go up into the sky in a machine that looked like the big dragonflies in the high grass.*

Mike stood up from his chair. *We can find where the dry land is if we go to the city of the light and sound.*

Poo said, *I can feel Lovey Grace. She is in the city and she wants her blue dress.*

Travis looked at Poo and then back at Mike, who smiled and patted both their heads. *Let's go to the city and see Mother.*

Mike spread his arms to expand his finned wings, and floated up into the wet atmosphere. When he reached what was once his wife's sweet garden, Mike turned his head and gestured to his two friends to follow. Travis and Poo lifted off the porch just like their master and swam to his side. Together they took off with great speed into the green haze.

CHAPTER THIRTY-FIVE

The Emerald City

The three friends only knew this new world from the restricted vantage point of the island they were on. Since the shower of lights that night, the world was in a transformation that the inhabitants of the land only became aware of after the Green Storm.

The sea had been terraforming and changing for over eighty years. It was an isolated and gradual adjustment. The first shifts were in the deepest canyons and valleys that went to the core of the planet and the few life forms that existed at those depths.

In the last thirty years, the process and expansion accelerated with the warming of the oceans. The alien life form was brought to earth inside the tiny crystals that joined and evolved with everything in the oceans.

On the night of the Green Storm it expanded its reach beyond the seacoasts. The thick, wet air extended more than a quarter mile into the atmosphere and over four hundred miles inland. The farther the mist was from the oceans, the thinner it became. The creatures that easily floated in the thick air over Plover's Island couldn't swim or breathe in the outer borders of the mist.

Each day, massive tubeworms functioned like huge factory chimneys rooted at the base of the sea. They pumped more of this liquid fog, allowing it to expand its reach into the air and over the dry land. All the elements that the new life forms needed to thrive upon were contained in its mixture.

The composition was lethal to all living things on dry land. At first, not knowing what they were up against, the inland survivors hadn't fought back against the expansion. They huddled in cramped cities and towns away from the mist that was spreading toward them. The earth had become a planet of pale green clouds with patches of color that indicated the existing dry sections of the continents that were losing their real estate every day.

*   *   *

Mike led Travis and Poo into the thick liquid below the mist. Far out to sea and deep below was the city where the strange arthropods, which now joined with their bodies, came from. The big dog easily followed Mike as he glided through the water with great speed. Poo on the other hand, carrying Lovey Grace's blue dress in his mouth, had trouble keeping up.

When Mike saw this, he doubled back and the three friends descended together. On the way they met other altered pilgrims on the same journey. Schools of creatures, once human, glided through the water, using their finned wings to give them speed and stability. Some traveled in small assemblies while others formed dense illuminated shapes that moved as one unit.

Mike noticed random spots of color mixed within the groups of these transformed beings. When he realized what these anomalies were, he laughed to himself. More than two thirds of the mutated humans were wearing pieces of clothing. For most, like Mike, their modesty was not lost when their minds and bodies were transformed.

When Mike, Travis, and Poo reached the city, they were transfixed by its size. This metropolis was much bigger than the mermen city that once ruled at this depth and its inhabitants were now, like the altered humans, part of the collective. It was similar to the organic city Mike's ancestor William had seen so many years ago and where Emily, Thomas, and January once lived. Unlike the mermen metropolis, this one and the others like it were still growing and expanding.

Mike and the dogs watched as the arms of the city stretched out like roots of a tree. Chamber after chamber subdivided and spread over the floor of the sea. The three friends felt and witnessed the vibrations of this development. This overwhelmed their senses until they were able to focus again on their mission.

Mike paused outside one of the huge tunnels. *I can feel our mom is here. I can feel her in every creature, every wall and chamber. Boys, she is here and we will find her.*

They swam through the clear walls of the city, and like the mermen's huge township, it had no doors. The gossamer barriers gave way when they passed through them and then quickly resealed. As the three traveled from chamber to chamber, they felt the multitude of voices and vibrations contained within the walls of the undulating metropolis.

They worked hard to keep their concentration on the search. Above them, huge jellyfish lit the ocean sky. These monsters were like cities unto themselves. Inside were smaller life forms that were part of this living structure, performing functions essential to its existence.

Whales that had transformed into gigantic, shell-covered mammoths with tendril dorsal crests looked insignificant next to these colossal beasts, as they passed peacefully by. Schools of transparent white sharks and fluorescent squid grouped for protection as they swam around, beneath, and through the colossal jellyfish's tentacles, to avoid being eaten. Travis finally met the creatures that were at the top of the predator chain. Even Mike's kind could be breathed in for food, as easily as they did with the mouthwatering lightning bugs.

The three friends traveled from chamber to chamber until Poo suddenly stopped, smiled, and almost dropped his blue bundle.

The little dog felt his mistress so strongly that nothing else could be sensed.

A figure swam toward them, gliding through the walls and into where they were. It was Lovey Grace. She looked like herself, but she was also a being like Mike. She still wore the nightgown she had on the night she walked into the sea, but the garment was tattered and ripped.

Lovey Grace projected her greeting to her little friend. *My Poo Bear, I said we would be together again.*

She swam up and hugged him tightly. Lovey held Poo in one arm and extended the other to her son. Mike floated to her side and embraced his mother. Poo gave Lovey Grace the blue bundle. Delighted, she unfolded the garment and she kissed him. As the silk fabric floated in the thick water, the glowing light of the city made it appear the most vibrant of blues. It was not wearable by a creature like herself now but the color made her happy.

Mom, I never thought I would see you again, Mike cried in a sound only life forms of their kind could hear or sense.

Lovey Grace smiled and then asked, *Where are Claire and Brian? Why are they not with you?*

Mike hesitated. *They were taken away. They weren't changed and we've lost them forever.*

Lovey Grace looked at her son. *They'll be with us soon. Our world is growing and expanding. We are better and more than we were before. A life that always was, became part of us and soon all will be part of them. Our world was dying and now it will be new and alive again.*

She spoke in a way he had never heard her talk before, and in their new state, Mike felt closer to her than ever. They were more now than just mother and son. They were part of each other and part of the whole.

I am going back to find Claire and my son, he announced. *I want you to come with me.*

I'm staying here. She and Brian, like all the rest, will be with us soon. I'll wait for them here.

Well, I can't wait. I must find them now.

He looked at the two dogs. *Come with me boys.*

Travis nodded his approval, but Poo swam to his Lovey Grace and she took the little dog in her arms.

Mike kissed his mother and patted Poo.

Travis swam to Poo and nudged him with his nose. *See you soon, my friend.*

Let's go find them, boy, Mike said to his big dog.

Travis and he swam through the wall of the chamber and up past monsters too immense to even comprehend a sense of their size. They glided between the field of tentacles attached to the city-sized behemoths and watched the residents of its enormous arms swimming inside.

Near the canyon walls that grew out of the earth's core, towering tubeworm factories expelled nutrients and gases targeted to enrich the mist. The two friends had to swim with great skill not to be swept away by the massive currents created by these powerful entities.

As they got closer to the surface mist, they passed more groups of newly transformed beings wearing their crazy quilt of garments from their former lives. This was their new world now, full of huge cities, fantastical creatures, multitudes of voices, and the odd polka dot and plaid.

CHAPTER THIRTY-SIX

Fire and Water

When the two friends arrived back at Plover's Island, the mist was so thick that the original shoreline no longer existed. They swam to the bungalow that was once their home and discovered that it was overgrown by plants and large tubular worms that swayed from their bases. Mike and Travis watched as the great creatures reproduced by ejecting small tentacle offspring into the wet atmosphere. The new babies floated upward into the mist until they disappeared into the opaque haze.

Mike witnessed his home disappear under the growth of the encroaching vegetation. All the memories of his family and the island were swallowed up before his eyes. The other two houses were under the same, slow methodical attack.

He noticed in the distance that the carnival had been devoured too. The skeleton of the Ferris wheel was now a trellis of dark green and purple growth, with vines snaking around its circumference and supports.

Mike knew that what was occurring had to be, but he wasn't ready to let go of his past. The new world could not be a place he was at peace with until he found his wife and son. Mike and Travis turned their backs to their island home and swam to Ridgewater.

They arrived at the old ferry pier and glided through the park and entrance, past the benches Lolly and Lynette sat on when they were invited to their last party.

They continued down the main street of the town. Its buildings were covered with plants, tubeworms and tall sea grass swaying in the thickness of the ever-growing mist. The street was filled with creatures traveling up and down its thoroughfare like townies shopping and going about their way. Mike saw only a few transformed humans. He assumed there would be more beings like himself.

Of the two he saw, one was a woman floating in front of a dress store window. Another, was a man with a dog, a scaled covered Boston bull terrier. The dog swam up to Travis and greeted him with a sniff that was happily returned. The transformed man was older than Mike and wore black pants held up by red suspenders. Mike thought that bad taste, like modesty, was also not lost in their new evolution.

He didn't know the man whose body was shorter and less muscular than his. He had a puffy, scaled belly that made him look like a large green-and-silver goldfish wearing bulging crimson braces. He also held securely in his sharp teeth a large ivory pipe with a face carved into it. The few others, like Mike, that he encountered were also different. It seemed that humankind, even after their transformation, kept their distinctive shapes and their old personalities.

Why are there so few of us here? Mike asked the man with the dog.

He removed the pipe from his mouth. *Most people were evacuated the second day after the storm. By the fourth day only a few of us who were blessed with the rain, stayed. Most have gone to the cities beyond the mist, but they will be back soon. The blessing reaches us everywhere.*

Mike was shocked that a term like blessing was used for their new transformed state. *Why didn't you go with them?*

I stayed with my wife while she changed, but she died before her evolution was complete. After that, my little friend and I were blessed.

We decided to stay in Ridgewater. This is our home.

Mike empathized with the man. *I am so sorry for your loss. Why was her change not completed?*

She was already sick with cancer. The blessing could not cure her and she died. We gave her to the plants, they took her in and she was finally made part of us all. I feel and hear her all the time in the ripples of the mist, he thought with reverence.

Mike paused. *Where did the ones who were evacuated the second day go?*

I heard the man in the protective suit tell my neighbor and his wife, when they were taking them away, that they were relocating to Ohio. The mist that blesses us was not there yet.

As Mike was listening to the man, an explosion of fire burst far above their heads at the edge of the green haze. It caused a shockwave that created strong ripples in the wet fog. When the powerful undulations reached them, they were knocked to the pavement along with Travis, the bulldog, and the woman that was window-shopping on the opposite side of the street. Many other creatures along the street were slammed to the ground or into the sides of plant covered buildings. Some survived the trauma. Others exploded and split apart. The dead were quickly grabbed by the plant tendrils and devoured beneath their leaves and flowery beds.

This explosion and the aftermath of ripples also caused the two nearby buildings to collapse. Windows shattered, causing sharp pieces of glass to float in the mist and pierce the jellied flesh of several floating beasts. Mike saw that the woman across the street was injured. When the man with the pipe and he recovered from the blast, they swam to her side. Mike lifted her up as the goldfish man used his healing hands to close the wounds on her side.

Mike pointed to the fire above them. *What caused the explosion?*

The man looked up into the haze. *It's the military. They are trying to dry the mist and push it back. They've discovered that the blessing, even though it is made of the sea, can burn. They are trying to destroy it, but that won't work. Everything will be one soon. All will be blessed and connected to us.*

How long have they been doing this?

They started on the edge of the mist near Ohio then went north and south of its perimeter. It caused the mist to recede temporarily, so now they are exploding firebombs from above. It stops the blessing for a moment, but then the expansion continues again.

How do you know this? Travis asked.

The man smiled at Mike and the big dog. *I feel the vibrations of our kind near the edge of the border. They can see the men with the fire and bombs. Some of our kind have died, but they will be replaced by the ones outside the blessing very soon. Listen and you will know I am telling you the truth.*

Travis and Mike focused hard and listened. The man was right. But neither of them felt this "blessing" he talked so much about.

Mike and Travis were about to leave when the man spoke up again. *You will feel the blessing.* He laughed. *And red suspenders are very tasteful, my friend.*

Mike, now very aware of the oneness the man and his mother spoke of, smiled. *I hope we will and I'm sure they are.*

Mike and Travis swam to where the Guillory shop and store was located. Like all the other buildings, the vegetation took over their Ridgewater place of work.

They swam through the back window into the office. Everything was covered in green and purple plants. Mike could barely see his desk or Claire's craft table. The family pictures on the wall were practically invisible. Aunt Cleo peeked out from behind a leaf, while a translucent tendril caressed Lovey Grace's and Michael senior's cruise photo. The thick liquid of the mist still hadn't blurred all of the old photos but the moisture was slowly working its way under the glass of each.

Mike looked at the map of the United States on the opposite

wall. *We've never been to Ohio, old boy.*

Travis smiled. *Which way do we go?*

West. We go west.

They swam out of the office window. Mike looked back at the family photos for the last time as the moisture and plants consumed them. *Goodbye.*

* * *

Mike and Travis traveled through the wall of mist, dodging the many floating monsters, food-seeking plants, and huge tubeworm towers that were shooting more of their offspring into the air. They also discovered that reproduction wasn't their only purpose.

When they swam near the upper level of the mist, Mike and Travis witnessed one of the newborn jelly creatures propel itself out of the haze and attack a passing plane, destroying it on contact before it dropped a firebomb. Expansion of the mist was not the only weapon the new life was using to make this world its own.

The trip was difficult. On several occasions, explosions of fire dented the barrier, causing the same deadly ripple effect they'd experienced in the town. Both of them were pounded and bruised from the blasts. At one point, Travis was hurled into the side of a huge tentacle monster that looked like a large squid. He would have been devoured if the thing had not been more dazed by the ripple than he was.

A few miles from the edge of the perimeter of the growing mist, they stopped to rest and get their bearings. They paused in front of a group of buildings that looked like an industrial park. They swam to a structure that only had double glass doors and no windows. Above it, a sign read: *Bob's Designer Outlet.*

Let's go inside and rest. Maybe I can find a nice pair of designer pants. Mike laughed as he motioned to Travis.

They opened the unlocked double doors. No large life forms were inside; just the tiny tasty ones that Travis loved to eat. He took his time, feeding on them with great gusto. Mike also breathed in his fill of the luminous things and then went looking for pants made of a stronger material to replace the tattered ones he had on. Eventually he found waterproof rain trousers that would do the job. He then tried on a poncho, but it was too hard to swim in and slowed down his gliding speed considerably.

Well I guess it's bare-chested for me the rest of my life, he joked.

This brought up a question he had not thought of. How long will a transformed Mike or Travis live? He posed the query to the liquid cosmos that was now their new world but only got the same answer he had gotten from the man with the red suspenders. *All are one and we are all connected forever.* He understood what the "all are one" meant but the collective didn't answer his question.

He asked Travis the same thing.

The big dog answered without any hesitation. *You eat until you are eaten.*

Travis continued to breathe in as much of the lightning bugs as he could.

The simple logic of Travis' answer made Mike laugh. *You eat until you are eaten.* This is the time you have left. It made perfect sense in the world they now lived in.

Mike swam to his friend, rolled him over and rubbed his belly until the dog laughed, lost control, and peed. It floated in the thick mist. Mike was almost sprayed with it as the glowing liquid floated by.

He chased Travis around the store knocking over displays and clothing racks until they tired out. They settled behind a counter, closed their eyes, and floated next to each other. It was the first time they had slept in their new altered forms.

When they awoke, it was dark. They looked outside the double glass doors and the only light came from the bright blasts of red and yellow explosions at the edge of the burning mist. The building was strong and shielded them from much of the shock.

Once the explosions stopped, the two felt it was safe to continue their journey.

Mike looked at Travis. *Time to go find Claire and Brian, my friend.*

Mike opened the double glass doors, letting in a few of the larger floating beasts searching for shelter after the latest fiery assault. The luminous beings lit up brighter as they passed, almost as a thank you for the chance to enter the safety of the store.

Mike and Travis swam upwards, to avoid the crowd of larger creatures and then glided toward the edge of the slowly expanding mist in search of Claire and Brian.

ABOUT THE AUTHOR

BUD SANTORA

Bud Santora is a versatile designer and illustrator. For his work as a costume designer he's won an Emmy Award and two nominations. As a holiday designer he's worked for companies such as Sears, K-Mart, and Silvestri. He has created covers for several novels and also illustrated the children's picture book, *Wise Bear William: A New Beginning*. Currently he does freelance design and resides in New York City. *The Green* Storm is Mr. Santora's debut novel.

www.ingramcontent.com/pod-product-compliance
Lightning Source LLC
Chambersburg PA
CBHW021957170626
46808CB00001B/187